TAMARISK ROW

# TAMARISK ROW

*Gerald Murnane*

SHEFFIELD – LONDON – NEW YORK

First UK edition published in 2019 by And Other Stories
Sheffield – London – New York
www.andotherstories.org

9 8 7 6 5 4 3 2

ISBN: 978-1-911508-36-6
eBook ISBN: 978-1-911508-37-3

Proofreader: Sarah Terry; Typesetter: Tetragon, London; Typefaces: Linotype Swift Neue and Verlag; Cover Design: Sarahmay Wilkinson. Printed and bound by the CPI Group (UK) Ltd, Croydon, CR0 4YY.

A catalogue record for this book is available from the British Library.

This book was supported using public funding by Arts Council England.

# FOREWORD

*Tamarisk Row*, my first book of fiction, was first published in 1974. I was already thirty-five years of age at the time, and I had been trying to write such a book since early 1964, ten years before.

The earliest abandoned fragments hardly resemble the published text. Sometimes my projected book had a title quite unlike *Tamarisk Row*. That title first occurred to me in 1968, and almost at once I was able to foresee the contents of the book and to outline the shape of it. For the first time in five years, I felt confident of completing a work of fiction.

During the five years when I was able to write no more than a few thousand words before giving up, I sometimes supposed I was incapable of writing a book-length work of fiction. I believe nowadays that I was incapable of writing what seemed to me a conventional book of fiction: a novel with a plot, with characters deserving to be called credible, and with numerous passages of direct speech.

As a boy at secondary school, I had had much trouble writing critical essays about novels. Ten years later, as a mature-age student of English at university, I had, if anything, more such trouble. Even after I had seemed to myself to have grasped something of the literary theory then fashionable, that theory remained wholly unrelated to my experiences as a reader of fiction, let alone a would-be writer of it.

I cannot recall having believed, even as a child, that the purpose of reading fiction was to learn about the place commonly called the real world. I seem to have sensed from the first that to read fiction was to make available for myself a new kind of space. In that space, a version of myself was free to move among places and personages the distinguishing features of which were the feelings they caused to arise in me rather than their seeming appearance, much less their possible resemblance to places or persons in the world where I sat reading. I seemed to have sensed also from an early age that some of my experiences as a reader would change me more as a person than would many an event in the world where I sat and read.

The personages that I seemed to move among while I was reading were not only what other readers would have called characters. Often the personage whose presence most awed me would have seemed to me to exist on the far horizon of the place where the fictional events were taking place. (And yet the awesome personage sometimes seemed to loom beside me – we two were looking out from almost the same vantage point.) The awesome personage, as I might have called him or her long ago, I call nowadays the Narrator or the Implied Author, and I still find myself often nowadays as much affected by him or by her as by any fictional character alleged by him or by her to exist.

The notebooks or journals that I kept during the early 1960s include pages of speculation about the way in which I ought to write the latest draft of my first book of fiction. A recurring question was 'How much should I claim to know?' Another matter that troubled me was the distance that should lie between myself-as-narrator and the nearest character in the fiction. While I was writing about these matters, I sometimes thought of myself as dithering or as needlessly agonising over a task that I ought to have set about long before. Today, however,

I feel somewhat proud of my much younger self, he who might have borrowed his way of writing from any of the authors then fashionable but who would not – could not do so.

I have my own term for the sort of narration that I used in *Tamarisk Row*. I call it considered narration. It might be said of some works of fiction that they bring to life certain characters. I would hope that the text of *Tamarisk Row* could be said to have brought to life the fictional personage responsible for it: the narrator through whose mind the text is reflected.

Some persons have supposed that the image on the dust-jacket of the first hard-cover edition of *Tamarisk Row* shows a part of the planet Earth. In fact, the image is of a part of the surface of a coloured glass marble. It was not my decision to have on the dust-jacket of my first book of fiction an image of a glass object the defining features of which lie within the object. And yet, I believe no image could have been more apt. The text of *Tamarisk Row* may seem to a hasty reader to be an account of so-called actual events on the surface of a well-known planet, but my hope was always, from the time nearly fifty years ago when I made my first notes, that an appreciative reader of my book would seem to be viewing fictional scenes and personages as though through coloured glass.

The text of the first edition of *Tamarisk Row* contained several misprints, and these have been corrected for the new edition. As well, the last two sections of the book have been restored to their original positions. 'The Gold Cup race is run' is now at the very end, where I had always intended it to be. The editor of the first edition insisted that the book should not end with the account of the race. I, still unpublished, meekly gave way to her.

Over the years, several readers have told me that they consider 'The Gold Cup race is run' an example of so-called stream-of-consciousness prose. It is no such thing. What is

9

now the last section of the book consists of five very long compound sentences, each comprising a main clause and numerous subordinate clauses, together with a description of part of a horse-race. These six items are interwoven, so to speak. The first sentence begins; soon afterwards the second sentence begins; later the third begins, and after it the fourth followed by the fifth. Finally, the race-commentary begins. Soon afterwards, the first sentence continues, only to be interrupted by the continuation of the second sentence, followed by the continuation of the third sentence, and so on. In due course, the five sentences come to an end, one after another. The race-commentary, however, does not quite come to an end. The very last words of the book are the words of the race-caller as the field of horses approaches the winning post.

*GERALD MURNANE, 2007*

# TAMARISK ROW

## CLEMENT KILLEATON LOOKS AT A CALENDAR

On one of the last days of December 1947 a nine-year-old boy named Clement Killeaton and his father, Augustine, look up for the first time at a calendar published by St Columban's Missionary Society. The first page of the calendar is headed *January 1948* and has a picture of Jesus and his parents resting on their journey from Palestine to Egypt. Below the picture, the page is divided by thick black lines into thirty-one yellow squares. Each of the squares is a day all over the plains of northern Victoria and over the city of Bassett where Clement and his parents set out and return home across the orange quartzy gravel of footpaths and the black strips of bitumen in the centres of streets, only seldom remembering that high over a landscape of bright patterns of days the boy-hero of their religion looks out across journeys of people the size of fly-specks across paper the colour of sunlight in years he can never forget.

## BASSETT HEARS MUSIC FROM AMERICA

While the calendar for 1947 hangs out of sight beneath the new one, Clement Killeaton lifts a sheaf of pages and sees in the yellow squares the familiar shape of late-afternoon sunlight that he crosses to reach Mr Wallace's corner store. All around the blistered weatherboards of the Wallaces' shop and attached house are brightly painted signs whose consistent colours and unwavering lines are the work of a people who live far away beyond the blur of dust or haze at the farthest end of Killeaton's street, in the labyrinthine mansions with peacock-studded lawns that slope down towards dark-blue ponds. There in a room with enormous windows a man with a polka-dotted bow tie broadcasts radio programs to listeners all over the plains of northern Victoria, telling them about America where people are still celebrating the end of the war. He plays for his listeners a record that has just arrived in Australia. The last words of the song are – *in the hills of Idaho in the hills of Idaho.* While the record is still playing, the man walks to a window through which someone, perhaps an American soldier, once looked out, across a great distance, towards a few faint ridges of the real Idaho. Tears fill the man's eyes. When the music stops, thousands of people in Bassett and the country for miles around hear him blowing his nose and clearing his throat.

## THE WALLACES' MARVELLOUS AVIARY

Clement opens the door of the grocer's shop and almost catches Mr Wallace doing something shameful behind a stack of biscuit-tins. The boy buys groceries for his mother and then asks politely may he look at Mr Wallace's aviary. The man shows him out through the back door. Past the crates of empty soft-drink bottles and the brittle tops of dead spear-grass are the towering walls of fine wire-netting. Behind the wire the dense shrubs and trees are planted in the shape of landscapes from every part of Australia. Hidden among the grasslands and scrub and forests and swamps and deserts are the nests of nearly every species of Australian bird. Somewhere past the dangling black and yellow of regent honeyeaters and the elusive crimson and turquoise of paradise parrots Margaret Wallace, a girl no older than Clement, is building a bower like the satin bowerbird's – a velvety resting-place enclosing more secrets than any dome-shaped nest of wrens or burrow of pardalotes but open to the sky so that whatever is done within its walls will be remembered as happening by sunlight. But Clement is not able to search for the place. Behind him in the yard Margaret Wallace calls out to him to visit her in her playhouse made of boxes and cardboard. She sits under the sign *Old Dutch Cleaner Chases Dirt*, cramming into her mouth the lollies she has stolen from her father's shop. Clement peers through the door into the dim playhouse. He still hopes that one day the two of them will pull down each other's pants and stare at each other in a secluded place like an aviary. Margaret is more friendly than on other days. She offers him humbugs, musks, and Tarzan jubes. Her hands are brightly stained and sticky with sugar. Clement asks her has she noticed any birds mating and breeding in the aviary lately, but Margaret wants to talk about how soon her parents will have saved enough money to buy a house in a better part of Bassett and get away from their shop.

## CLEMENT BUILDS A RACECOURSE

One Saturday morning in 1946 when the unsteady posts and rusted wire-netting of the lean-to back veranda at 42 Leslie Street are buried deep beneath a blue hill of wistaria blossoms, Clement Killeaton walks out through the back door and begins to collect small twigs and chips from all round the yard. When he has gathered a small bundle he takes them to the space between the lavatory and the lilac tree. Kneeling, he uses the sides of his hands to level and smooth the fine dirt and gravel.

With a piece of brick he hammers the first of the tiny lengths of wood upright into the hard earth. By lunchtime he has marked out an elliptical shape with two straight sides. After lunch he surrounds this with a second circuit of little posts parallel to the first. Late in the afternoon he searches for a longer, regular piece of wood. He chooses one of several likely pieces and drives it firmly into the ground at one end of the straight sides, between two posts of the inner series. As the shadows of the dense suckers of lilac reach the far side of his cleared space, Clement forms loose dirt into a long low mound beside the straight that is marked by the one taller post. Just before his mother calls him inside for the night he scratches with his fingernails in the hard-packed earth at the edge of his cleared place, shaping the first few yards of a road that will lead from the racecourse under the lilac tree, by way of leisurely loops and confusing junctions, past many unkempt shrubs and through tangles of weeds to the farthest corner where the tamarisks lean. He gouges out something that he thinks at first is a lump of gravel. It proves to be a whole round marble that must have been lying in the ground since before the Killeatons came to live in Leslie Street. While Clement is washing the marble at the gully trap, his mother calls him in for tea. He asks who might have owned the marble. She supposes that some boy who lived there before Clement must have lost it or just left it outside and forgotten it until the rain or the dust came and covered it up for all those years. Clement takes the marble to the kitchen window and holds it up against the setting sun. Far away in the heart of a silvery-white skein that seems to have no beginning and no end is an orange or scarlet glow. Next morning Clement shows the marble to one of the Glasscock boys from next door. The boy says – yes I remember that alley all right – it belongs to Frankie Silverstone the big kid that used to live here before you shifted here – he used to have hundreds of precious alleys and that one was his favourite – if you give it to me I'll ask my mum where the Silverstones shifted to and post it to Frankie. Clement refuses to hand over the marble, but because he is frightened that Silverstone may hear about it he lets the Glasscock boy choose ten alleys to keep in return for saying no more about the one that turned up in the yard. Clement spends a long time near the lilac tree, wondering which parts of his yard he ought to build his roads across in the hope of turning up more marbles on the way from the racecourse to the tamarisks.

## THE PEOPLE BENEATH THE TAMARISKS LIVE FOR RACING

One hot day after his racecourse has been built, Clement walks across his backyard towards the corner where the tall horny trunks of the tamarisks curve upwards from lumpy boles. On the lee side of the very last tamarisk, Clement conceals one of the farmhouses he has prepared for the owners of racehorses. The people who first settled years ago on that farm chose the row of tamarisks because someone had told them how of all trees that are famous for their hardiness the tamarisk can endure the fiercest heat and the driest desert soils, and how people who are setting out to cross desert country always know that when they have passed the last tamarisks they are entering the most desolate land of all. The lonely place beneath the tamarisks is the farthest of all farms from the racecourse. The husband and wife who live there look up every day at the brittle green spikes that give no shade or the pink wisps of blossom that they sometimes mistake for dust drifting in from the reddish land farther out. They remember how their grandparents, who must have travelled over great distances, stopped at last at a place from which their children and grandchildren could still look further out but only towards a place that they dared not settle in. If the children and grandchildren wanted to go to live in places even lonelier than the land of the tamarisks, they would have to retrace the journeys of their ancestors, hoping to discover pockets of desert or bush that the first travellers did not notice or perhaps a district that they crossed and marked with roads but which has since been neglected or forgotten and lapsed back into a wilderness. On the walls of their lounge-room are coloured photographs of the finishes of races. In one photograph a powerful black stallion thrusts his massive head with gaping nostrils and unseeing eyes out from between a bunch of brown and chestnut geldings. High above a confused mass of coloured silken jackets and caps the right arm of the rider of the black horse is raised in what might be a gesture of triumph. The green silk of the sleeve has fallen away from the man's frail wrist. Gripped between his knuckles is a thin whip of dark leather that has curled itself backwards into a perfect arc. The writing under the picture explains that *Journey's End*, a black horse six years old, was beaten by half a head in the Gold Cup of that year. Late on a summer afternoon the parish priest knocks at the door. Although the day is hot and the house is almost wholly hidden by trees and hedges, the husband and wife are both decently dressed. To show that they have nothing to hide the man lets the priest in at once. The three people soon begin to talk about racing. The married couple tell the priest about the horse named after their prop-erty Tamarisk Row. He is the son of the old unlucky stallion *Journey's End* and they are training him carefully in secret for this year's Gold Cup. The priest reminds them that racing is neither good nor bad, that it neither pleases nor angers God to look down and see His children spending all their time and money in planning to win a big race, that racing is only sinful when people are not content with the joy of seeing their horse get up in a close finish but use their winnings for other pleasures like eating and drinking huge meals in expensive hotels and night clubs or undressing their girlfriends or boyfriends in luxurious houses bought from the proceeds of successful plunges. The husband and wife assure the priest that they take their pleasure only from the racing itself. The husband even suggests that a married couple might get more joy from sharing in the ownership of a promising galloper than from any other pleasure of marriage, but the priest thinks that this would be giving to racing more importance than it really has in God's plan for the world.

### AUGUSTINE REMEMBERS HIS FOREFATHERS

Every afternoon hundreds of years ago a gentle breeze blows misty rain across the many chimneys of the great house whose shape is beginning to fade at last from the silver watch-case in the leather stud-box in Augustine Killeaton's wardrobe. Augustine's grandfather arrives in Melbourne from Ireland and travels northwards until he reaches a town where the afternoon sun is an awesome orange colour behind the dust from the goldfields. Drunken Scotsmen and scheming Englishmen trick him out of his money just before he dies in a town the miners are leaving for other places where the veins of gold run more truly. Augustine's father straightens his back and looks across grey-green paddocks in south-western Victoria and watches Irish rain drifting in from the ocean. He quarries pale sandstone from a coastal hill and builds within sight of the cliffs that are the southern boundary of his farm a large house whose front gable is copied from one wing of the house in Ireland that his father was supposed to have lived in. Augustine Killeaton at the age of twenty-five still lives in the Western District where he was born. He works on his father's farm on the coast near Kurringbar. He has never tasted strong drink or wanted a girl or been on a racecourse. Each summer when the first north winds arrive he plans a journey in the only direction that has ever attracted him – north across the miles of grazing lands, then past the sheep and wheat districts, and last through the dusty Mallee to the great inland zone that is coloured orange-red on maps. One morning Augustine sets out to see the annual Cup meeting at the Kurringbar racecourse. All the way from his father's farm to the races he sits tensely in the windy back seat of a neighbour's motorcar, fingering the leafless trees around the silvery house that his ancestors might have gambled away.

## AUGUSTINE MEETS A PROFESSIONAL PUNTER

After the Kurringbar Cup has been run, many of the dairy-farmers from outlying districts quietly leave the course to be home in time for the evening milking. Augustine Killeaton stays on at the races. His brothers, who have never been to a race-meeting, have agreed to let him off the milking in return for a shilling each from Augustine's share of the wages that their father pays them all each month. Augustine's racing bank for the day is five pounds, all saved from his wages for months past. He makes no effort himself to pick winners, but follows unobtrusively a small group of men from Melbourne. The Kurringbar Cup meeting has attracted many Melbourne stables and their followers, but Augustine has singled out one little band of punters as the smartest of all. He tries to master their trick of whispering a bet to a bookmaker and then melt-ing into the crowd to avoid being noticed, and he admires their way of watching each race impassively while the crowds around them yell and gesticulate. After the last race Augustine has won nearly fifteen pounds, while the Melbourne punters have won hundreds between them. Augustine walks boldly up to the leader of the band and introduces himself. The punter shakes hands coolly and says his name is Len Goodchild. Augustine says – I was wondering Mr Goodchild Len if I could be of any use to you and your friends as an agent at Western District meetings. Goodchild thanks him and says – see me some Saturday at the races in Melbourne. As he walks away, Augustine hears two of Goodchild's men talking. The men call Goodchild the Master. That night when his brothers ask him about the races, Augustine says – I won a few pounds myself but the Master told me he won a couple of hundred.

## AUGUSTINE REACHES BASSETT BY
## WAY OF INLAND AUSTRALIA

Augustine visits Melbourne and stands at a discreet distance from Goodchild in the betting ring at Mentone. Goodchild beckons him over and pencils a few faint crosses in Augustine's racebook. One of the marked horses wins. On the following Saturday Goodchild questions Augustine until he satisfies himself that Augustine is not connected with any other racing men in Melbourne or the Western District. A few days later at a country meeting Goodchild asks Augustine to stay out of the betting ring all day because a man that even Goodchild sometimes takes orders from is going to surprise the bookmakers with a cash plunge and the sight of Goodchild's men in the ring might give the game away. Augustine realises he is being tested. He stays all day in the bar sipping lemonade. After the races Goodchild offers him a seat in his car. The other men in the car talk of the hundreds they won that day. Augustine admits to them that he won nothing but he knows he is now one of Goodchild's men. For two years Augustine lives in boarding houses in Melbourne and goes to the races sometimes two or three times a week. About once a month he helps Goodchild to place a commission and the book-makers accept his bets on credit because they know he is one of Goodchild's men. At other times he backs the horses that Goodchild assures him are fancied by their connections. On mornings when there are no track gallops to watch, Augustine goes to Mass and communion at St Francis' church in the city. He spends his evenings alone and tells people he has no time to be interested in women. He knows that Goodchild and at least two others of his men are bachelors who still live with their parents. One day Goodchild introduces Augustine to a beautiful young woman who has just become his fiancée. Augustine goes back to Kurringbar for a few days to make sure that his father and brothers do not need his help on the farm. His brothers are surprised that he has managed to live off the races for two years and save nearly a hundred pounds as well. Augustine travels north. One hot day he approaches a small town in the Victorian Mallee. Dazzling silver-white wheat silos rise out of a lake of heat haze. On the edge of the town is a racecourse. The north wind from the far inland flattens the tawny grass between the white-railed fences. Augustine decides that even if his travels lead to nothing he can at least look forward to a day when he arrives at an unsuspecting town with a horse of his own in the float behind his car and a roll of banknotes in his pocket, and goes home again that evening hundreds of pounds richer. He does not know what the name of the town will be, but the horse will be named Silver Rowan after the most conspicuous tree in the pale dripping garden of a mansion that might have belonged to the Killeaton family. A few years later Augustine returns to Victoria from the north.

22

He crosses twenty or thirty miles of plains scarcely different from those that he has crossed for years past. Then he reaches the city of Bassett. He is still nearly 200 miles from his home in the Western District and he knows no one in Bassett. He sends a telegram to someone in the Riverina district of New South Wales. A week later a three-year-old gelding arrives at the Bassett railway station, consigned to Mr Gus Killeaton. The horse from the north and the man from the Western District walk along the unfamiliar gravel footpaths of Bassett towards the loose-box that Augustine Killeaton has rented from a man recommended by the parish priest of St Boniface's. Augustine finds a job as assistant farm manager at a mental home and decides to stay in Bassett until his horse wins a race and earns him enough to return home. He registers the horse's name as Clementia because he is grateful to God for bringing him back alive from the north. He saves the name Silver Rowan for years to come, when he can afford to buy a well-bred yearling from some stud in New South Wales or Queensland. Whenever he looks at Clementia's golden-brown eyes, Augustine remembers obscure stopping-places on his journey north and counts himself lucky that at least he has a young racehorse to show for all his years away from home.

### CLEMENTIA WINS A MAIDEN HANDICAP

Golden balls of dung splash in the dust. A few children stop and stare. Augustine Killeaton, a young man and not yet married, stops and waits while his small black gelding drops his turds in the exercise yard of the Bassett racecourse. Then he bends over and looks into the cracks that have opened in the four flattened spheres. As far as he can see into its bright depths the dung is crisp and fibrous. He reads the dense yellow strands as a sign that the horse is much fitter than even he, the owner-trainer, has suspected. Augustine hands the bridle to his friend Norman Brady who goes on leading the horse quietly round the exercise path. Augustine moves nimbly into the crowd around the bookmakers' stands. He takes out of his pocket two ten-pound notes, which is all the money he has with him. He asks one of the rails bookmakers for five pounds each way Clementia at 25 to 1. He puts the betting ticket and his remaining note into his pocket and turns towards the saddling paddock. One of the last bookmakers that he passes has Clementia at 33 to 1 win only. Augustine asks for the odds to five pounds. With his change of five pounds in his hand he pushes back into the crowd, looking up at each bookmaker's board. Smartly-dressed commissioners, many of them from Melbourne stables, keep up a barrage of bets on the short-priced horses. Augustine hears not one bet laid against his own horse. He finds another board showing 33 to 1 win only and hands over his last note. He waits to see the bookmaker wrench the knob beside the name Clementia. When the man turns the horse's odds down to 16 to 1 Augustine walks proudly away pretending not to notice that a few people are looking curiously at him. He collects the horse and tells Norman Brady that he only had a few bob on him because the odds were so tempting but that he still doesn't think he'll stand a chance having his first start in a race against a smart field of maidens, some of them well backed with Melbourne money. In the mounting yard he looks between the huddles of owners and trainers and jockeys for Harold Moy. A voice says – here we are Gus. Augustine turns and sees the little man with Chinese features standing conspicuously alone. Augustine and his jockey stand close together looking silently at Clementia's legs. Augustine says – you know all about him Harold and his weak legs – I have to try all the time with him in case he breaks down for good – I've specked

24

him at bolter's odds so you'd better ride him right out if he looks like he's got any sort of a chance – still if he doesn't go well in the first couple of furlongs drop him right out – there'll always be some little race up north somewhere that we can save him for one day. Harold says – I'll look after him Gus – I won't knock him around. As Augustine hoists him into the saddle Harold whispers – I made my wife have three quid on him at thirty-threes – that's what some of them were betting you know. Augustine says – I know – I got a little bit of it myself. His hand brushes Harold's yellow hairless hand and without thinking he squeezes the little man's fingers and pats his smooth wrist. Harold screws up his eyes and looks out at the straight where some of the other horses are already cantering past. Augustine walks alone through the whispering secretive knots of owners and trainers and out of the yard. He finds a place on the crowded slope overlooking the straight and stares towards the line of trees at the far side of the arid racecourse. The whole of the great bare elliptical course wavers in the heat. A bunch of horses crowds against the barrier strands, and the starter pulls his cord. Several horses wheel or shy and miss the start hopelessly. Augustine deliberately sets the muscles around his mouth and scans the field for a sight of Clementia. He looks first at the stragglers then at the main bunch. Near the middle of the field Clementia's colours, emerald green, silver-grey hoops, orange cap, catch his eye. The horse is moving at least as freely as any other. The field bunches on the sharp home turn. Clementia's colours are lost in the ruck. The leader begins to tire. Challengers emerge from the pack. Two horses draw clear. Their riders swing their whips awkwardly and desperately. A confused roar or scream goes up from the crowd as the leaders draw level with the grandstand. Augustine presses his lips together. Absurdly wide on the hard almost grassless track, Clementia feels soft well-watered turf beneath his frail legs.

Harold Moy throws himself prostrate in the saddle. His legs twitch frantically behind him. The crowd still screams at the two leaders. Augustine Killeaton does not open his mouth. Clementia passes him, almost up against the outside rail, with little more than the orange cap visible between the heads of the crowd. The leaders pass the post. Clementia is out of sight under the judge's box. The spectators argue among themselves. No one is sure which horse has won. Some people did not even notice Clementia. A number is hauled up over the judge's box. The name Clementia travels fitfully through the crowd. The people around Augustine pronounce it wrongly. Augustine strolls calmly back to the mounting yard and leans on the rails of the winner's stall. The steward has to glance at his racebook to discover Augustine's name. He calls out – A. C. Killeaton owner trainer isn't it? Augustine nods. Some of the other owners and trainers look hard at Killeaton. He keeps his eyes on the gate through which the clerk of the course is leading Clementia. Harold Moy in green and silver does not smile. One or two people in the crowd clap briefly. Augustine takes the bridle, and Harold slides down from the saddle. He whispers – I'm sorry Gus sorry – I should have known how good he was – Jesus if only we'd known we could have been set up for life. Harold goes off to the scales. Augustine notices a swelling on the horse's weakest leg. Clementia limps a little on his way back to the stalls. Norman Brady comes running up. He says – Gus Gus it's a tragedy – I had thirty bob each way on him – we'll never get a chance like that again as long as we live. Augustine points to the horse's leg and says – we mightn't even get another race out of him. Norman takes the proppy horse back to his stall. Augustine finds the first of his three bookmakers. The clerk takes his ticket and counts out 166 pounds 5 shillings. Augustine stuffs the notes into his trousers pocket and keeps his hand around them. He collects from the other two men and then walks to the galvanised-iron lavatory away from the hum of the crowd. He goes into a cubicle and leans against the door. He counts his money slowly and whispers aloud – 506 pounds 5 shillings. He divides it into two rolls and puts one in each side pocket. He sits down heavily on the toilet seat and starts to make the sign of the cross but instead leans forward and pumps his clenched fists backwards and forwards through the air ahead of him, hissing through his teeth as Harold Moy does when he rides a horse out. He pumps with his hands and jerks his knees until suddenly he sobs just once and a shudder crosses his body. Then he gets to his feet, sets his face into its usual shape, touches the pockets where his money is, and goes outside. That evening, when Augustine and Norman walk the horse down the ramp behind Brady's truck they find him lame and stumbling. Later Augustine visits the untidy weatherboard house on the edge of Bassett where Jean Glossop lives with her parents. A racehorse snorts and scrapes in its straw in a loose-box beneath pepper trees at one end of a trampled dirty yard beside the house. Joe Glossop and his wife only nod to Augustine when he walks into the kitchen where they sit around their wireless set. Jean Glossop takes Augustine out to sit on the broken cane sofa on the front veranda. He tells her the story of the maiden handicap. He persuades her that they now have more than enough money to get married on, even after he has paid his feed bills for Clementia and a few other odd debts to Norman Brady and a bookmaker here and there. They decide to arrange for their wedding as soon as Jean has finished her instructions in the Catholic faith and been baptised. They walk past the horses' sheds and into the small paddock which is all of her father's property. Near a horse trough overhung by faintly rattling kurrajong trees they sit down on short dry grass. Crickets cry not far away. Scattered street lights shine through distant motionless trees. Jean Glossop stretches herself flat on the ground. Augustine half crouches, half lies above her. He has waited for years for an event like this and he cannot believe that these few moments on this unheralded evening may be his best chance yet. There is not time to wonder why it is this night and these few yards of meagre grass rather than one of those many other afternoons on deserted grasslands when he might have made elaborate plans for a triumph that was a fitting reward for all his years of afternoons that came to nothing. The shapes around him threaten to sweep past. When it seems almost too late he throws himself forward and lies like Harold Moy on Clementia, thrusting his hands and knees towards the noise of the crickets. He sees no more of the post as he passes than a blur of white among a throng of his rivals. There is no one to tell him whether or not he has got up to win. He knows that even if he has brought it off he will wonder for years about that other race that was going to bring him all that he could want.

## AUGUSTINE BECOMES A HUSBAND AND FATHER

Each weekend Augustine takes Jean Glossop to the local presbytery to be instructed in the Catholic faith. In the last week before she is to be baptised he takes Clementia to the Bassett racecourse at daybreak for his first hard gallop since he broke down after his win in the maiden plate. Clementia tries to jump the long wide shadow of a clump of trees at the back of the course and breaks a leg. Augustine runs to the course ranger's house and brings back a rifle and shoots dead the horse that raced only once for one great win. Harold Moy struggles to unfasten the bridle and saddle from the dead body. Augustine puts one arm around the man's thin shoulders. Harold says – now we'll never know what he might have been Gus – what he might have done for us. Augustine says – I'll take home the bridle and gear at least and keep it hanging in his loose-box – you never know – we might get another one half as good as him one day. After Jean is baptised she tells Augustine she feels as if she has a new body of creamy-yellow silk that no one has ever seen or touched. Before she makes her first confession she tells him she might be going to have a baby after what they did that night when Clementia had just won his race, which was the only time they committed that sin together. He explains to her how they can use each day of their married life to do small penances for their past mistakes and to earn treasures of grace for the future. He plans to have a horse in training always. He will potter around the backyard carrying buckets of oats and forkfuls of straw, whistling softly between his teeth to coax the horse to pee or leaning on railings for hours in the quiet sunshine far from the crowds and the dust of racecourses, knowing that each little task in his backyard is one small step towards another day like Clementia's day at the Bassett racecourse. He will hang the photograph of Clementia's win in the lounge-room. Jean has already bought for the bedroom the picture that she loves of Our Lord in red and white robes with his satiny sacred heart bleeding where the thorns made by sins of impurity have pierced it. When they kneel together at the altar-rails on her first communion day he asks God to help him explain to her something about the long journeys that have made his life so different from other men's and the wide strange places that he may still have to go on looking for even after they are married and he has explored all over her body, and to make her patient and strong enough to live in a cheap rented weatherboard house while her husband waits for a message from the inner circle of professional punters in Melbourne or lays his own careful plans for a fierce plunge at long odds on a distant windy racecourse. A few weeks before their marriage they buy some cheap new furniture for a house that they plan to rent in a newer part of Bassett. There is still plenty left of the hundreds of pounds that Augustine won on Clementia. Augustine has a long talk by telephone with Len Goodchild in Melbourne. He tells Len about the wedding and says what a good thing it would be if he could have a decent win to give him a start as a married man. Len tells him about a horse that his men are going to back in Melbourne. Without worrying Jean about it, Augustine takes a hundred pounds from the bank and puts it on the horse. It leads almost to the post, but a lightly-weighted horse that Augustine himself has seen racing around the Bassett district gets up and beats it. There is still enough money left for Jean and Augustine to spend a week in Melbourne after the wedding. They go to Mass and communion every morning at St Francis' church. Each of them buys a candle and lights it and sets it among the blazing rows on the brass stand. Jean whispers that now she is a proper Catholic they can go to the same heaven at last. Augustine asks her what she thinks heaven will be like. She says – there's a huge staircase or a sort of grandstand on a steep hill that shines like brass or gold and after that a wide smooth place like a green carpet where we'll all wear colours like priests' vestments. Augustine watches his candle on the blazing ridge. Its flame flickers and falters but somehow keeps going while others that were lit later die down and go out. Outside the church he tells Jean that even his candle gave the others a start and went on to win at long odds. On their last day in Melbourne Jean asks to go to the races just for a day's fun. She reminds her husband that she has never once been to a race-meeting. Augustine politely refuses to go and explains that the races are a waste of time and money unless you go to back a horse that you know something about or to see your own colours carried in a race. Soon after Clement Killeaton is born his father decides to move to a cheaper rented house. His wife urges him to ask Len Goodchild or his other old friends in Melbourne for a small loan so that they need not leave their comfortable house. Augustine tells her that although he mixes with Goodchild and his men on the racecourse, it may be years before they admit him to their inner circle. These are the men who share his joys and sorrows. Augustine supposes that these men might ask each other for a loan sometimes when things are tough, but he tells his wife she must never talk like that again about loans as if her husband's racing colleagues are just a bunch of mates dipping into each other's pockets.

## SILVER ROWAN WINS A GREAT RACE

When Clement Killeaton is five years old his parents visit a doctor in Melbourne to see why they have had no more children. One afternoon while his wife and son are shopping in Melbourne, Augustine visits Len Goodchild and asks the Master to keep an eye out for a horse that Augustine can buy cheaply and race around Bassett. He tells Goodchild he will phone him each week from Bassett to keep in touch like the old days. As soon as he is back in Bassett, Augustine waits until his wife and son are out for the day. He locks the front and back doors of his house and pulls down the blinds against the late afternoon sun. He takes off his shirt and singlet and puts on the green and silver racing colours and takes a whip in his hand. He gathers the pillows from Clement's bed and the spare bed and heaps them on the double bed where he and his wife sleep. He forms the pillows into the broad powerful back and the rump and withers of a racehorse. He rides his mount out of the barrier with the whip to show it who is master. At almost every stride during the long race he has to urge the horse with his heels and elbows. As they near the turn Augustine glances back and sees the moist green shape of Ireland already far away. The straight leads past a coast of high cliffs in western Victoria. When he looks for the winning post the rider sees instead the raggedly forested hills around Bassett. As soon as the field straightens up he begins to swing his whip with an emphatic rhythm that matches the horse's galloping action. Again and again he brings it down with all the force of his arm onto his mount's hindquarters. He hears distinctly among the roars of the crowd the voices of people he once knew. One stride past the post he collapses, gasping and sweating, on the horse's neck. Someone calls out that Silver Rowan has done it again at last. Someone else says – that's the same trainer who once had a champion called Clementia but the horse broke down before he had a chance to prove himself. A crowd of thousands looks up at the winning jockey who has just ridden the race of his life but who, as he leads the field back to scale, affects a look of dignified sorrow to suggest that this race has only brought him back to square after many years of narrow unlucky defeats and that the people he wanted most to see his triumph are far away.

### STERNIE NAMED FOR A MIGHTY PUNTER

For nearly four years after Silver Rowan's great win, Augustine spends nearly every Saturday at a race-meeting, sometimes in the Bassett district but more often in Melbourne backing horses that Len Goodchild recommends. From time to time Goodchild says to him – I haven't forgotten I'm supposed to find you a horse of your own Gus, and Augustine says – all in your own good time Len – I can wait. Then, one afternoon in 1947 Goodchild takes him to the backyard of a strange house in Caulfield and offers to sell him for next to nothing a big ungainly chestnut gelding named Sternie that is still a maiden. Augustine agrees and says he will take the horse back to Bassett, give him a long spell, and then try to win a race with him at some weak northern meeting. Then he asks about the gelding's history. Goodchild looks round to make sure that they are alone and tells him a little about Mr Sternberg. In a suburb of Melbourne where people walking along the footpaths can only guess what a great blank expanse of windows lies hidden behind the massed foliage of shrubs and trees, lives a Jew named Hyman Sternberg whom Augustine has never met. Augustine has occasionally seen a pudgy man in a crumpled suit talking to Goodchild at the races, but he has never dared to ask Goodchild afterwards whether the pale man was the Jew that they sometimes speak about. Mr Sternberg hardly ever goes to the races. Two or three times a year Augustine hears a whisper among his racing friends that the Jew is coming to back a certain horse. The horse is always a short-priced favourite but the Jew reckons that any price is a good price about a certainty. Someone says that Mr Sternberg hates going to country race-meetings because he feels uncomfortable away from the few miles of suburbs where he travels between his home and the factory that he owns. Only the greatest of certainties tempts him away from Melbourne, and then he sits well away from the windows in the back seat of someone else's car glancing almost fearfully at the harsh paddocks and scrub that keep slinking past and taking up a position between him and the city. Augustine has spent years getting to know Len Goodchild, but much of the Master's life is still a mystery. One of the things that Augustine never discovers is just how Goodchild is connected with men like Sternberg. Augustine is sure that the Jew is far more powerful and cunning even than Goodchild but Sternberg belongs to a secret inner part of the racing world where Augustine might never be admitted. The Jew boasts for years that he will never own a racehorse because it is cheaper to back other men's horses, but at last after a run of successful bets he buys a well-bred yearling. Even before the horse starts in a race Sternberg decides that it is not worth keeping and sells it, not caring in the least that he will never have the pleasure of seeing his own colours carried on a race-course – a pleasure that thousands of other people cheerfully pay hundreds of pounds to enjoy. The man who buys the horse is an acquaintance of Goodchild, one of what he calls his outer circle, but does not understand how secretive even those men have to be and how closely they must guard their privacy. The new owner thinks it is a good joke to name the horse Sternie after Mr Sternberg. Goodchild does not smile as he tells Augustine how angry Mr Sternberg was to think that even that much of his name would be printed in racebooks for people to stare at, how he cursed the horse and its new owner and said he hoped the vucking mongrel would never win a race, and how so far the curse seems to have worked because the horse Sternie is still a maiden. Augustine laughs and says – there are dozens of small races up north that he could win – curse or no curse. Every morning before daylight he trots the horse behind his bike for a couple of miles. Once a week he takes him to the racecourse and Harold Moy gives him a fast gallop. Every afternoon after work he leads the awkward chestnut for miles through the least-frequented streets around the edges of Bassett. The sun goes down and the inland frost gathers over the city, but Augustine keeps on walking. He plans to give Sternie two races and to get Harold Moy to keep him so far back each time that the northern district bookmakers and punters come to think of Sternie as a hopeless hack that someone races just for the fun of it. A stranger stops to admire the horse Sternie as Augustine leads him back towards Leslie Street. The stranger asks – what's his name mate? Without stopping, Killeaton says – Silver Rowan.

## AUGUSTINE HAS A BAD DAY AT FLEMINGTON

Early on Saturday morning Clement meets Augustine bringing Sternie through the front gate after his exercise. The boy asks his father – will Sternie have a race today? Augustine says – he's not ready to start in a race yet – I have to make sure he's properly fit before I give him his first big race. Then the man hurries inside and puts on his best suit and prepares to go by train to the Melbourne races. On the evening train from Melbourne back to Bassett Augustine sits in a corner of a crowded second-class compartment. He peers through the window at the shapes of the sparse northern forests that gallop past in vying packs and straggling files, still far from home in some interminable race. A half-drunk man talks loudly about his big win at Flemington that day and asks Augustine if he went to the races too. Augustine says – I'm sorry mate but I don't know the first thing about racing. At the Bassett station Augustine finds a seat in a crowded taxi. A man in the front seat asks to go to Americans' Gully. The car travels through deserted city streets between cumbrous facades of shops and hotels that were built seventy years before, when Bassett was being hollowed underneath by the tunnels of gold-mines that are now abandoned. Near Americans' Gully the shapes of mullock heaps blot out whole fields of stars above the rows of old flimsy cottages that were first built for renting to the miners. The passenger opens the front gate and steps straight onto the veranda of his house. The taxi skirts the city by way of the shuttered windows and leaning balconies of Chinatown and then heads vaguely towards Leslie Street through streets where on even unimportant corners there are small squat hotels hardly bigger than the houses around them with only the word BAR glowing faintly green or orange against some covert light bulb to distinguish an occasional window. Killeaton tells the driver to stop in front of a row of small houses that were built with a few feet of front yard so that the clerks and shop assistants and tradesmen who first lived in them might plant a rose or a lilac between the parlour window and the picket fence. He finds his wife sitting by the stove in their kitchen. In his darkened bedroom Clement lies listening. Augustine refuses the meal that his wife has been keeping in the oven, and asks for just a cup of tea. He asks her – what did I tell you on Friday morning was the bet of the day at Flemington? She says – I'm sorry I can't remember. He says – you must remember – I should have written it down so I could show you now to prove it – anyway you can guess what happened – I started the day off badly but I'd fought my way back almost to square by the second-last race – Goodchild's men were pouring money on a thing I knew nothing about so of course I had to be with them. It was a good thing beaten if that's any consolation – well to cut a long story short I had just two quid left to put on Tamburlaine in the last – as I said on Friday morning it was the bet of the day – It won with its ears pricked but I still came away a few pounds down on the day instead of sticking to my own judgement and having a decent win. Mrs Killeaton asks – do you mind telling us how much we owe at the moment? Augustine says – I'm too sick and tired to work it out now. Then he explains that in future he will stay away from the Melbourne races unless he sees one good bet sticking out like Tamburlaine. He will concentrate on getting Sternie fit to win a small local race. The money that he saves by not chasing Goodchild's tips in

Melbourne will make a nice little stake to put on Sternie when he has his first try. Augustine finishes his cup of tea and walks up the passage whistling between his teeth. Clement throws himself around in bed, pretending he has only just woken up. Augustine comes in and asks the boy is he all right. Clement says – I was just wondering what will happen if Sternie never wins a race. Augustine sits on the edge of the bed and tells his son about a racecourse that encompasses all the folds of hills and prospects of plains that the boy has ever seen from high places in Bassett. At its farthest side there is still a horse, obscurely placed near the tail-end of a big field, whose rider has only just begun to urge it forward with tentative thrusts of his arms, and whose owner, if its long run from that seemingly hopeless position brings it home too late after all, will send it around still another course which reaches even farther back, whose far-flung curves and stupendous straights allow even the least likely straggler to come from behind and win, and where a race sometimes takes so long to be decided that many of the crowd who came to watch have left and are far away before the leaders come into view but the truest stayer will always win.

## CLEMENT FIGHTS THE SON OF A BOOKMAKER'S CLERK

One morning as Clement Killeaton hurries along McCracken's Road on his way to St Boniface's school an old man with a dirty beard rushes out towards him from the doorway of Corcorans' butcher shop. Clement turns and runs back towards the corner of Leslie Street. Warm urine sprinkles the inside of his thigh. He runs a few yards further and looks back. The old man is not chasing him. The boy walks the rest of the way home with his legs held wide apart. His mother gives him a clean pair of trousers and he sets out again for St Boniface's. He reaches the school gate with a few minutes to spare. He finds the boys from his grade all playing the game called snatchers. Sometimes they forget about snatchers for weeks on end until one morning before school a boy from Barry Launder's gang, which rules Clement's grade, cups his left hand over his cock and balls, runs silently at some boy who is staring in another direction, and with his right hand wrenches the fellow's balls until he screams and drags himself free. The boy who has been snatched puts his left hand over his smarting privates and runs at some other boy who has not yet realised that snatchers is on again. The boy who started it runs at someone else, and within a few minutes every boy in sight has one hand between his legs to guard himself while he creeps or sidles or dashes without warning towards someone whose left hand has strayed from its place. The game goes on all day. No boy dares to put his left hand on guard while a nun or a lady teacher is watching, but many a boy stands in line and marches into school with a hand poised high on his thigh ready to ward off the dreaded snatch between the legs from behind him, or the sudden attack from the boy in front who may wheel around when the teacher is not looking and snatch boldly in sight of the girls. Even in school the left hands are kept ready for the boy who saunters down the aisle as if to borrow a rubber but in fact to snatch under cover of the desk-tops. This morning a boy named Ronald Fitzgibbon sees Clement walking through the gate and calls out to him – look out for snatchers. Clement puts his left hand up at once and during the few minutes before the bell stays close to Fitzgibbon who seems to be the only boy he can trust not to snatch at him. When the bell rings, Clement is so fond of Ronald that he walks towards the assembly with his free right hand around the other boy's neck and shoulder in the way that best friends always walk in St Boniface's schoolground. Clement tells Ronald that he has a secret place under a lilac tree in his backyard and that Ronald can enjoy it too if he likes to visit the Killeatons' place after school. Then he tells Fitzgibbon how he wet his pants that morning. By now they are standing in line. Just before the nun blows her whistle for silence, Ronald Fitzgibbon turns around and whispers to the boy and girl behind him – pass it on – Killeaton piddled his pants this morning. They giggle and pass it on. The message travels down the line. Clement turns to Ronald Fitzgibbon and punches him hard on the jaw. Fitzgibbon punches Clement twice quickly about the nose and mouth. Clement feels blood flowing out of his nose. He howls loudly and the nun sees him. Some of the girls tell her which two boys were fighting. She promises to strap both boys as soon as everyone is inside and morning prayers are over. She tells another boy to take Clement to the taps and hold a wet hankie over his nose. At the taps the boy teases Clement about his wet pants. He puts his hand between Clement's legs. Clement fights him off, and the boy says – I wasn't snatching – I was only trying to feel the wet piddle. That night Clement tells his father that he has had a fight with the Fitzgibbon boy and lost. A few nights later Augustine says to his son – I've been making inquiries and it turns out that your mate Ronnie Fitzgibbon is the son of Jim Fitzgibbon the man who works for Horrie Attrill the big bookmaker – Mr Fitzgibbon and I had a good laugh together when I told him about your fight – I want you to shake hands like a man with little Ronnie when you see him tomorrow – you should know by now that all bookmakers and their men are our enemies but there's no harm in you inviting the boy home after school to play some afternoon as long as you never speak to him about racing or our horse Sternie or the racing men in Melbourne that you might hear me talking about sometimes.

## CLEMENT RACES THE STATE-SCHOOL BOYS

Clement's mother makes it a rule that the boy must be home from school by four o'clock every day. In the late afternoon, long after he has changed into his old patched pants and gone out into the yard to play until tea-time, Clement still sees groups of children dawdling along Leslie Street on their way home from school. The children stand staring into any yard where someone may have devised a game that lasts for more than a few minutes. The biggest boy from one straggling group unfastens the Killeatons' front gate and comes in to see what it is that keeps Clement contented for so long behind his cypress hedge. The others follow the boy through the gate. Margaret Wallace remains leaning on the front gate. One of the boys is her brother. Clement persuades the boys to call the worn dirt track around his house a racecourse for horses or men and the panel of greenish-gold glass in his front door that glows with late sunlight the winning post. He lines the boys up beside him and asks the girl standing beside Margaret to clap her hands and start the field on a race of twenty laps. Clement calls to the girls to keep a count of the laps and judge the finish, but they do not answer. The bigger boys sprint from the start and vie for the lead. They swing on the blistered posts of the veranda and tear off branches of twigs from bushes to stop themselves veering off the little circuit of their course. Clement drops far behind them, breathing easily and conserving his strength. He soon loses sight of the boys ahead. As he passes Margaret and the other girls he glances at their faces. They look with pity or contempt at the tail-ender. Clement still runs deliberately slowly. After two or three laps the girls are ready to give up watching the race. Clement tightens the muscles of his face and pumps his arms harder. He believes he is starting to gain on the leaders, who are still out of sight ahead. The girls suddenly seem interested again as they notice the outsider making his long slow run. Their faces show first sympathy and then admiration as Clement gains a few more yards during the next few laps. Soon afterwards the reckless leaders hurtle off the track and into the thick front hedge where they wrestle and tumble and laugh among the dust and dead twigs. Clement sets out on another lap but they order him to stop. One boy asks what the prize would have been anyway if they had bothered to keep going. Clement turns his back so the girls will not hear and whispers that he thought the winner might have been allowed to go down with one of the girls to the big drain under the McCracken's Road bridge on the way home from school next day and look at or touch or play with or tickle those white shapes of skin that he is sure the boys are always looking for on all their rambling walks after school among the dull front fences and pebbly footpaths. A boy tells Clement that that prize is no good because he and his gang have been coming home along the creek and through that drain for years now. The others are already tired of the Killeatons' yard. They peer out through the fence into Leslie Street. As they are all leaving, Clement calls Margaret Wallace back into the corner between the hedge and the fence. He makes a sign that he hopes will tell her he is still waiting every afternoon for her to come with him into some shady corner where they can pull down each other's pants. She tries to kick him in the shins and then runs off to catch up with the others. Clement is relieved to see that at least she does not tell them what he wants to do with her.

## CLEMENT CONCEALS TAMARISK ROW

Clement takes a week to establish a farmhouse and stables in every sheltered nook and neglected corner of his backyard. Then he spends several days collecting small stones of distinctive shapes and colours. To each farm he allots a certain number of stones. Every Wednesday and Sunday he reads the Sporting Globe newspaper after his father has finished it and chooses from it attractive names for horses. He writes names such as Gold Watch, Night Life, The Trapper, Icene, Scaramouche, Hiatus, Orthodox, and Rubantine in the back pages of an old exercise book. His mother discovers him writing names and snatches away his book and the racing paper. She tells him to stop playing racing games for good and to go outside and smash up the racecourse behind the lavatory and never to mention racing again to his father. He walks around the backyard, carefully concealing the farms and their stables and scraping with his bare feet to wipe out all trace of the roads that once connected those places to the racecourse. He takes the greatest care to hide the spacious house and the tree-lined paddocks in the corner beneath the ragged tamarisks. He pulls up the lines of tiny stakes around the racecourse but leaves for anyone to see the smooth paths of its straights and curves. His mother finds him loitering around the lilac tree and says she will buy him a packet of seeds so he can plant a little flower garden and water it himself where he tried to build an old racecourse. On a lonely road that is almost obscured by trees the priest stops to talk to the owner of Tamarisk Row. The priest says – I've decided that perhaps you shouldn't think about racing so much for a while – how about you and your wife forgetting about that big race you're always trying to win and ask God to give you a baby instead – and then when your little boy is growing up you can let him watch you training your horse and racing will be just good fun whether you win a big race or not.

## CLEMENT VISITS THE RIORDANS' PALATIAL HOME

On a Saturday morning late in 1947 Augustine takes Clement for a walk to the home of Stan Riordan, half a mile away on the edge of Bassett. After his father has gone inside to talk to Stan in his carpeted office, Clement wanders across a courtyard of flagstones on the cool southern side of the big stone house. Creepers with green leaves like drooping silk ribbons cover the trellis high above him. He enters a fernery with walls of damp logs and searches for a hidden doorway among the trembling fronds and the rigid pale-green spikes as dense as sheaves and behind the cascades of dark feathery stuff that spill down from hanging wire baskets. Outside the fernery he discovers behind a palisade of tall irises a fishpond overlaid with water-lilies. A green lattice tufted with moss bars his way and he turns back. He finds at last a path to the front garden, which is hidden from the road by a towering hedge of cypresses, green with a golden sheen all down it. An abrupt colonnade of pillars fluted with granular cream-coloured plaster draws him towards the front doors of the house. They are double doors with great panels of flawless glass and nothing visible behind them but the abundant folds and flounces of pale satin draperies. From behind him on the lawn come the sounds of girls' voices. He walks down resilient laneways between tall shrubs until he finds Therese Riordan, about twelve years old, and another girl of about the same age whom he does not know. The two girls are playing a game with small red and orange berries. They take no notice of Clement. Sometimes as they stand up to reach for more berries or fling themselves down on the deep cushion of buffalo grass Therese Riordan's skirt slips up high above her knees. When she is busy counting her berries she does not bother to pull it down to cover her thighs. Clement walks quickly round her but her pants are well hidden. The other girl guesses what Clement is looking for and reaches across to pull down Therese's skirt. Clement asks the name of their game, and Therese answers – how many eggs in the bush today. The other girl invites him to play it with them but he finds the rules too confusing to learn. They tell him to go away and come back when he can play properly. He finds his father and Stan Riordan talking earnestly together. Before they see the boy approaching they agree that Stan will lend Augustine fifty pounds and won't be in a hurry to get it back. Stan says – I'm genuinely surprised that you're in so deep with your bookmakers Gus and I wish you'd have come to me earlier about it – I always thought you were doing well with the information you got from that chap Goodchild and his team at Caulfield. Augustine sees Clement standing in the spacious shade of a loquat tree. He lowers his voice and says – they're having a lean trot at the moment Stan but they're still my best chance of getting out of trouble again. Augustine leads Clement down the front path past Therese and her friend who are looking down to discover how much of Therese's thigh the boy might have seen. Even before the boy and his father are outside the front gate the girls are playing with the berries again, hiding them behind their backs, guessing how many there are, prising open each other's fists to see them again, and laughing quietly about the true meaning of the handfuls of glossy red and gold fruits.

### CLEMENT AND AUGUSTINE TALK ABOUT MARBLES

One Saturday afternoon Augustine stays for a long time in one of his fowl sheds. Clement looks for him to ask why he is not listening to the Melbourne races. He finds his father sitting with one of his purebred Rhode Island Red pullets in his lap. Augustine stares vaguely ahead while he gropes with one hand between the bird's legs. If he can fit three fingers between the pelvic bones it is a sign that the pullet will soon begin to lay. When Clement asks him about the races he explains that he is thinking of giving up betting altogether and just keeping Sternie in training as a hobby. Clement tells how his mother has forbidden him to keep a racecourse behind the lilac tree. He asks his father may he start building one again because it is lonely in the backyard without some sort of racing each Saturday to train for. Augustine says – it might be an idea if you just played with your marbles behind the lilac – you could call the marbles men and race them in heats of the Stawell Gift – there isn't as much gambling on foot-running as horses and your mother mightn't be so upset if she sees you. Clement tells him about the strange marble that was buried under the racecourse and asks whether the boy Silverstone could have run races with his marbles when he lived there years ago. Augustine says he doesn't think so because not many boys nowadays are interested in professional running although a few years back you would often see a young chap marking out a track for starting practice in his backyard.

## TAMARISK ROW IS NARROWLY BEATEN

Clement takes his jar of coloured marbles to the place between the lilac tree and the lavatory where his racecourse once stood. He arranges a dozen marbles in a ragged line at the place where the six-furlongs barrier used to be. If his mother had not told him to destroy his racecourse he would have been able to close his eyes and push the marbles carefully around the track with his fingers to decide the Handicap Maiden Plate at a small inland town. But now that the fences of twigs are gone there is only a patch of gravelly Bassett soil to stare at while the story of the Maiden Plate unfolds. The owner of the property that lies out of sight beneath the far cloudy tamarisks fastens the door of the float behind his utility truck and kisses his wife goodbye. He reminds her that she has promised to walk around naked for an hour after Mass tomorrow if Tamarisk Row wins the Handicap Maiden Plate at a small town many miles inland. She smiles and says she will offer up a prayer for their horse when she hears from the wireless that the barrier is down. The man drives carefully for hours across plains and through infrequent towns. At noon he parks his truck and float in the shade of some untidy trees near the curve of white rails on the turn out of a straight. He meets his best friend who has travelled many miles to the course from another direction and gives him a thick roll of notes to put on Tamarisk Row. As the field walks out onto the track for the Maiden Plate the owner of Tamarisk Row sees how each set of coloured silks has been designed by the horse's owner and his wife or girlfriend to tell the story of their lives, to remind people of the hardships they once endured before they met each other and went to live among comfortable paddocks, or to hint at the peculiar pleasures that they enjoy after their horse wins a race. He looks proudly at the single pink stripe, pale and pure like his wife's naked skin, that is protected on all sides by the wide dark-orange of the shadeless soil in the districts he has travelled during all the years since he was a boy among the gravel streets of Bassett, then at the sleeves and cap of acidic light-green, the colour of the unvisited places that he and his wife will discover in heaven after they die in the state of grace or that they see past the corners of their farm when they stand on their veranda in the late afternoon and half-close their eyes, remembering the under-sides of leaves in corners of the backyards where they first wondered where they might be standing one day in the late afternoon after they had found a person to love and go naked with. As the barrier strands go down he notices how one owner's defiant purple is contradicted by a colour that grudgingly admits that he will probably never find after all the contentment that he once sought so eagerly. Another man's wife has used their colours to boast unasham-edly that she enjoys naked games and mating in sunlit places even more than her husband likes touching and kissing and grasping her. One man's discreet colours say simply that for most of his life he has had no friend or wife but that he would feel a sort of lonely satisfaction if ever his horse came home ahead of the strident reds and flaunted blues. Tamarisk Row is forced back almost to last as the closely grouped field rushes to the first turn. His owner watches undismayed as the black colt, galloping with long easy strides, drops well behind the leading bunch in the back straight. He grows a little alarmed as the leaders approach the turn with Tamarisk Row still many lengths back. The lead changes and changes again while the black horse is still out of sight somewhere in the middle of the field. Between the brilliant sashes that boast of pleasures and the diamonds and stripes that tell of memories or hopes, a streak of light-green appears at last. Tamarisk Row's jockey tries frantically to find a clear passage for the horse that is only now beginning to stretch his powerful legs. When the leaders are almost at the post a gap opens in front of him. With a few great strides the black horse bursts clear of the whole pack of struggling horses and reaches the line with just two horses ahead of him. The owner says almost nothing to his best friend as they lead the horse into the float for the long journey home. Around them in the car park other people with weary faces are preparing for long silent journeys. From only a few cars come the sounds of cheerful talk and the laughter of women. It is almost midnight before the float arrives back at the property named Tamarisk Row. The owner spends a long time making sure that the horse has a clean bed of straw for the night and the correct amount of oats and molasses in his feed-box. When he finally goes into the house he finds his wife still cheerful despite their loss. She tells him how she sat all afternoon in the lounge-room while a north wind thrust through the cracks under the doors. The sound of branches sweeping the walls and windows was the only noise in all the wide space between the empty back paddocks and the road where no car passed all day. Wind or a far thunderstorm crackled in the wireless as Tamarisk Row's race drew near. The horse's name was mentioned only twice during the brief time while the race was run. She understands without being told that the horse was unlucky and should have won easily. She takes off all her clothes and leans backwards with her legs wide apart just as she promised she would if the young black horse had won. Her husband touches between her legs for a few minutes but then tells her quietly that her little pink lump cannot console him after all he has lost that day. She puts her clothes on and they talk of waiting patiently, perhaps for many months, until Tamarisk Row has another chance to prove himself. They agree to sell one of their promising young unraced horses to get the stake for the next bet on the black horse. Clement Killeaton puts the last of his marbles back into their glass jar. His mother walks past on her way to the lavatory and asks – were you doing something sneaky just then? He tells her he was running a Stawell Gift with his marbles. She says – look out if I catch you with that racecourse again. Clement sits for a while and wonders whether, if he had been allowed to guide the field around the rails of a real racecourse, he might have been able to clear a passage through the field so that Tamarisk Row would have been able to win as he deserved.

## CLEMENT TRIES TO FIND OUT ABOUT GIRLS

Clement keeps watch on the aviary every afternoon until he sees Mr Wallace close the door carefully behind him and walk off into the dense scrub of wattles and banksias, startling a pair of olive-backed orioles as he goes. Clement hurries through the door of Margaret's playhouse. She backs away from him into the farthest corner as if she knows what he has come for. He stretches his hand towards the space between her thighs, but too cautiously. She picks up an old china soup-bowl full of black cats and tries to tempt him with it as she edges towards the door. He dodges around her arm but upsets a baby's pot full of chocolate balls and falls to his knees. As Margaret reaches the door she lifts her dress high over her head and does a few quick steps that she must have learned from watching a child tap-dancer in a film. Clement sees only a smooth white slope stretching down from her belly. By the time he is on his feet again she has run to the door of the aviary. She locks the door from the inside and prepares to do another little dance beneath the nest of a pair of cockatiels. But she hears her father coming and pretends to be studying the nest. When Clement arrives home he calls softly through the fence to the youngest Glasscock boy. He tries not to notice the crust of egg-yolk, which has probably been stuck on Nigel Glasscock's top lip since breakfast that morning, as he leads the younger boy into one of the Killeatons' fowl-sheds. Clement asks Nigel about his sisters. The boy admits that he sometimes hops into the bath with one of them on Sunday nights, but he cannot describe clearly what they look like naked. He soon grows tired of Clement's questions and presses his moon face against the wire-netting at the front of the shed. Just when he is about to leave Clement gets him to take out his cock. Clement takes out his own at the same time. Clement gently twists Nigel's into many different shapes and asks the boy each time whether it reminds him of what his sisters have between their legs. Nigel Glasscock grows tired of this too and tells Clement to let him put his Tommy away and he will tell him what Mr Glasscock's looked like when he was lying naked in bed late one Saturday morning. Clement almost asks was Mrs Glasscock naked in bed too, but changes his mind when he remembers the two sack-shaped titties that flop around on the woman's chest and belly under her greasy dress. He feels a burning pain in his legs and clutches his calves. The smooth greasy black tail of his father's razor strop curls back from his skin. Before he can tuck his cock safely away he has to grab at his legs again as the black strap crashes around his thighs. Nigel Glasscock tucks his Tommy out of sight and runs towards the front gate. Clement's mother lifts the razor strop again. The boy's cock dangles helplessly as he skips and leaps to dodge the blow.

## CLEMENT WATCHES A GIRL IN A STRANGE COUNTRY

Early on Saturday morning Clement goes with his mother on the bus into the main streets of Bassett. When his mother has finished her shopping she tells Clement he can choose a small book from the shelves in Gunns' Newsagency for his sixth birthday because he seems to like books. Clement chooses a book called Little Jacky Hare. When they arrive home he puts the book on his dressing-table beside his other books, My First Book of English Birds, which he chose on his fifth birthday, and Little Brother Jesus, which was sent to him by his aunt who is a nun. Far away from the parched trees of Bassett a girl sits in a walled garden. Through the gateway in the old mossy wall she can see a river that has flowed past Great Yarmouth and Golders Green and Tunbridge Wells and many other wooded inland towns miles away from McCracken's Road where a boy who wants to see some birds has to walk for hours on Sunday afternoon along gravel footpaths past straw-coloured lawns towards the ill-defined edges of an inland city before he glimpses among dusty branches the obscure grey-green plumage of one of the birds that is illustrated in the few smudged colour-plates of his father's copy of Leach's Australian Bird Book. After Clement has closed the book he sees the girl walking down between reed-buntings and water-wagtails towards the low grassy cliffs where the lawn meets the stream. While she is taking off her dress to bathe Little Jacky Hare scampers into the grass near by. He is fleeing from hunters and dogs who have separated him from his mother and sister and driven him out of the green tussocks where he has lived all his life on a hillside within sight of the girl's home. The girl sees him trying to hide near the river bank but does not disturb him and goes on undressing. She bathes knee-deep in the placid dark-blue water, listening to the sounds of willow-warblers and nuthatches in the trees and fields all around. With one quick glance she fixes in her mind an expanse of green more broad and luminous than any corner of lawn or garden that a boy in a tawny city thousands of miles away might assemble from the precious streaks and tints in the pages of books that he chooses each year for his birthday. When she has dried herself she sits on the pleasant lawn not far from Jacky's hiding-place and begins to dress, pausing often to watch a pair of stonechats flitting above her. She arranges her clothes prettily as if she knows that one day a few people in countries that she has never even read about will stare at pictures of her and the place where she once lived and wonder what it was like to be a girl in that green garden where so few people ever came that birds and animals frisked without fear all around her and where the colour of a single leaf or the sheen on a single feather was brighter and more lasting than great sheets of sunlight on their own plains. She hears the sounds of the hunters moving further away and beckons Jacky Hare to come out into the open. Clement asks his father whether there are any hares in Australia. Augustine tells him about the huge hares that used to lie all day in tall clumps of grass on the farm where Augustine was born. The hares had no burrows to hide in and their young ones had no other way to protect themselves than by crouching low in the thick grass as the men and dogs approached. A boy flees from his home in an inland town and tries to live like a hare in the sparse grass on the hard dry hills. Each day he watches the chestnut-tailed heath-wrens and lilac-wattled honeyeaters and thinks of names that everyone might call them by, but the birds are already moving farther back away from the towns and farms and some kinds are disappearing altogether from the land so that no one will ever know them by name. Boys in the towns of Australia who look in books for stories about the Hareboy and his blossoming shrubs and flitting birds see instead a pale smiling girl beside a far-off river. After living for a few years among unsatisfying rocks and dull-coloured leaves and elusive birds and knowing that few people will ever read about him or see his picture in a book, the Hareboy comes back to his friends and does not even bother to argue with them when they say that the yellow-breasted shrike-robin is not a real bird, or that the common beard-heath is not a real flower.

### CLEMENT LOVES BARBARA KEENAN

Clement Killeaton sees again a trellis heavy with green creepers that hides the back garden of a house at the better end of Leslie Street and thinks once more of Barbara Keenan, the girl he has loved for more than a year. One Saturday he walks for half an hour through strange streets past the northern railway line and the deep drain that everybody calls the creek. He stares for a minute at the view along Barbara's street but turns back so that he does not see at last through the side gate of a weatherboard house, a little neater than his own, a backyard where on Saturday after Saturday a girl is content to go on playing the same few trivial games while only a mile away on the other side of the creek a boy draws in the dirt of his backyard maps of squares in which one square is shaded with tufts of grass and enhanced by a few low hills that he has scraped up with his hands from the otherwise level dirt. For a long time, as he wriggles on his belly along the bare ground from the farthest corner of his yard, the boy cannot even see the town where one square of streets is distinguished so clearly from those around it. The dwindling voices of American women have almost ended their song – *in the hills of Idaho in the hills of Idaho* – before he glimpses the low hills blurred with foliage above a vista of grove-like streets. He approaches the end of a long journey across a country that he may never see towards hills that he can only guess at where he might have seen some clearer sign of whatever it was that he wanted to love when he saw and could not afterwards forget such things as the peculiar arrangement of three pale-golden freckles on the unsmiling face of a small girl who never spoke to him and who played her most private games behind leaves that he had never parted. After years of travelling he has almost reached the end of a journey that he first began when he heard on the wireless the songs Red Sails in the Sunset, When It's Springtime in the Rockies, or In the Blue Ridge Mountains of Virginia that are much older than the songs on the new hit parade programs that everyone in Bassett is now listening to or when he saw coloured pages of old National Geographic magazines with captions like *Oregon-bound wagons once caused traffic tie-ups in this lonely pass*, or *Grass-grown ruts still show where plucky pioneers once passed*, and knew that somewhere, so far away that no gaping child or adult who might peer into the corners of a backyard in Bassett may even begin to search for it, is a country deep inside what people who live near its borders call the country. Only the imponderable expanse of its treeless grasses is huge enough to encompass the months-long trek towards a hint of foothills, which is what he sees before him whenever he vows to go on loving Barbara Keenan. Almost every day at school he catches sight of the clean pink skin above her knees that are marred by no scabs or sores from falling on gravel footpaths and schoolgrounds, yet still he refuses to wonder about her thighs and pants and sets his eyes instead on a line of violet just above the farthest horizon. A man knows that there, at the very end of an almost-empty landscape, his little sweetheart of the mountains is safely hidden from other men and boys until the day, almost at the beginning of summer and just as she is about to give up hope, when he arrives back and surprises her dressed in modern American bathers and standing in a clear mountain stream. On the afternoon of the first Friday of the month the children of St Boniface's school march in threes to the church for Benediction. They swing their hundreds of pairs of feet under the seats and finger the varnish, sticky from the heat, on the railings of the seats in front of them, while the massed gold spikes of the monstrance and the extravagant creamy folds of the cope and humeral veil do honour to the tiny stark white disc of Our Lord in the Blessed Sacrament. Clement sees, a few seats ahead of him, Barbara's white socks turned down neatly over her ankles and, when she stands up for the last hymn, Hail Queen of Heaven, part of the gradual curves of her calves. He reminds Our Lord present on the altar that he has never tried to see beneath her skirt and asks Him to protect her always from boys or men who may want to do impure things to her. In answer to his prayer he is allowed to see how the man who goes home to the Rockies sometimes makes out through gaps in forested cliffs and beyond tenuous valleys the true country of Idaho where it trembles, faint and unapproachable, in the last sounds of a song.

## BASSETT ENJOYS AMERICAN FILMS

Perhaps no one now remembers the song of Idaho in all the streets of Bassett where every Saturday afternoon hundreds of children from Catholic and State schools walk towards the Tasma or the Liberty or the Miami to watch Tim Holt or Gene Autry riding back through miles of unfenced grasslands to claim the ranch that was always his by right although few people would believe him. A girl with flawless white skin waits to welcome him in front of the homestead that is miles from any road. The trees and flowers and birds are still newly discovered and too strange for the people to know by name but when the children of Bassett have gone back to their homes the men and women will spend their spare time learning the differences between each kind and giving them original names like searcher's home, American skin and lonely Angeline. Clement studies his atlas to learn the names of the places where those people live. His father discovers what he is doing and tells him that some of the first Killeatons in Australia were pioneers who rode out looking for land in places where there were no crowds to cheer them on. They rode on, not needing people to watch who could not even tell which of the two places, the one that the pioneers were riding towards and the one that the watchers could turn around and go home to, was the real country and which was only a place that people watched others riding towards.

## THE GLASSCOCKS, THE BARRETTS AND THE MOYS

Clement tells a racing story to the Glasscock boys from next door. They ask their father to have a race with them but he misunderstands them and only chases them round the house with a broomstick held between his legs for a horse. Clement watches them through the fence because Augustine has forbidden him to go into the Glasscocks' place. Clement's mother laughs at Mr Glasscock from behind the curtains in the side window. She says – it'll be a different tune when Lloyd Glasscock comes home on Friday night the worse for wear from the Clare Castle. On Friday night Augustine is late home because of the phone calls that he has to make to Melbourne. Clement's mother locks herself and her son in their house and then peeps through the curtains at the Glasscocks' house. Mr Glasscock arrives home at dusk. Minutes later he drives all his children out into the backyard. When some of them creep back onto the back veranda he chases them with a broom. While Mrs Glasscock prepares his tea the Killeatons hear him in the front bedroom tearing up a floorboard. For a long time after Augustine has arrived home the Killeatons hear Mr Glasscock banging his board against walls and doors. Augustine says – it's none of our business and anyway Lloyd never hurts anyone and the eldest boy always stands up for his mother and nails down the boards on Saturday while Lloyd is away. After Clement has said his prayers and climbed into bed Augustine comes in and reminds him how lucky he is not to have a father like some of the men in Leslie Street. Augustine talks about Cyril Barrett who never drinks or smokes but goes off on gambling sprees and leaves his family alone for days with no money in the house, and Mr Wallace the thin-faced grocer who makes his sons help him for hours in the shop after school and makes his wife unhappy in other ways. Clement asks whether Harold

Moy the jockey is a good husband. Augustine hesitates then says – yes I suppose he is in his own way. Harold Moy is half-Chinese. His wife has lustrous olive skin but her eyes have an Australian shape. She stares through sun-glasses across glaring racecourses while her husband urges on his mount to please her. While she watches her husband, Clement sees, in either of the bright tunnels where her eyes should be, a diminutive man in a jacket of rich colours. Behind the man's half-smiling wrinkled face a blank plain stretches back from streets of tiny wooden cottages in Bassett's Chinatown, built by people who found their way by sea and land to a country whose name they could not even pronounce and stayed for so long among people whose language they did not know that no one remembered them in the land they had left, where the blinds are always drawn but whose rooms contain only bare walls and unwavering lights, towards not a sky but a smooth sloping golden rim beyond which the God of the Catholics and all His angels and saints never pass on any of their journeys around the edges of their misty lawns and forests. Harold has no children because he is selfish and wants to discover with only his wife beside him the streets and rooms in another city that a few of his people may have reached in their travels hidden in the harsh light from that golden wall that seems to Clement so cheerless and unpromising.

### AUGUSTINE BACKS SKIPTON IN THE MELBOURNE CUP

Clement's mother locks all the doors and windows whenever her husband is away from Bassett. A warm wind rattles the windows, and the drawn blinds sway faintly during the afternoon of Melbourne Cup Day, 1941. Clement's mother cannot explain what she is trying to keep out of the house. She tells

Clement to play quietly among the coloured lines and patterns on the rug in the lounge-room. Towards three o'clock a huge yellowish shape bumps against the house and waits to be let in, but the boy has learned how to sit quietly and pretend that no one is at home. When the place is quiet again Clement's mother tells him that his father has had a lot of money on a horse in the Melbourne Cup. It is the most important race since Clement's mother and father were first married. Clement is too young to understand a race broadcast. His mother stands up with her face pressed against the wireless. She whispers that Skipton is last but there is still a long way to go. Clement asks her what Skipton means and she says – it's the name of a town a long way away somewhere on the way to your grandfather Killeaton's farm. A little later she tells him that Skipton is going to win after all. She listens a little longer then turns off the wireless. She kneels down and makes Clement kneel beside her to pray. He repeats each few words after her to thank God for letting Augustine win enough to pay all his debts and take them on a proper holiday to Kurringbar so that Clement can see his uncles and aunties and grandparents at last. His mother prays silently while Clement listens to the wind in the hedges along the side streets of Skipton. He tiptoes to the window and peeps around the blind. Big slow plains are creeping sadly away from the house. A haze of dust from the north makes a sign in the sky and tries to reach Bassett, but the blinds are pulled down all over the city and no one sees the silent empty places where they may all be going. But the northern sky comes home in the end and even the Killeatons' walls and windows might not stop its long searching run. Clement's mother takes him to Wallaces' shop to buy a family brick of ice-cream and three bottles of creamy soda. On the way they hear the roaring of the men in the bar of the Clare Castle. She tells the boy how lucky he is that his father doesn't come home drunk and chase him like Mr Glasscock. Late at night Clement wakes up as Augustine comes home. The boy hears his parents counting out hundreds of pounds on their bed. Augustine tells his wife that their holiday might have to wait a little longer. He didn't want to worry her but his debts were more than he told her, but now Skipton has just about cleaned them all up.

### CLEMENT FIRST HEARS OF THE FOXY GLEN

Augustine takes Clement up the hill to Stan Riordan's big house. Augustine talks to Stan Riordan on the back lawn near the fishpond. He pays back ten pounds of the money he owes him and asks Stan to write a short note that he can show to the other big starting-price bookmakers in Bassett if he should want to get some big money on for his Melbourne friends in the next few weeks. Stan warns him kindly not to get in too deep but agrees to write the note to say that Augustine's credit is good. Augustine says that his mates in Melbourne never miss with their really big bets and there could be one coming up. Clement goes off quietly to look for Therese. He finds her with her friend again. The two girls are unpacking things from a box decorated with transfers of flowers. They try to stop Clement from looking too closely at the things. He sees a small tin that is kept locked and asks what is in it. Therese says nothing but the other girl says – all these things are Therese's treasures and that's her Foxy Glen. On the lid of the tin is a faded picture of an animal. Clement tells them it looks more like a dingo than a fox but they ignore him. The girls take some of the treasures to the front garden and Clement follows them. As they climb astride the lowest branch of a willow tree he sees several inches of Therese's white pants and sees that she sees him staring at them. The girls talk in whispers as they pass things between them. Clement slowly moves closer to their branch. He asks Therese does she have any young brothers, although he knows she has none. He asks her does she know what a boy looks like without his pants on. Therese tells him not to be so rude or she'll slap his face and tell his father. The other girl says – Therese knows all about that stuff – she even keeps pictures of things like that in her Foxy Glen. The girls whisper together. Therese still does not smile. Clement tries to learn more, but Mrs Riordan calls the girls and they run inside, taking their treasures with them. Clement goes looking for the Foxy Glen but it is not where he first saw it. While he is wandering around the garden the other girl comes up quietly behind him. She is alone. She asks him where he lives. When he tells her in Leslie Street she tells him that her boyfriend used to live there. Clement asks her was his name Silverstone, and she says that it could have been. Then she tells him that her boyfriend knew everything about girls and the things that men and women do in their bedrooms or in the long grass beside the creek on Sundays. Clement asks what those things are, but she tells him she cannot explain if he does not know already. He asks whether Therese Riordan knows, but the girl tells him to look in the Foxy Glen if he wants to find out. She tells him she would like to have a young brother to talk to sometimes, and offers to tell him about some hair that some people have between their legs. Clement asks her to persuade Therese to join in their talks, but the girl thinks Therese might be too shy. Clement asks her again about the Foxy Glen. She agrees to tell him more if he comes to Riordans' next Sunday. He explains that his father only comes when he has lost at the races. His father calls for him to go home. As he leaves, the girl reminds him that they might have some fun in the fernery together one Sunday. He asks her again to get Therese interested. When he reaches home he clears a space in a paddock of a remote stud farm and writes in the dust the names of all the clean and pretty girls whose pants he has seen. In an unfenced place on the edge of the desert country he starts a list of girls who may soon agree to take down their pants for him. He puts Therese Riordan first on this list and Margaret Wallace second. He does not write Therese's friend on this list because her face is ugly when she grins. Then he takes a marshmallow weed and sweeps it across the plains where the names are written until the ground is as bare as it seemed to be when the Silverstones had gone away and the Killeatons came to live there and little Clement was still too small to go digging and scraping in the backyard for signs that another boy might have left behind.

## CLEMENT SEES STRANGE CREATURES IN COLOURED GLASS

When the sun is low in the sky west of Bassett a peculiar light shines in the panel of greenish-gold glass in the Killeatons' front door. Creatures neither green nor gold but more richly coloured than any grass or sun try to find their way home through a land where cities of unpredictable shapes and colours rise up on plains of fiery haze, then vanish just as quickly while some of their inhabitants flee towards promises of other plains where cities may appear whose glancing colours will sometimes recall for those few who reach them certain glimpses of the places that have gone, and others still make their way across familiar vistas not knowing that the towers and walls they are looking for no longer stand. Past all towns and plains is a region where the green of the peopled countries can barely be recognised among richer nameless colours and towards which a few creatures sometimes set out, mostly alone but sometimes in little bands that are often driven apart but always try to come together again, struggling to keep their own distinctive lines and outlines, even near the last edge of the land and sky where they used to belong, where the boy watching them suspects that for all the luminous expanses before them, where whole mountains or countries unfold within tinctures that were no more than single roofs or tree-tops in the cities far away or from behind brief coruscations that may once have been sudden gestures among the wandering creatures, those creatures far from home still try to carry into that place whose every landscape seems to lead back to countless places farther off, each as vast as the land that is supposed to contain them all, traces within them of some almost-spent glow that recalls a play of light on a few inches or miles of a plain that may never be seen again. One evening it happens again that a creature, whose radiance has persisted through many lands and whose journeys have taken it across levelled hills and buried valleys where it alone might have paused and wondered about the true history of those deceptively empty places, keeps the boy watching and hoping and urging it almost aloud through pale-green insidious mists and past tranquil hinterlands until, as it nears the land that may not really be a land where he has wanted it to go, he sees it waver and flicker and has to narrow his eyes and tilt his head but cannot see it across those last slopes or cliffs and loses sight of it, so that he will never know whether it is lost forever in some capricious wilderness that was never its true destination or whether, like a few others that he has watched on other afternoons, it has turned back after all towards lands it may still remember, and if so whether he may one day catch sight of it in a strangely altered shape arriving back among places that resemble those where he first discovered it and trying to enact again some of those first great journeys that now no longer have any purpose. While

Clement watches the creatures, the sun moves away from Bassett but not before it has exposed across every plain and beneath every hill and through every city and within every creature, and even perhaps in the inaccessible region beyond all countries, streaks or tinges of a colour that none of the creatures seems to have seen although it alone might easily obliterate them all and countries they love. As the very last light leaves his front door the boy realises that if only the creatures had discovered this colour things might have gone differently with their journeys.

## BERNBOROUGH COMES DOWN FROM THE NORTH

Long after the war is over, the people in Bassett and inland Victoria go on looking northwards towards America where the Yank servicemen are home again kissing their sweethearts on porches or in drugstores or night clubs and singing without missing a single word the songs Shoo Fly Pie and Apple Pan Dowdie, I've Got My Captain Working For Me Now, Mares Eat Oats and Does Eat Oats and Little Lambs Eat Ivy, My Dreams Are Getting Better All the Time, Give Me Five Minutes More, that the people of Bassett have to learn as best they can by listening to the hit parade program on Station 3BT. While they stand looking, a small cloud of dust comes south towards them. A huge field of horses is racing on an immense track whose curves sweep inland, enclosing hundreds of miles of arid country, and whose mighty straight runs down the western slopes of the Great Dividing Range parallel to but out of sight of the east coast and all its cities. Bernborough, a six-year-old stallion from a provincial city in Queensland, gallops easily at the very rear and so far back that the leaders are out of sight of his rider. Along the farthest back stretches of the course a mob of wild brumbies tries to keep up with the field. Augustine points them out to his son and reminds him how much stronger and faster they are than the stunted ponies that pass for wild horses in American films. But even brumbies are not meant for racing, and the riderless horses soon give up chasing the racehorses and go back to their waterholes. Clement shows his father two photos on the front page of Wednesday's Sporting Globe. One picture shows more than twenty horses strung out around the turn into the straight in the Doomben Ten Thousand. A white arrow points to Bernborough, barely distinguishable among the tail-enders. The second picture shows the finish of the same race with Bernborough clearly in front, having passed twenty and more horses in the short Doomben straight. Clement puts his hand over the arrow in the picture and asks his father to guess which horse is Bernborough. He hopes to astonish Augustine with the sight of the horse's incredible finishing run. But Augustine has already studied Bernborough's history and announced to his racing friends that a greater horse than Phar Lap is coming down from the north. He has backed Bernborough to win the Caulfield and Melbourne Cup double and keeps his eyes on the dust cloud which is now crossing western New South Wales. Clement asks his father how the race is going. Augustine describes how the field sweeps down into northern Victoria and tells Clement that the boy will probably catch a glimpse of the horses on the turn into the straight which will take them not many miles from Bassett. He warns the boy to look for Bernborough near the rear of the field, just beginning his famous finishing run. Clement sees boys playing racing games in St Boniface's schoolyard. As usual they all try to lead all the way in their races. Many of them have called themselves Bernborough after the horse whose name their fathers have probably mentioned to them.

## CLEMENT WATCHES A PLAY ABOUT GYPSIES

Clement goes to school again and sits in his desk that has a map of a desert in the grain of its varnished top. He grips the iron bar near his knees to take his mind off his thirst and the heat. He stares at the occasional patches of green in the pictures in his reader, then at the long trailing fronds of maiden-hair fern in the pots along the window ledge. Two girls who are the nun's pets stroll out to the taps to fill the watering can with cool water for the plants. Through the open door Clement sees the girls in the shady shelter shed drinking daintily from the bubble taps and dabbing at their mouths with their crumpled white hankies. He stares for a while at the blackboard, where precisely ruled columns and paddocks enclose what the nun calls their most important work. One Friday afternoon Clement hears the nun say that she will probably put up a whole lot of new work over the weekend. All Sunday Clement looks forward eagerly to the Monday morning when he can spend his hours in school exploring a maze of coloured streets and yards, loitering with pleasure by green and blue pools and following admiringly the perfect arcs and circles of the rarer numerals and letters. On Monday he marches to his desk, lifts his head slowly and deliberately, and sees the same old pattern of work with its usual film of dust. He puts up his hand at once and asks the nun what happened to the new work, but she tells him not to worry about it. In December Clement realises that the blackboard will keep the same pattern until the very end of the year. He traces well-known pathways among dots of yellow, brown, orange and a lime-yellow that he tries to believe is true green, looking in vain for some unexpected thicket that might disclose a tunnel or a clearing as refreshing as cool water. After lunch his skin is still so hot from the running he has done in the yard that every new place he rests on along the smooth wooden seat only chafes and irritates him more. The nun tells the grade they are going to the Albert Theatre to practise for their Christmas concert. Outside, the whole school is lining up in pairs on the gravel and stirring up a cloud of fine white dust. The long file of children moves off down Lucknow Street past a view of the creek between pepper trees whose green branches sweep the dirt, then steeply uphill between the huge elms of Cecil Park, where there is little trace on the bare ground of the grass that looks so green in the coloured postcards of Bassett the City of Gold. They pass fewer people as they near the top of a great hill. By the time they reach the first of the long flights of wooden stairs that zig-zag up the rear wall of the theatre they seem to have come a long way from the frequented streets of the city, although those children who know that part of Bassett say that on the other side of the theatre is one of the best-known streets of the city. Just before he goes in out of the sunlight Clement turns and discovers that he is looking down on Bassett from its highest hill. Before the press of children forces him inside he has a glimpse of motionless tree-tops standing against the slow onset of a far-reaching yellow-grey plain of haze, and wonders how many hours or days it might take him to read from their rows and clumps and scattered groups the shape of the hot city out of sight beneath them. In the unvarying twilight of the cavernous theatre Clement slips out of his place in the line so that he can sit next to Desmond Hoare, the boy he has chosen only that morning to be his best friend. While a troupe of girls sways to and fro on the stage high above them holding baskets of vivid flowers and sing-ing – *as I was going to Strawberry Fair*, Desmond Hoare whispers to Clement that as soon as school has broken up he is going to Melbourne for the whole of the long summer holidays. In a long street in a Melbourne suburb named after a tree or a flower, in a house with lawn between the footpath and the gutter, his little sweetheart waits for him. Desmond will play every afternoon with her between the shrubs on the lawn. On the hottest days they will catch the tram to the beach. An old nun with networks of wrinkles all over her face overhears Desmond Hoare whispering and tells him fiercely to be quiet. She says – talking about girlfriends when you're hardly out of the cradle. Clement tries to hide his face from her but Hoare does not seem embarrassed. The girls in white leave the stage and a group of girls from the seventh and eighth grades comes out to rehearse their play Little Gypsy Gay. Therese Riordan, dressed in fiery green silk, is Gay's mother. Her skin is a faultless golden-creamy colour in the subdued light. From where he sits Clement sees the first few inches of smooth pale skin above her knees, but it worries him to think that every other boy in the hall can see it too. Therese steps to the front of the stage and speaks in a voice that carries to the obscurest corners of the theatre, so that even the dull-eyed drowsy grade-one children sit up to watch her. Clement whispers to Desmond Hoare that the big girl in green is his girlfriend and that he visits her in her big house on the hill near his place every Sunday. Hoare looks at him once briefly then turns to the boy on his other side and whispers to him to pass it on that Clem Killeaton loves the big girl with the green stuff on up on the stage. The message moves down the row to the aisle, then leaps back to the row behind. As it passes behind Clement someone kicks his legs beneath the seat. High up at the end of yet another hill, and far back in the great painted landscape behind the gypsies and the girls whose silken thighs have brought gasps from hundreds of drooping mouths, a lemon-yellow road leads past hollyhocks and festoons of crimson roses towards a tall marble fountain among lawns as perfect as green plush. There, in the country of Jacky Hare and the wheatear and bullfinch, after he has endured one last trying summer among harsh hills and leaves tasting of dust, a boy who has waited for years for a sight of his true home among cool lanes and hedges climbs to the last vantage point of all from which he knows he will see what he has always been hoping for. As she leaves the stage, and while the rows of children break off their whispering and fidgeting to applaud her, Therese Riordan carelessly brushes one white hand and wrist down across several acres of fields as cool and green as emeralds seen through water. A tremor crosses the lofty landscape, and even the far fountain seems for a moment like a mere layer of paint on a tottering screen of canvas. Someone in the seat behind Clement says quite audibly – wave ta-ta to your girlfriend Killeaton – the gypsies have taken her away.

## CLEMENT ORGANISES A CONCERT

It is summer again as usual in Bassett, the largest city for a hundred miles in any direction. Under the one tall gum-tree among the fowl sheds behind 42 Leslie Street, Clement Killeaton arranges a concert. He calls on Gordon Glasscock to present the first item. The tall boy stands awkwardly on a platform of palings and logs from the wood heap. His almost-white hair stands out stiffly from his head where his mother has clipped it short for the holidays, and on his top lip is a weeping scab that he calls his cold sore and that Clement's mother has said will not heal properly because the Glasscocks don't get the proper foods to eat. Gordon mumbles to his audience that he will recite a poem. He takes a deep breath and says with barely a pause for breath The Land I Love by Cecilia Ballantyne *My mother loved a gentle land with dove-grey drifting sky with woodlands green beneath the rain and flowers that soothed the eye – she saw beneath her favourite hill the fields as trim as lawns and through the bosky coppices she heard the hunters' horns.* Clement stops him and asks where he found the poem. Gordon says – it's in the grade six reader at school. Clement tries to explain that the words have a sad hopeless sound there beneath the ragged strips of bark and the moistureless leaves in an obscure corner of Bassett, Victoria, Australia. Someone has mistakenly included in the school reader a poem about places that no boy with running sores on his mouth and dangling patches on his pants will ever discover among lonely trees in backyards that the far green world has never heard of. Gordon argues feebly that the thing is only a poem and not true or real anyway. Clement allows him to start his recitation again. Near the top of the last of all the hills that surround a few shallow gullies where a spent creek lies between beaches of flaking rocks and pebbles of a hundred nameless colours, a band of exhausted Englishmen hears no sound of chaffinches or great tits as they struggle upwards. They console each other with descriptions of a land not far ahead where birds with garish feathers but traditional names come down tamely to rippling watercourses. One of them describes a park-like city named Hartlepool or Basingstoke where cocka-toos dangle from elm twigs and passing children look fondly into the birds' cosy nests. Another tells how he has heard the peculiar silence of a whole district of uncomplicated hills that few people have ever passed but where someone will one day stroll at ease, giving a name to every dell and gap and edge and thorp and combe and crag so that the next people who pass by may spend hours guessing why such a name was given to such a place and in what order the man who named them all passed over the cluster of hills and discovered their peculiar features and the differences between them. Still another talks of how his children will teach their children a thousand stories about the towns that they can see on what was once a dull plain and put into their hands books with pictures of a country they may not return to but which they will never forget is the place where robins and scarps and Glastonburys are seen in their true shapes. Gordon Glasscock stumbles on until he reaches a turning point in the poem – *such was the land she wandered in and neath whose soil she lies here within stark horizons I scan far different skies – I watch the parched ranges where cattle roam at will in damp green ferny gullies I stand and look my fill.* When Gordon has finished, Clement asks him whether the poet was Australian or English but the boy cannot say. Clement asks whether he prefers Australian or English birds and Gordon answers without hesitating – Australian birds of course. Clement asks him to name his favourites. He names magpies and blackbirds. When Clement tries to explain that blackbirds are not Australian birds Gordon Glasscock challenges him to put on an item of his own. Clement mounts the platform of palings and sings all the words he can remember of two of the most beautiful songs that he has heard on the wireless – There's a Bridle Hanging on the Wall and Home on the Range. Clement's sweet girlish voice compels the others to listen. As he sings he half-closes his eyes and tries to see the blue-green immensity of America and the heroic journeys of its horses and men.

## AUGUSTINE KEEPS IN TOUCH WITH PROFESSIONAL PUNTERS

On Friday Augustine comes straight home from work. He leans his bike against the back veranda and reminds Clement not to wheel it inside because he will be riding it to the post office after tea. He reminds his wife that it is only half-past four and here he is home with his family while the men he works with have rushed off to the nearest hotel to fill their bellies with beer. He spends the hours before tea with one of his pens of

Rhode Island Red pullets and hens. He hooks a long piece of wire around a hen's leg and stands for a long while with the bird in his arms examining it for faults. When he finds a bird with a crooked bone or an eye of the wrong colour or a head and comb not of the quality that judges look for in poultry shows, he fastens a coloured plastic ring around its leg. He uses rings of several different colours. A red ring shows that a bird will be killed and eaten as soon as it is needed. Yellow means that a bird will be packed in a crate and sold at the market in Bassett. Outstanding birds get a blue or even a purple ring. Each of these pullets is given a girl's Christian name which is then written in pencil in some blank space on the fibro-cement wall of their pen. Later they will be moved to another pen where an outstanding rooster will be allowed to mate with them. Augustine has told Clement many times that he is not interested in taking his Rhode Islands to shows even though they belong to one of the purest strains in Australia. The man who first sold him these bloodlines is getting old now, and when he dies his farm might be sold up and his breeding stock scattered anywhere. So Killeaton goes on breeding Rhode Islands year after year in shabby pens in his backyard where no one else but himself admires the one or two birds from each year's hatching that are nearly perfect in colour and shape and proportions. Augustine eats his tea with the Club racing paper spread out in front of him. As soon as the meal is finished he goes to his bedroom to put on his best suit and tie and hat. He folds the Club neatly into his inside coat pocket, checks the lead in his propelling pencil, fastens his bike clips around his shins, checks the lights on his bike, and sets out for the main streets of Bassett. One Friday night Clement goes with his father, sitting astride the parcel rack behind the saddle of the bike and holding onto Augustine's waist. Augustine leaves the bike chained to a post on the footpath of Fleet Street and

enters one of the dimly lit trunk-line telephone booths on
the shadowy pillared veranda of the Post Office. He has to
wait while the unseen switchboard operator books his call to
Melbourne. He makes Clement stay inside the booth out of
the cold. The boy reads all the printed signs, then begins to
fidget. When his call is ready Augustine spreads out his Club
on the narrow ledge and holds his pencil ready in his hand.
He tells Len Goodchild 120 miles away that he hadn't intended
going to Melbourne this weekend but that he'll be available
if he's needed. He laughs affectedly into the receiver and tells
Goodchild that he has brought his young colt with him to the
phone tonight. He has to repeat his words and laugh again
because the line is bad between Melbourne and Bassett. He
asks his friend are they expecting any really good thing to
go off in the near future. He says that he is not in any serious
bother financially but that he would be glad of a good win to
clear up a few troublesome little local debts. He asks is there
any mail for tomorrow and holds his pencil poised. Goodchild
uses a code to give Killeaton his selections in case anyone is
listening to their conversation. While they are talking about a
horse whose name starts with the same letter that begins the
name of a man they both know who drives a dark-green Dodge,
Killeaton has to pay more money for extra time for his call,
but he does not complain. When they come out of the phone
booth Clement asks to be taken home but his father tells him
there is one more important call to make. He takes Clement
into an almost-empty Greek cafe. They walk past the tables to
a glass-walled compartment where the proprietor sits at a desk
covered with racing pages. The man nods at them and goes on
muttering into a telephone. Killeaton whispers to Clement –
listen to Nicky talking in Greek – that's what he uses for his
racing code but Mr Goodchild's code is safer. When the man
finally puts down his telephone he and Augustine talk quietly

together for a long time. Clement sits beside a radiator and begins to doze. On the way home Augustine tells his son that far away to the south beyond the dark bulges of the central Victorian hills in a certain unremarkable square of light within a pattern of squares and rows of lights too vast and complex for any one mind to comprehend, a little band of men sits up until almost midnight talking in subdued voices of their daring schemes. They drink only tea or milk and few of them smoke. Several are bachelors. Others have left their wives safely at home in distant suburbs. The man whose house they sit in lost his wife many years ago and has no time to waste on the complicated business of finding another. Some of them have jobs or businesses that keep them busy on weekdays. Others, the most dedicated and courageous, rely entirely on their cunning and their years of experience and their banks of perhaps a thousand pounds to live for year after year from racing. One or two of these look forward to a series of brilliantly-planned plunges that will earn them so much money that they will never again have to bet for a living, but the others are content to spend the rest of their lives as professional punters, devoted to the game and looking forward to the continual challenge of the Friday night racing papers with their lists of names and predictions of odds that are mostly to tempt the mugs but may yield just one or two value bets.

## CLEMENT AND KELVIN BARRETT PLAY NEW GAMES

On Saturday morning while trucks and floats are still travelling from secluded corners among the knotted roots of trees or from behind thick tangles of weeds towards famous racecourses, Mrs Killeaton calls her son to the front gate and warns him to behave himself while she goes into Bassett on the bus. Clement watches until the bus has turned the corner into McCracken's Road. When he turns back towards his yard a boy named Kelvin Barrett comes to meet him. Barrett refuses to tell how he got into Killeaton's yard, but Clement insists that he must have climbed the fence from the yard of the Presbyterian church hall next door and scrambled down through the tall tamarisks. He knows that Barrett sometimes goes to the Presbyterian Sunday school in the old hall and peers through the picket fence of a Sunday morning to see what games Killeaton plays when he is alone. Clement looks around quickly to make sure there is no sign of any road or farmhouse to suggest to Barrett that all around him just out of sight is a countryside whose centre is a racecourse where crowds are already gathering. Kelvin Barrett lifts a few branches of shrubs and peeps around the corners of a few fowl sheds. He tells Clement that a long time before, when the Silverstones lived there, the boy Silverstone used to have a secret hide-out where he played special games with many of the children in Leslie Street. Kelvin himself was invited into the hide-out once, but he cannot remember where it was. He crosses the backyard and opens the Killeatons' back door. Clement follows him inside. In the lounge-room each boy slips his braces down over his shoulders and lets his trousers fall around his ankles. They shuffle backwards and forwards, facing each other and jerking their hips to make their cocks and balls swing. Clement tells the other boy to wait a minute. He runs to his father's bookcase and grabs a certain magazine. He is so anxious that he tears some of the pages as he turns them. He finds the bloodstock pages and points out to the Barrett boy a picture of a stallion, one of the ten most successful sires of winners for the current season. The horse stands proudly near a tall white-painted fence between whose railings are glimpses of small paddocks protected by dense plantations of trees where dozens of his mares graze peacefully. Clement runs his finger along the stallion's belly, then down the powerful drooping thing beneath that his father calls a sheath. Then he looks up into Barrett's face. Barrett is not sure what Clement means. Clement prances around like a stallion preparing to mate with his mares, and tugs at his own sheath. He takes Barrett's cock in his hands and tries to shape it into a stallion's sheath, but the other boy roars with pain and grabs savagely at Clement's cock to pay him back. Clement runs from room to room with Barrett after him. In the front bedroom the State-school boy starts to climb onto the bed to bounce on the springy mattress. Clement begs him not to mess up his parents' bed, and has to submit to having his sheath twisted and tugged before they finally shake hands and go back to the lounge-room. This time Clement allows Barrett to decide what game they will play. He has to lie on his back while Barrett lies on top of him so that their things rub together. The other boy presses too heavily on Clement. He pleads with Barrett to get up and go but the boy pins him down and bounces up and down on top of him. Kelvin Barrett tells Clement that their fathers and mothers sometimes do things like this to each other on hot afternoons while their children are away at school. Clement has to pretend to hear the bus coming to make Barrett get off him at last. Barrett pulls up his trousers, strolls outside, scrambles up through the tamarisks, and jumps down into the yard of the church hall.

## THE SECRETS OF THE STATE-SCHOOL CHILDREN

Almost every afternoon Clement sees Kelvin Barrett going home from the Shepherd's Reef State school. He never talks to Barrett because he (Clement) is usually with the crowd of children who dawdle home together from St Boniface's school. Several of the Catholic children have friends at the

State school, but they do not play with them until they have reached home and broken off from the mob of Catholic children. One afternoon when he is walking home alone, Clement hears Kelvin Barrett calling to him to wait. The Shepherd's Reef boy crosses the street to walk with Clement. With him is another State-school boy. This boy has a pale, almost spherical, head and colourless eyebrows. He says his name is Dudley Earl and that Kelvin Barrett has told him all about his friend Killeaton from the Catholic school. They walk a little way in silence. The round-headed boy chuckles to himself and Clement begins to fear him. The two State-school boys discuss whether to tell Clement something special that they heard the other day at their school. Clement pretends to be unconcerned, but longs to know something of what they learn in their school, where, so he has heard, no prayers are said and no catechism is recited and where for one period each week the children study Australian birds and animals in a subject called nature study. Dudley Earl stops at a corner where a side street branches off McCracken's Road. He points out to Killeaton a newly painted cream weatherboard house a little neater than its neighbours. Earl tells him that Mr Wormington, a teacher from Shepherd's Reef school, lives there. The boy asks Clement would he be game to go down and peep into the man's front garden, but Clement says he has to hurry home. The Shepherd's Reef boys tell him he is scared because he has never been taught by a man teacher. Near the corner of Leslie Street they decide to tell Clement the special poem they have been whispering about. Dudley Earl recites it, but Barrett has to prompt him at several places. Earl says – *John had great big waterproof boots on John had great big waterproof hat John had great big waterproof coat on and that said John was that.* He shouts the last few words at Clement and a bead of spit flies out of his mouth onto Clement's forehead. Clement does not dare wipe it off while the others are looking at him, waiting for him to comment on the poem. Clement finally laughs and says he enjoyed the poem and understood it very well. The State-school boys walk away very pleased with themselves. When they are out of sight Clement hurries back to the corner of the schoolteacher's street and creeps as near as he dares to the cream-painted house. The front blinds are pulled down against the hot afternoon sun. The front yard is deserted. In a little round window a magpie of royal blue and white stained glass emerges from a thicket of green and gold leaves and fronds. Clement hears a faint cry from inside the house, where the light must lie in green or gold pools behind the glowing glass leaves. In a silent twilight, coloured like the innermost parts of a forest, people who know the secrets of the Australian bush instead of the mysteries of the Catholic religion are enjoying the true meaning of a poem.

### CLEMENT TELLS THE STORY OF KENNIE TEAGUE

At lunchtime a new boy arrives at St Boniface's school. The boys in Killeaton's grade stop their games and gather round to stare at the stranger. He backs up against a brick wall and starts to howl. A mob gathers round him. The children at the back press forward so hard that those in the front are pushed up against the new boy. He covers his face with his hands and tries to turn to the wall. Some of the boys at the front start to punch and wrestle the boys just behind them. Somebody punches the new boy. The nun patrolling the yard blows her whistle but it is nearly a minute before the sound reaches the noisiest parts of the mob. The nun asks the new boy what is the matter, but he cannot speak for crying. She sees his nose running with snot and his face streaked with dirt and tears and tells him that at least he can use his handkerchief. She gathers from noises and signs he makes that the boy has no handkerchief. She looks around the crowd that has formed again a few yards away. She beckons to Clement Killeaton and tells him to lend his hankie to the new boy and then to keep him company until the bell goes. Clement gives the boy his clean hankie and the nun goes away. When the new boy has rubbed the hankie a few times across his wet snotty face Clement tells him to come to the taps and wash the hankie clean. A small group of boys still follows at a distance, hoping that the new boy will start howling again. Clement takes his hankie between two fingers and drops it into a washbasin. He tells the new boy to have a guzzle at one of the other taps, but he forgets to warn him not to go near Teague's tap, the basin that has been disfigured with blue stains ever since the day when a big girl Teague, the sister of Kennie Teague in Clement's grade, asked to be excused on a hot afternoon and instead of going to the girls' lavatories went out to the row of taps at the end of the shelter shed, took down her pants, which were filthy and ragged like all the clothes that the Teague family wore, climbed up onto the basin at the end of the row, and did a great soupy yellow flood of piss all down the white sides of the bowl, and which no one else has touched ever since except her little brother Kennie who gets bashed up if he dares to go near any of the clean taps. When Clement looks up from washing his hanky he sees the new boy with his head bent down deep into Teague's basin drinking with his lips around the tap. The boys who have been following him are so shocked that they let him finish his drink before they start to yell – he drank out of Teague's tap – the new kid drank out of Teague's tap. A crowd gathers again and Clement slips back into the second or third row. They force the new boy up against the blue-mottled basin and he starts to howl again. No nun comes to scatter them, but after a few minutes the bell rings and the crowd of boys runs off reluctantly, spreading the story about the new boy as they go. During the next few weeks the new boy keeps trying to find a friend but the others avoid him. Sometimes he tries to talk to Killeaton because Clement was the first boy he met when he arrived at St Boniface's, but Clement runs away for fear that the others will see them together. At last, when it seems to Killeaton that the other boys have forgotten about the day when the new boy sucked at Teague's tap, Clement stands still and does not run when the new boy comes up to talk to him. The new boy says – remember how I drank out of Teague's tap that day when I was still new at St Boniface's – well what's up with Teague's tap anyway? Clement looks round to make sure that no one else is listening, because although he started on the first day in the bubs' grade at St Boniface's and has been at the school for just as long as Teague or any of the other boys, he only knows that the reason why everyone hates and avoids the Teague family is something filthy that the Teagues did a long time ago in a part of Bassett where Clement has never been. Only a few boys in Clement's grade seem to know the true story of the Teagues. Clement has never been privileged to hear it from them. He tells the new boy that the Teagues are a dirty family as anyone can see from Kennie's long unwashed hair and the patched pants that reach below his black-grained knees and the food stains on his shirt and the scabs and pimples on his big sister's face and the smell from their pants because they never wipe their bums properly in the lavatory. Then he tells the boy about the day in Sister Canisius's grade when some girl couldn't find her lunch money and the nun asked – was any person in this room at playtime while I was out? and a boy said – I think Kennie Teague was Sister, and the nun said – hands up anyone else who saw our Mr Teague in here at playtime, and nothing happened for a minute until Clement put up his hand and said – please Sister I saw him too, and thought that perhaps now he might learn what really did happen in some old shed strung with cobwebs or on a back veranda heaped with rusty tins at the Teagues' disgusting house to make the whole school hate the boy with the flopping hair and his sister who wore her mother's old dresses to school. And because the new boy follows him around begging to hear the rest of the story, Clement tells how Sister Canisius said – well now we've got at least one trustworthy witness, and told Kennie Teague to stand on the platform and turn out all his pockets and show the grade and how Teague clutched his desk with both hands and bawled out in his funny voice that some people said he couldn't help because he was tongue-tied – I nair stow no muhhy, and some of the girls giggled because he was shouting in school. And because Clement is still proud of the important job he was given that day, he tells how the nun said – I'm sorry Mr Teague but you're acting like someone with a very guilty conscience, and made the rest of the class go to sleep on their desks while four of the strongest boys dragged Kennie's hands away from the desk, carried him by his hands and legs to the empty space at the back near the piano, and held him there blubbering and thrashing around while Clement pulled out of Teague's pocket and held up for the nun to see the old rag that Kennie used for a hankie and some scraps of paper that looked like a note from Mrs Teague that the boy had forgotten to give to his teacher, and how when they found no money in his pockets the nun told Clement to pull off Kennie's shoes, which were rotten old sandshoes, and peel off his socks, which turned out to be an old pair of woollen khaki army socks tucked under his feet to fit him, and shake them out thoroughly in case the money was hidden in them. And because the new boy seems just as disappointed as the nun and all the children were when they found that Teague had no money hidden on him, Clement tells him the end of the story – how Kennie kicked and struggled so much that he forgot he was in a schoolroom with the statue of the Sacred Heart only a few feet away on its altar decorated with flowers and let off two loud farts that everyone in the room could hear, how Clement and the boys who still had a grip on Kennie's arms and legs could tell from the bubbling noise of the farts that Teague was shitting his pants, and how the nun said – whatever next – get the dirty creature out of my sight this minute and don't bring him back until he's respectable again. But because Clement is not yet sure whether the new boy is one of those who enjoy talking about such things he does not tell how when they got Kennie to the lavatory his pants fell down and they all made snatches at his cock and balls and he lay there without even trying to protect himself until they got tired of punishing him and went outside. And because Clement hardly ever talks about such things to anyone, he says nothing of how when he saw the thin black sausages of dirt in the crease between Kennie's balls and his thighs and the tiny tattered ribbon of brittle yellow stuff trailing from the loose skin of Kennie's cock he thought of a tumbledown house almost crushed by the weight of vines with sticky blooms and sap that left brown indelible stains on fingers and a family whose parents were always out in hotels and never home to feed and wash the children. The boy never complains about his hard lonely life but tries to find a boy who could be his friend and come home to the untidy house and hide under a bundle of rags in the girl's bedroom and spring out and overpower her and tear her clothes off while her brother keeps watch at the door. But no boy listens to Kennie Teague. The clean boys punch and torment him while he howls and lies helpless because there is no hope of explaining to them what he might have offered them.

## CLEMENT PLANS A RACE THROUGH HALF OF BASSETT

Few children from St Boniface's school live in Leslie Street. Hardly any of the boys in Clement's grade know where he lives. The two or three who have played in his yard have never noticed among the untrimmed shrubs the signs that promise that an event which once took place in a far distant shape like an amphitheatre, so that the crowds who watched it could study each of the thousands of stages in its elaborate unfolding, may one day be revealed to the people of Bassett. The people who walk up and down Leslie Street thinking of places like Melbourne or America or England far away past the low stony hills that enclose their city have seen nothing in all the quiet length of that strip of worn bitumen edged with gravel and fallen gum-nuts and leading only to other even quieter streets of gravel and dust to suggest that one day there might be flags and pennants hanging from its gate-posts and coloured arrows painted on its tar for days before the start of a great race which is open to every boy at St Boniface's school and for which there are no handicaps, so that more than a hundred milling boys have to form two ragged lines across the width of Lucknow Street outside the school gate to start. Nor are they prepared for the sight of hundreds of girls from the school, together with nuns and lady teachers, perhaps a thousand parents and relatives of the boys competing, and crowds of men, women, and children from the houses along the way who might gather to watch the race under every tree along Lucknow Street, Cordwainer Street or McCracken's Road. But when Clement's father brings home one afternoon from the mental asylum where he works a big ledger with dozens of unused pages at the back, the boy rules up the book ready for the day when the largest crowd that has ever been seen in that part of Bassett gathers near the corner of McCracken's Road and Leslie Street to see the leading bunch, gasping at the end of their journey of almost a mile, wheel around the last corner and force themselves to sprint the last hundred yards up the slow hill to the finishing tape that stretches from the front gate of 42 Leslie Street to the gum-tree across the street. Men with cameras will wait at short intervals along every street. The films that they take will be combined afterwards to show clearly the position of every competitor at every point of the race. The complete film will be projected in slow motion on a large screen so that a group of specially trained artists can prepare hundreds of coloured sketches and diagrams which will be printed in a book about the race. Anyone reading the book will be able to spend days or weeks following the progress of any one of the competitors from a place of obscurity to one that seemed to promise success and then through the ordeal of the last few hundred yards, when at different moments it seemed likely that now one and then another and then again still another might go on to win if only he did not falter and in a few strides doom himself to a failure that was all the harder to endure because of the triumph that had seemed briefly within his reach, from a prominent place that seemed to assure him of a leading part in the great final battle slowly back until even the most loyal watcher had to admit that all his early hopes were of even less worth than the hopes of the plodding few whose dogged runs took them at the finish only as far forward as the middle of the field, or from the most despised of all positions to one that was scarcely noticed at the end but still gave a wry pleasure to a discerning watcher because it placed him forever ahead of a few who in the exhilarating run towards the first corner had seemed assured of so much more than him.

## A GYPSY VISITS THE KILLEATONS

When Augustine arrives home at the house in Leslie Street his wife and son notice at once that he has no crayfish wrapped in newspaper under his arm and no cake of chocolate bulging his coat pocket. They know better than to bother him with questions about the races. He sits alone at the table eating a small part of the meal that has been kept in the oven for him. He chews his food with the slow rhythmical movements that he sometimes tries to teach to his son because they promote a regular loose bowel action. There is a knock at the front door. The sound startles the family because they have so few visitors. Sometimes Augustine promises his wife that when they can afford a decent house and some respectable furniture he will invite some friends home every Sunday. Then his wife asks him what friends is he talking about because he admits himself that most of the racing men he mixes with can't get through the day without making pigs of themselves on beer, that some of them are not good-living men, and that even the good Catholic racing men are mostly paying off their own homes and would only turn up their noses at the Killeatons' shabby rented place. The knock sounds again. Clement's mother takes off her greasy apron and goes to answer the knock. At the kitchen door she turns and makes a face at Clement to warn him against peeping at the visitor like an ignorant slum kid. Mrs Killeaton comes back to the kitchen and whispers to her husband that the man at the door is foreign-looking but doesn't seem a bad type and says he has tramped all day around Bassett selling medicines and health drinks to support his wife and children. She asks her husband should she buy a small bottle of something because she feels sorry for the man. Augustine asks in a loud voice – how much is the stuff? She says – only a shilling for a small bottle. Augustine says, loudly and cheerfully so that

the man at the door will hear – we've lost so much lately that
a shilling can't make much difference to us. He gives his wife
a coin, and she goes back to the front door. She brings back
a small brown bottle whose yellow label has only the words
*Guaranteed Worm Mixture Best For Children Take One Spoon After
Meals Or At Other Time.* She opens the bottle and sniffs at it, then
pours the milky liquid into the sink. She turns on the tap to
wash every drop down the plug-hole. Then she carries the bottle
and its lid outside to the rubbish tin. When she comes back
she washes her hands carefully with sand-soap, peering down
into the drain where the worm mixture has gone. Augustine
says – I suppose you've got to feel sorry for chaps who have to
travel round from door to door selling things. On Monday at
St Boniface's school some of the boys say that the gypsies have
come to Bassett, that houses are being burgled and girls are
being chased down lonely streets. That night Augustine reads
aloud to his wife a story from the Bassett Standard telling how
police have been called to intervene in domestic arguments at
the Bassett camping ground, how several men believed to be
gypsies have been convicted of being drunk and disorderly, and
how police have warned residents of Bassett to take precautions
against strangers selling doubtful goods or stealing poultry.
Clement asks his father who the gypsies are and where they
come from. Augustine tells him that long ago, before the time
of Jesus, a tribe of people from a land that was probably Egypt
were driven out of their true country and forced to wander
through poor countries like Armenia and Transylvania until
at last they scattered into little bands, each going in a different direction and wandering so far that after many years they
no longer remembered the way back to their homeland but
lived cheerfully in whichever country they found themselves,
except that something still kept them from settling for long in
any one town or city and compelled them to go from place to

place travelling along little-used roads and grassy tracks because people often persecuted them. At last, after many centuries of travelling, a small band of gypsies reaches Australia. They spend their lives journeying between towns in the sunlit arc of country that stretches for more than a thousand miles, out of sight of Melbourne and Sydney and Brisbane, from inland Victoria to outback Queensland. Camped at sunset beside a grassy back road that approaches an isolated town from an unexpected direction, the gypsies stare across a landscape that no Australians have noticed because although people have lived there for years no one has looked out before from the gypsies' vantage point. Pausing at corners where no signposts stand, the gypsies decide on a route that no one before has attempted. The country that they set out to cross is marked on hundreds of maps but their journeys are circuitous and unpredictable. Resting in the heat of the day somewhere between two roads that have been neglected for years because they run parallel to the main routes, the gypsies discover a tract of country, perhaps only ten miles wide and enclosed on all sides by roads between towns, where the sound of the breeze in cypress boughs or the rattling together of grass-seeds reassures them that even on journeys within a populous land there are places as secluded as they could wish for. Their leader tells the gypsies that they can always expect to find, in corners of districts that Australians believe to be well known and thoroughly explored, sheltering places like the lonely thickets their people once found on the road away from Egypt.

## THE GYPSIES GET GARRY BRODERICK

Every afternoon half a dozen boys who live around McCracken's Road saunter home from St Boniface's school in a straggling group, stopping to drag down from the kurrajong trees pods of itchy powder that they poke down each other's backs, slithering down the steep banks of the creek to piss across the wide drain at the bottom, and creeping through the dark drain beneath the embankment of the northern railway line where State-school boys are believed to take their girlfriends to a secret hide-out for rude games. Clement Killeaton would like to follow these boys home every night, but his mother has forbidden him to dawdle or to go out of his usual route. One morning he hears groups of boys in St Boniface's yard whispering that the gypsies have got Garry Broderick, one of the boys who walks home with the McCracken's Road gang. Their teacher tells them in school to say a little prayer for a special intention for someone in their own class. Broderick is missing from his desk. As soon as prayers are over a boy asks the nun whether Garry Broderick is dead. She puts on her stern face and says – little Garry will be back with us in a few days when he has recovered from a nasty experience that he had. In the yard at playtime Clement hears that Broderick was stabbed, that his clothes were torn off by a madman, and that he was tortured by the gypsies because he refused to say God was mad and to kiss a picture of the Devil. That afternoon Clement's mother meets her son at the school gate. On the way home she tells him that sometimes men who are sick in their minds or very drunk sneak up on little children and do dreadful things to their bodies. Augustine promises his wife that he won't go away to any more race-meetings until she feels brave enough to stay alone in the house again. Clement sees his parents whispering together over a certain page of the Bassett Standard. When he finds the page afterwards he sees that a column has been cut out and removed. At school next day several boys turn up with a column that they have cut from the Standard. Clement reads that a thirty-five-year-old labourer of no fixed address has been remanded without bail for trial on a serious charge involving a schoolboy. In their chasing and shooting games the boys call their enemies gypsies instead of Japs and Germans. That night Augustine announces that the police have been out to the camping ground and ordered all the gypsy families to leave and go where they like but never come back to Bassett as long as they live. Several days later Garry Broderick arrives at the door of the classroom. A priest stands beside him, holding the boy's hand. While the children scramble to their feet and cry – good morning Father and God bless you Father, the nun leads Garry to his seat. He grins around at his friends. At playtime the nun patrolling the yard continually scatters the circle of boys that gathers around Broderick. Still grinning, he tells everyone that he has been talking to policemen every day, that his father is going to give him a shilling pocket money whenever he wants it from now on, and that a dirty gypsy is going to be put in jail for five years because of something that he (Broderick) saw him doing beside the creek. Another boy says that his father was working out near the camping ground the day before and saw a mob of gypsies going back north to where they belong and looking very ashamed of themselves.

## AUGUSTINE TELLS THE STORY OF EUROPE

Clement is curious to know the exact route that the gypsies followed to Australia. In an old National Geographic magazine that Augustine has brought home from the library of the Bassett Mental Hospital, under the heading *By Iron Steed to the Black Sea: An American Girl Cycles Across Romania*, a gypsy woman, swathed in greasy shawls against the wind and the forbidding skies and with her baby tied to her back, sets out along a gravel road that leads past uninviting marshy grass towards a cluster of shadowy forested mountains. The caption names the grey gravel the long long road of vagabondage. This road, like others that the gypsies must travel on through that land, which for all its strangeness is still miles from their homeland, passes first among steep hillsides where villages of houses roofed with hay brace themselves against the giddy slopes. Strange sheep with dark stringy hair instead of wool come home each evening to yards with crude brushwood fences. Clement asks his father about the barefooted dirty shepherds and the miserable dairy-farmers with their bony mongrel cows. Augustine tells him that, just as the boy suspected, these are not real farmers. They were following their useless animals out to their scanty pastures in the morning and driving them back to barns and folds at night for hundreds of years before the first bushmen were born in the snug little huts that their pioneer fathers hewed by hand from the towering Australian trees. While the pale peak-faced Europeans went on copying their ancestors' methods of farming, tipping their caps to the local baron or grand-duke as he rode away from his turreted castle to spend the winter in Venice or Rome, and marrying their first cousins from the same village so that their stupidity and lassitude became thoroughly bred into their children, the bushmen of Australia were choosing great tracts of a land that had never been touched by a plough and crumbled like rich fruit-cake when they drove the corner posts of their boundary fences into it, droving overland the mobs of sturdy sheep and cattle that bred with zest under the proud gaze of their owners and filled the enormous properties with meaty full-blooded progeny, and devising for themselves, with only their native intelligence to guide them in a country that was hindered by no senseless traditions or customs, those farming methods that would make Australia the world's greatest producer of wheat wool beef and milk, even though the Americans would always boast in their infuriating accent that they were the world's best farmers. In countries where gloomy pine-shaded valleys recede endlessly back like the pages of calendars whose pictures are of mysterious scenes coloured in unhealthy greens and disturbing reds, the Europeans call themselves Catholics but know little of the mortification and self-discipline and resistance to persecution that are the marks of a true Catholic. Their cheerless cathedrals grow gradually empty of people while, in clearings where the clinking of parrots sounds instead of the jangling of green-encrusted bells, the little weatherboard churches built by the sweat and sacrifices of a few families of bushmen are crowded to their back porches on every Sunday of the year. Second- and third-generation Catholics go on felling trees and splitting posts and quarrying stone for their sprawling farmhouses that will stand for a century and more, glancing up for reassurance towards the broad yellow unbroken arcs of their horizons or the few ponderous golden leaves of their calendars, the last of whose pages may have been lifted quietly out of view not long before Clement first peered up behind his kitchen door and tried to understand why now instead of one great sun-coloured canopy that drooped for years at a time above his father's journeys he could see only a few rows of sharply ruled squares that would soon be up-ended and put away, along with the vague outlines and sober colours of the religious scene above them, in a twilight that was already thick with layers of such things. Far away in grey shadows behind a stark wall of hills someone goes on turning the Europeans' dreary pages so rapidly that a cold breeze begins to blow. Ghostly-white Jews in streets that the sunlight has never reached go on with their centuries-old task of wrapping gold coins in greasy cloth and mumbling to a God who was paid in full in blood two thousand years ago and has no more claim on the world. The servile peasants, who have spent too much time in the damp alleys and pestilential niches of their absurdly complex cathedrals when they might have been kneeling attentively on the bright slopes around the high altar assisting at Mass, begin too late to pray in earnest and speak truthfully to God. Advancing down the long long road to meet them is a war so terrible that not even a good Catholic can tell which side is right and which is wrong. Soon only the windowless walls of churches and monasteries are left standing. Outrages are committed against the Blessed Sacrament and even against nuns. Thousands of innocent people suffer along with millions who have been heedless or guilty and deserve to suffer. Peace settles like dust on the rubble of stones and hills, but things are no better. In the valleys around the ruined towns the listless survivors of the war try in vain to feed themselves from the stunted cattle and hairy sheep and the cramped misty fields. In places with long harsh names people chew the gristle of dead rats. Before long, thousands of once-proud townsmen and farmers are lining up for parcels of nourishing food sent from the distant farms where the pioneers' grandchildren have already doubled or trebled the yield of their land. Some of the Australian farmers have never even seen a Japanese bomber in all the sky above their properties. But far out in the silver and black maze behind the calendar-coloured stacks of National Geographics that have lain safely for years in a sturdy bookcase in the lounge-room of some comfortable home hundreds of miles inside the cliffs of the island continent of Australia, the gypsies are still travelling.

## CLEMENT LEARNS FROM HILLBILLY SONGS

Every weekday morning Clement's mother turns on the wireless to Station 3BT while she is lighting the fire in the stove. Clement always wakes up when the Hillbilly Half-hour begins, then lies in bed listening for a few songs that are the most beautiful music he has ever heard – except for Santa Lucia and the Skye Boat Song. Sometimes many weeks pass without his hearing his favourites, and he has to be content with songs like I've Been a Fool Too Long in which a man stands awkward and shivering while the woman whom he tried to please by taking off all his clothes sits laughing in a train about to leave town with all his clothes in her suitcase, A Soldier's Last Letter in which a man calls his mother his darling before he dies because he has no proper girlfriend, The Blind Girl in which a man's words are impossible to make out because his face is trapped in the thick cobwebs hanging all around a poor girl's tumbledown hut, and Don't Leave the Old Man Boys in which a ragged newsboy takes pity on an old man because the boy once had a father who used to look at himself in the mirror every morning as Augustine Killeaton does and sing as Augustine does You'll Miss Me When I'm Gone so loudly that his wife and son laughed at him and mimicked him until the day when his song suddenly came true. Four songs in each Hillbilly Half-hour are requests from listeners, but few people in Bassett or the country around love the same songs that Clement loves. At last the boy persuades his mother to send in a request program for him. He asks for I Am Thinking Tonight Of My Blue-eyes in which a man whose girlfriend has grown up and gone to live in a country like America stands trying to see the hills that are all he knows of that place, It Makes No Difference Now in which a man who found a wife after years of travelling around country race-meetings arrives home late one Saturday night but discovers no one waiting to hear the story of his horse's run that day because his wife has fallen in love with the owner of the horse that has beaten his own in a famous race, There's a Bridle Hanging on the Wall which always brings tears to Clement's eyes and

in which a man's horse breaks down in a Cup race and has
to be destroyed and a man comes home and puts the horse's
gear away in the empty loose-box, and The Blue Velvet Band
in which the same man sells his remaining young horse to
pay his fare to America and reaches a certain small town of
white-walled houses and yellow-and-silver poplars among a
blue haze from the cliff-like hills around only to learn that
his darling has died a few weeks before still wondering what
he was doing during all those years in the far country that she
scarcely remembered. Months pass. Each morning Clement
hears the name of someone from a distant street in Bassett
whose request program has been chosen from the huge bag
of letters that rustle emphatically as the announcer dips into
it. Out of the jostling throng come such popular favourites
as Old Shep, When the Rain Tumbles Down in July, and The
Overlanders, and Clement sees a tedious grey-brown colour
spreading across a city that might otherwise have been cut
through by a green pathway down which the waiting people
would peer for the first sight of unknown outlandish colours
and horses with evocative names and histories of promises
still not yet realised. But one day someone called Miss Shirley
Hazelwood from Honeysuckle Street North Bassett requests a
program that ends with the song about the empty stable and
the horseshoe nailed above the door. A horse gallops up and
down on the one spot inside Clement Killeaton's skin, trying
to find a way out. The boy jumps out of bed and runs to the
kitchen to hear his song. His father listens to it for the first
time. When it is finished Augustine reminds Clement that
it is only an imitation Yank song and that Australian men
and horses have done things that would make fools of the
soft Americans and their fancy stunted ponies. That evening
Augustine urges his son to listen to some genuine Australian
entertainment. A Musical Families session has just begun on

Station 3BT. A man is singing The Wild Colonial Boy while his son accompanies him on the piano accordion. Augustine makes Clement sit down beside his mother, who is reading the serial in the Australian Journal, and tells him that this is the way a family should enjoy their evenings. When Musical Families ends, a program called You've Got To Laugh is relayed from Sydney. The compere Chuck Hoobin calls himself The Boy from the Ozarks. In his native American accent, which Augustine refuses to believe is genuine, Chuck Hoobin invites people from the audience to compete in quizzes on stage. The losers have their faces pressed into apple-pies or their clothes pelted with ripe tomatoes or water poured over them, or they are made to jitterbug on stage. Augustine turns off the wireless not long after this program has begun and begins to add up sums of money in the margin of his newspaper.

## MR GLASSCOCK ILL-TREATS HIS FAMILY

Clement is woken by the sound of someone sobbing. It is Saturday morning and the sun is already hot. Clement peers through the curtains and sees Mrs Glasscock sitting on her front veranda sniffling and shuddering. Behind the greasy floral dress that she has been wearing for weeks, her huge slack titties roll wearily and aimlessly against her belly. Her youngest son Nigel stands on the dirt path beside the raised veranda. One arm is around his mother's neck and his face is close to hers. During the morning Clement plays quietly near the Glasscocks' fence and learns that Mr Glasscock has locked out of the house all his family except the eldest girl Dorothy, who has to get his meals for him. The other children have gone away to play, although Nigel comes back now and then to sit with his mother in the woodshed where she is spending the day. At lunchtime Dorothy sneaks out with a sandwich and a cup of tea for her mother and some money for Nigel to buy a Boston bun at Wallaces' shop. A little later Clement catches sight of Mr Glasscock going off to the Clare Castle for the afternoon. Clement's father too is spending the day in a hotel but the boy knows that Augustine drinks only an occasional lemon squash, that he hates the smell of the drunken crowds in the bar, and that he only goes to the hotel to talk to a few racing men and to hear from the starting-price bookmakers in the dim back lounges the betting fluctuations on the Melbourne races so that he gets the best odds for his bets. In the evening while Clement is buying a family brick of ice-cream in Wallaces' because his father has had a small win, he hears the grocer saying that Lloyd Glasscock is a disgrace to the neighbourhood and that someone ought to give him in charge. After tea the Killeatons listen through the laundry window to the noises from next door. Mr Glasscock sends his wife and Nigel out to the woodshed for the night. The other children have still not come home. Mr Glasscock tries to belt Dorothy because his tea is not cooked properly. The man who lives on the other side of Glasscocks' place knocks softly on the Killeatons' door and asks Augustine to go with him to phone the police. He too has been drinking, but he looks seriously at Augustine and says – it's not right for that big well-grown girl to have to stay in the house with that beast – even if he is her own father you never know what he'll be up to next. Augustine says he'd rather not interfere, but the other man persuades him to go. The two men climb over the Killeatons' fence and sneak through the long grass in the yard of the church hall so that Lloyd Glasscock will not see them. When the men have gone Mrs Killeaton tells Clement to get straight into bed without turning the light on, to leave his pyjamas off for just this night, and to say his prayers lying in bed because God will understand. The bedroom is stuffy and hot. Clement is too frightened to peep around the blind. He throws off his sheet and lies naked on his back. He listens for sounds from the Glasscocks' house, but hears only the occasional thump of a chair falling as Mr Glasscock chases Dorothy from room to room threatening to lift up her dress and tear her pants off and belt her until he raises big red marks all over her white bottom and the tops of her legs without caring how much of a certain other white thing he might happen to see between her legs as she kicks and struggles. Just when Mr Glasscock has her trapped in a corner and she offers to cook his tea every night and make his bed and wash all his clothes and pretend to be his young wife if only he will let her off the belting and let Mrs Glasscock sneak into the back room to sleep, Mr and Mrs Killeaton creep into Clement's room. Augustine whispers that everything is all right now in the Glasscocks' place. The boy's mother warns him as usual not to sleep on his back or he will have bad dreams.

## A BOY TEACHES CLEMENT SOME CATHOLIC DEVOTIONS

During afternoon playtime at St Boniface's school, Clement persuades Kevin Cuming, a boy with long bony legs, to run short frantic sprints and long tiring stayers' races up and down the narrow laneway between the main yard and the back gate of the school. Cuming only narrowly beats Killeaton in the shorter races but in every long race he leaves Clement far behind. Clement asks the long-legged boy to train him as a runner and improve his stamina. That afternoon Clement jogs beside Cuming as the tall boy leaves the schoolyard.

When Cuming, still jogging, veers off the footpath and into St Boniface's churchyard Clement follows him. They stop to a walk at the church door. Cuming dips his fingers three times into the holy-water basin, making the sign of the cross first on his forehead then on his lips and last over his heart. Clement does the same, although he has never seen his father make more than one sign of the cross at a church door. Cuming falls to his knees in the back seat on the epistle side of the church and buries his face in his hands. Clement kneels beside him. The taller boy looks around the church, sees only two old ladies kneeling near the altar-rails, and moves towards the gospel side. As he crosses the axis along which the tabernacle lies, he goes down on both knees, touching his chin to his chest and striking his fist three times against his belly. Clement follows him, doing as he does. Cuming prays again on the gospel side then walks slowly, with his hands pressed together in front of his face and the tips of his thumbs resting under his nostrils, towards the altar-rails. The old ladies take no notice as the two boys kneel briefly on the sticky leather cushion, bowing their heads and fingering the starched altar cloth that dangles on the inner, forbidden side of the wooden railing. Cuming leads the way to a side altar. He pulls his rosary beads out of his trousers pocket and twines them through his fingers as he looks up at the statue of Our Lady crushing the head of the Devil disguised as a snake. He leads Clement down the side aisle, crossing himself hurriedly as he passes each station of the cross, then into the rear part of the church beneath the choir gallery. He kneels in front of the life-sized crucifix in the corner, then tiptoes forward, clasps his arms around Our Lord's crossed shins, and kisses the nail that pierces His feet. Cuming waits while Killeaton kisses the sacred wound and even guides Clement's head so that his mouth touches the drops of dried blood on Our Lord's instep. After glancing around the church,

97

Cuming enters the confessional through one of the side doors. Clement hears him kneel down and murmur the short act of contrition, but he himself only peeps inside one of the empty booths. Cuming next leads Clement up the narrow stairs to the choir gallery, where he sits for a few moments on the stool in front of the organ. Then he returns downstairs, goes out by the same door through which he entered the church, blessing himself three times as before, and jogs towards the street. Clement jogs most of the way home. On the way he passes Margaret Wallace arriving home from Shepherd's Reef State School. She tells him that her father always lets her into the aviary for a few minutes as soon as she has put on her apron and eaten a double-header ice-cream from the shop. Clement gets home ten minutes late. He tells his mother that he wants to pay a visit every night after school. She speaks to Augustine about it that night. Next morning the parents announce that Clement may pay only a very brief visit to Our Lord in the tabernacle because He doesn't expect long-winded prayers from little boys. They warn him about talking to strangers, even in the churchyard, which is a favourite place for wicked old men who want to get hold of children. Each afternoon Clement sprints ahead of Kevin Cuming to St Boniface's church. After sprinkling himself three times at the holy-water basin he stands still for a moment, looking up at the lowest fringe of the colossal system of delicate golden tracery that reaches down through the dusty rafters and encloses in its barely visible web the rows of thickly varnished seats, the impassable altar-rails, and beyond them the pink and cream turreted altar itself. Alternately drifting down towards the levels of air where the whispered prayers of kneeling people pass on the first stage of their devious journeys through its baffling network, and billowing up towards the colourless slopes where the elaborate robes of the least of the angels and saints might sometimes trail carelessly past, the maze of filmy pathways, one remote corner of which is more complex and multifarious than the pattern of streets in any unvisited city or the tracks of cattle or hares or people of long ago through the grasses of inland plains or the sequences of coloured silks at successive intervals of fifty yards in famous staying races on broad racecourses or the whereabouts year after year of the well-knit nests of birds cunningly lodged among dense thickets in a thousand narrow gullies, tempts anyone watching its diffuse pulsating glitter to order his own steps or the involuntary shifting of his features or the spilling over of his unruly thoughts into a semblance of the first irregular but compelling arrangement of laneways in a long vista along whose farthest twinkling tracks not even the wisest or most saintly priest or nun may yet have travelled. Clement is allowed so little time for his visit that he is able to choose only one or two of the places that Kevin Cuming visits for his devotions. He kneels at the altar-rails or presses his mouth against the petrified blood of Our Lord or stares at the dusty wire grille inside the confessional before he jogs homewards, wondering at how little his stamina has improved since he first followed Kevin Cuming to the church and at the vast slope of changeable yellow haze that he still sees above the few systems of pathways that he has so far discovered and trodden devoutly around and the God who looks out and knows every pattern in it all. Each night Clement passes Wallaces' and sees Margaret at the gate of the aviary. After a week of jogging to the church and then home, Clement sees how little of the shifting sun-tinted maze he has so far crossed. That night he hurries straight from the schoolyard to the Wallaces' place, where he finds he has ten minutes to spare before his mother expects him home from the church.

## CLEMENT CONFESSES TO MARGARET WALLACE

Margaret Wallace stands on the other side of the fine wire mesh. The door of the aviary is locked, and the key dangles from her faintly freckled wrist. She boasts to Clement that she is going out of sight behind tall clumps of reeds surrounding a shallow grassy swamp that her father has copied from some coastal paddock in the far south-west of Victoria. As she disappears, Clement hears the flapping and splashing of startled dabchicks and moorhens. When she returns he asks her what kind of country lies inland behind the cold swamps. Margaret tells him that she has seen pleasant plains where the trees stand wide apart, where flocks of bustards cry out shrilly so as not to stray too far from the birds they may choose as their mates next spring, and clouds of green parrots rise up from the tall grass ahead of a traveller. Clement asks has she noticed places where people might settle and arrange squares of streets with clusters of gardens between, and she tells him that beyond the farthest place that she has reached the grass grows less abundantly and a huddle of low inviting hills sprawls around a vaguely defined creek-bed where infrequent rain-storms have exposed in the faces of boulders a close-set pattern of golden streaks. She claims that whenever she chooses she may go and make her home in that tempting place beneath the nests of honeyeaters and tree-creepers. Clement tells her that she will need a husband or a boyfriend. She answers that there may be a man already living there in a hut alone who will choose her for his wife and teach her all about the place, or that a boy whose father is a friend of her father may go on ahead of her and be the first man to explore the place and become the owner of it all and plant a lawn and garden and send for her to come and live with him, but that whatever happens no Catholic will be allowed to pry into the place and certainly not to kiss her or try to marry her. Margaret goes off again into the tall grass and low scrub and stays away longer than before. She returns with her hands full of brilliantly coloured feathers and claims that the birds are so tame in the places she has visited that they allow her to pluck a few of the finest feathers from their tails and breasts. When Clement asks her to tell him more, she says that beyond even the last inland place that she has told him about there may be a region so luminous that even her father who owns the whole aviary is not sure where it begins and ends because in certain weathers even the rocks and hills and bare grasses near the outer fences seem to flash for a few moments with its colour. Her father has crossed the aviary from one side to the other several times without seeing anything very remarkable but he still prefers to travel within the greener parts around its perimeter because he suspects there may be something too bright and powerful about the inmost area. Clement begs her to let him inside to see for himself whether there is something strange at the centre and whether birds or creatures still unnamed may live there. Margaret insists that no Catholics are allowed inside because they keep too many secrets from other people and dress up in coloured robes that no proper Australian would dream of wearing and speak in foreign languages when they pray. The boy offers to explain the mysteries of the Catholic religion to her if only she will let him explore the aviary with her. While she presses her surly face against the wire he describes the colours of priests' vestments, choosing feathers from the bundle in her hands to illustrate each sacred shade – green of eastern rosellas for the Sundays after Pentecost and the hope that God will change the drab pagan spaces around Bassett into small neat fields like those of Ireland where a man can travel from village to village within the one green vista, scarlet of gang-gang cockatoos for the feasts of martyrs and the Holy Ghost to remind people that God may one day send His messenger to inspire a small band of His faithful followers to set out for a vivid place that they have scarcely heard about, white of plumed egrets for great feasts and saints who were not martyred but died pure to urge some specially chosen people to live like priests and brothers and nuns spending all their time in walled gardens where only the tops of trees toss about in the north winds that tempt ordinary people to commit sins of thought about warm yellow-white plains where men and women play naked games together or rub the hottest parts of their bodies against the tickling grasses, black of clinking currawongs for the souls in purgatory to remind people of the dark grid of the edges of days that God has marked out on His holy calendars that are meant to warn Catholics and Protestants alike, and purple of paradise rifle-birds for Advent and Lent to remind people to press their faces in shame against the purple veil in the confessional and tell the truth about the things they have wanted to do with their wives and girlfriends because the grace that will pour back into their souls from the sacrament of penance shines with colours a thousand times more satisfying than the treasures that girls and women keep hidden in their playhouses and bedrooms. Clement persuades Margaret to weave her rifle-bird feathers through the wire-netting to make the shape of a purple screen. She agrees to turn her face away, and he murmurs – bless me Margaret for I have sinned this is my first confession Margaret and I accuse myself of – I have thought bad thoughts many times about a girl who goes to a State school – this is all I can remember Margaret and I am very sorry for all my sins. He looks over the screen and tells her in tones of ordinary conversation that she must now think up a punishment for him. She tells him to look his hardest through the wire, then teases him by holding aside the thick barrier of rushes that hides the inland parts of the aviary. He tries to make out the flat drier country behind her but a tall spike catches Margaret's dress and as it springs back into place exposes almost the whole of her pants without her knowing it. He calls her back to the wire and begins to teach her how to make her confession to him. She repeats the words after him but then claims she cannot remember committing any kind of sin. He urges her to recall the thoughts she has when she is alone in the farthest parts of the aviary, but she says she only feels pleased that her father owns the whole place and that if she feels like it she may explore all over it without any fear and without worrying whether anyone will catch her doing something wrong. Clement pushes a few times against the aviary door then turns around to go home.

## AUGUSTINE REMEMBERS CLEMENTIA'S WIN

A picture of the Sacred Heart and a framed photograph of the three-year-old gelding Clementia returning to scale after winning the Handicap Maiden Plate at Bassett on a certain day in January 1938 are the only decorations on the walls of the Killeatons' house. The racing print shows a solitary horse guided proudly towards a gazing crowd by a jockey with Chinese features and a silken jacket that highlights on many ridges and creases a light that might have shone white and dazzling on the circuit of closely cut grass that stretches back to a distant belt of trees marking the southern boundary of the great system of plains that stretches northwards to the river-border of Victoria and still farther into southern New South Wales. The crowd waits, the sun hovers, and the Killeaton family sometimes glance at the line of trees, but no sign comes towards them from out of the north. Augustine often reproaches himself for not daring to hope on the morning of that race that Clementia, the horse from the north, the almost untried gelding whose weak legs he had treated for hours in buckets of melting ice, had it in him to stride home with his ears pricked ahead of a field that included half a dozen smart horses from Melbourne stables. The line of northern trees tells him nothing on that day as he watches his colours, green for his ancestors, silver for rain as filmy and delicate as the prayers he once sent floating off over paddocks by the sea, and a few bright inches of orange for his hopes of something portentous that might arrive one day from far inland, moving towards the start of the brief race that he does not know is his last chance for at least ten years to back a winner at the unbelievable odds of thirty-three to one. No camera records the progress of the race. The result is printed in small type inside the back pages of a few newspapers and on one of thousands of cards in the records of the Victoria Racing Club in Melbourne. Few of the two thousand people who watch the race remember for more than a month or so afterwards the astounding burst of speed that carried the outsider from near last to first. Only the connections of the narrowly beaten horses wonder occasionally during the following year what became of the bush horse that brought their plans unstuck on that hot day up north at Bassett. Harold Moy, himself scarcely realising what he has just done, brings back to scale the horse that should have been Killeaton's greatest hope, that should have carried every penny of his savings and hundreds of pounds more that he could have borrowed from friends. Green and silver and orange come back triumphant from the unblinking north. Augustine Killeaton wins the race that he has waited all his life to win, and does not suspect that he may never win another. Colours too variable to fix in the memory have gathered at the edge of the northern plains, have run together into a thousand patterns that melted again as soon as they were formed, have assumed for an instant one fateful formation with his own device outstanding at its front, have massed themselves into a desperate gesture as if a finger pointed down from the north, and have scattered and will never again be assembled in that place.

## THE SKELETON IN THE CONFESSIONAL

One afternoon the McCracken's Road gang turns aside at the church gate instead of following the usual route home. Clement goes with them. The big boys whisper about some secret that has something to do with the church. Clement pesters them until they tell him that a woman's skeleton is somewhere inside St Boniface's church. They tiptoe into the church and pay their visit, kneeling in one of the back seats. They decide in whispers which of them will be the first to look. A boy creeps over to one of the confessionals and peeps into first one booth then the other. He comes back and says solemnly – they've taken her body away but you can still smell the dead smell. Another boy goes over and brings back the same report. While the other boys are searching around the baptistry and the crucifix corner for some sign of the dead woman, Clement hurries over to the confessional. He opens the door a few inches. A narrow shaft of sunlight reaches in ahead of him and picks out the last things the woman saw before she died – the smear of blood across the almost naked statue of Jesus hanging there to remind people that this is their last chance to be sorry for their sins, the close-set wires of the little grille, with thick grime around their meeting points, and all down one varnished wall a map of bare crumbling hillsides in a place like Palestine. As the boys leave the church Clement asks how the woman died. They tell him that she committed the worst of all mortal sins, the one

that Our Lord said in the gospels would never be forgiven. She
was going to try to get rid of it in confession but God or the
Devil killed her before she could open her mouth. That night
Clement asks his parents whether a woman really died in the
confessional. They ask him what he knows about it. While he
tells them some of the story that he has heard, his parents
make faces at each other. Then his father says gently – no one
has died in any confessional – a poor girl went out of her mind
with worry and fainted while she was going to confession last
Saturday night and now she's getting better in a rest home –
you can't go to confession when you're not in your proper
mind. Clement asks where the rest home is. They tell him it
is on the edge of a quiet little town near Melbourne. The girl
looks out of her window at streets that tell her nothing about
the district where she now lives or about the journey that she
must make one day back to the dark confessional where no one
will see her leaning her face against the mottled brownish hills
from behind which the priest will come to tell her whether
or not she was still in her mind when she committed that sin
and, if she was, whether he has the power to forgive her, and
where, if he says she was and neither he nor any other priest
on earth can take away the sin, there may be no way she can
save herself from hell, not even if she goes out of her mind
again or goes away to some city beyond hills as impenetrable
as the row upon row of sickly-coloured peaks that lead back
from just behind her head to no apparent sky, because even
though she never afterwards remembers Bassett she was still
in her mind in that city where she first committed her sin. For
many weeks the boys at St Boniface's talk about the girl who
died or went away, but no nun or priest ever mentions her.
Clement tells other boys all he knows about her. Sometimes
when he has made sure that no one is watching, he pays a visit
and looks quickly into the confessional and wonders why in

all those unexplored hills there is no place where someone might escape from a sin that was committed within the few gentle hills that thrust up through the dull surface of the city of Bassett.

## OLD BLUE NANCY

When the children drifting out from St Boniface's schoolyard into Fairbairn Street suddenly realise how much of the afternoon still remains and how little they might find to distract them behind the rotting picket fences of all the front yards, they look towards the gates of the church, hoping for a sight of Blue Nancy. Sometimes one of those children that the others dare not argue with points to an old lady, one of the many who live in the rows of old brick cottages between the church and the main streets of the city, and calls out – old Blue Nancy with blowflies in her pantsie, and starts to run as if the woman is chasing him. The other children squeal and claw at each other in their hurry to get away. They run for perhaps thirty yards along the footpath, calling out one of their rhymes – old Blue Nancy with maggots (her fingers, whiskers, her hankie, a dead cat, a stink bomb, lipstick, flea-bites, pepper, breadcrumbs, or soap-suds) in her pantsie, not caring whether the few grown-ups passing by overhear them. Sometimes Clement Killeaton runs with them, surprised to see how even the sweet-faced girlfriends or little sisters of the boys in the pack cry out without embarrassment the rude words of the rhymes. The children creep back a few yards to peer at the old woman. Many a time Clement is almost sure the woman is not the real Blue Nancy, or rather, not the woman he believes to be the real Blue Nancy and whom he once crept so close to that he is sure he would recognise her again. But someone calls out – Blue

Nancy's after us, and the children run off again, shrieking their rhymes. Sometimes when there is no old woman to be seen in all the street from the school to the Town Hall, a group of children, with Clement following them timidly, gathers on the footpath outside a certain house with drawn blinds and a tiny front yard full of dark leaves of arum lilies. One of the bravest boys pushes open the front gate, runs up to the front window, and raps on the glass until Clement is sure it must smash. Then the boy strolls back so slowly that the girls gasp at his courage. The children stand ready to run, but no sound comes from inside the house. Sometimes when Mrs Linahan from the shop nearby comes out to scold them, the children scatter as if Blue Nancy herself was after them, because Mrs Linahan is a spy for the nuns and sometimes comes to St Boniface's school to identify children who have misbehaved in the streets. At other times the leading boys stuff dirt and rubbish from the gutter or the dried turd of a dog or even lighted spills of paper through the slot marked LETTERS in the door. During all the years while the children of St Boniface's school claim to live in terror of Blue Nancy, Clement keeps trying to find out more about her. He never finds a boy who knows the whole story or who was present on the famous afternoon when Blue Nancy dragged a child screaming into her house and kept it prisoner until after dark and did filthy things to it. But all the different stories that he hears about Blue Nancy are so similar that he never doubts that there is such a woman, although he suspects that she may not live in the house with the lilies in the front yard. He often expects her to spring out at him from the shadowy corners at the back of the church or from the overgrown thickets in the corner of the churchyard where the former Bishops of Northern Victoria are supposed to be buried. Clement regrets that he was not privileged to be one of the children who saw Blue Nancy a few years before, when she was doing the deeds that made her famous. Yet he is never sure just who those children are. Just when he believes he has found one who was in the church on a certain afternoon when Blue Nancy attacked a group of children making the stations of the cross and herded them into a corner and spat at them like a cat, he learns that it was really an older brother or sister of that child, or another child who has since left St Boniface's. He pays many visits to the church in the hope of tempting her to show herself. He knows that every Sunday Blue Nancy goes to three or four Masses at St Boniface's and even to communion at each Mass, although this is forbidden, and that she dresses all in blue for Our Lady, although her clothes are so dirty that they could not possibly please Our Blessed Mother. She has been seen coming back from the communion rails munching on the Host, which is a shocking thing, but no one dares try to stop her. One rainy afternoon when she was too lazy to go out of the church to the lavatory she left a great pile of shit in a corner of a confessional and several inches of piss in the baptismal font. When she pays a visit she prays aloud in a voice that carries all through the church, and mentions the names of children in her prayers, asking God to make their Tommies turn black or drop off. Sometimes when Clement takes another boy with him on an afternoon visit to the Blessed Sacrament he sees an old lady loitering near the altar-rails or even changing the flowers on the altar itself and whispers to his friend – it's Blue Nancy isn't it? But the other boy only says – don't be stupid it's nothing like her. One day after he and a group of children have left the veranda of Blue Nancy's house covered in scribble and the letter slot stuffed with horse dung, Clement calls at the church to pay a visit. He walks alone around a corner of the building and buries his face in a cushion of dusty dark-blue stuff speckled with fluff and festooned with long white hairs. As the old lady thrusts him away from her belly he looks up and sees a wrinkled face wrapped in a long blue woollen scarf and topped with a blue hat with blue feathers. The woman's sunken mouth works rapidly as if she is chewing on something. Clement's legs go weak from fear. He runs down Fairbairn Street and keeps running all along Cordwainer Street. Next day he boasts to a few boys that Blue Nancy grabbed him outside the church and tried to put her hand up the leg of his trousers, but no one takes much notice of his story. As weeks pass he feels brave enough to go back each afternoon to the church and look for the old woman in blue, but he never sees her again. Sometimes when he is alone he doubts whether it was the real Blue Nancy after all, but whenever he is with a group of children on an oppressive afternoon and one of them starts to chant – old Blue Nancy with a pisspot in her pantsie, and he sees far along the hot dreary street the vague figure of an old lady, he joins eagerly in their game because he recognises the true Blue Nancy who might have killed him if he had not escaped from her clutches one afternoon at the church.

## CLEMENT LEARNS WHY A GIRL
## NEARLY DIED AT CONFESSION

One morning when some of the boys at St Boniface's school are talking about Blue Nancy and someone tells how he saw her the other night creeping out of the same confessional where the skeleton of the dead woman used to be, and someone else says that Blue Nancy probably had something to do with murdering the dead girl, and the others wait for someone to say that she certainly did and that he knows the true story of it, a boy named Alfie Brancatella, who seldom smiles or sees the point of any joke or tells a story that anyone is willing to

listen to, announces solemnly that he knows all about the girl
who nearly died in the confessional because she is a friend of
his auntie. Nobody stops to listen, but Clement waits until the
other boys have gone and then asks Alfie to tell him the story.
Alfie Brancatella says that his mother went to visit his Auntie
Teresa and his Auntie Teresa knows a lady in her street who is
looking after the girl whose name is Stella because Stella got
sick and had to go to Melbourne but she is a lot better now
and she might be getting a baby soon. Clement asks where
the girl Stella lives. Alfie says probably near his auntie's place
22 Jasmine Street Cornishtown past where the Cornishtown
trams stop and turn around. Clement tries to learn what really
happened that night in confession, but the boy only says that
his auntie says it was nothing to make a fuss about and Stella
only wanted to find a place where people wouldn't be nasty to
her or her little baby. Alfie promises to tell Clement if the girl
ever has a baby and to find out where she goes to live if ever
she leaves Cornishtown. On a hill that looks northwards away
from Bassett towards the useless grey mounds and scoured
gullies across which the ironbark forests are slowly making
their way back into Cornishtown, a girl who may never be
able to go to confession again sits during the long afternoons
trying to make out a vista that she might point to when her
baby grows up and say – that's the sort of country that will
have to satisfy you in place of the hills like Palestine's that
I once saw blazing all across the wall on the last afternoon
that I ever went to church or where we may have to go away
together like dingoes searching for a place where no one has
ever heard about mortal sins or which may turn out to be your
punishment because you will stare at it for years and still not
understand why everything is so grey and quiet because it is
no use telling you that there might have been other hills far
away for you to look at.

## AUGUSTINE TELLS CLEMENT HOW
## TO AVOID TEMPTATION

Augustine stands for a long time in the deep straw of Sternie's loose-box, rubbing first the wire curry-comb and then the soft bristle brush down the horse's shining coat. He hears children's voices through the galvanised iron wall. He stops rubbing the horse and listens, because it is some time since he has been able to take an interest in his son's games and hobbies. One of the Glasscock girls says she loves a boy from the Brothers' College who gave her a beautiful picture of the baby Jesus and his mother. Clement says he loves a girl but her name is a secret. A Glasscock boy claims it is Margaret Wallace, the grocer's daughter. Clement explains that Margaret is not his real girlfriend but only someone he kisses and hugs sometimes. The Glasscocks demand to know more about the secret girl, and he tells them she has never let any boy kiss her or look at her pants. Someone tries to frighten Clement by telling him that they all know the girl he means and that they will tease her about Clem Killeaton when they see her next. Augustine picks up a bucket and rattles it. The talking suddenly stops. The Glasscock children soon start talking again, but Clement says in a loud voice that he has to go and help his father and he hopes they enjoyed all the fairy stories he has just told them. That night when Augustine has finished his tea he invites Clement to sit down beside him. While the boy is sitting down Augustine glances at his wife. She goes to the sink and rattles some plates, pretending not to listen. Augustine says what a pity it is that he always has important racing business on Fridays and Saturdays otherwise the three of them could go to confession regularly as a family. He asks the boy whether the whole grade at school goes to confession before each first Friday and whether he, Clement, makes a fair dinkum confession. Clement answers solemnly that he does. Augustine warns his son that the nastiest sins of all are the ones that boys and girls or young men and women commit when they are alone together. Clement answers that he doesn't know anything about those things. Mrs Killeaton interrupts and says she is sorry to have to mention this because she was going to try and forget all about it but she has already once before caught Clement talking dirty stuff with young Nigel Glasscock. Augustine says sadly that he'll get the whole story from her later. He tells Clement not to go near the Glasscocks or any other State-school children for a while until he forgets all about their silly games and talk, that if he feels lonely sometimes because he has no brothers or sisters or mates that come and play at his place there's nothing wrong with him admiring some good little girl at St Boniface's from a distance, but that he will get into serious trouble if he goes near her or says anything silly to her. Augustine turns to his wife and says he supposes the kids used to go on with talk about boyfriends and girlfriends when she was a girl at State school. She says that of course they did a bit but she used to think it was a lot of rot and anyway they were big lumps of kids about thirteen or fourteen years old and Clement is still wet behind the ears. Later that evening while Clement is rolling marbles across the mat in the lounge-room Augustine warns him that he does too much dreaming on his own. Augustine looks over his little shelf of books, which he rarely touches, and takes down Man-Shy by Frank Dalby Davison. He tells Clement that Man-Shy is one of the greatest books he has ever read and that it will keep a boy's mind off that other nonsense that he probably gets from watching too many American pictures. Clement reads Man-Shy attentively during the next few evenings and weeps quietly over the last chapter. He spends the following Saturday alone in the backyard designing an enormous fenceless cattle station where a man goes on long rides each day with a woman who went to a State school in the bush but never showed any part of her body to a man before she met the one she loves. Together they get down from their horses and creep towards a waterhole that they have told their stockmen never to disturb because a herd of wild cattle comes down each night to drink there. They peer through the harsh prickly scrub to see which one of his cows and heifers the bull is preparing to mate with. They are careful not to let the wild cattle smell them because the cattle still believe that the whole of the Australian bush belongs to them. The man hopes that his girlfriend will learn from watching the cattle what he and she should do when they are married, because her own father and mother would never tell her and she is so pure that he does not like to talk to her about it. When the huge bull finally climbs grunting and wheezing onto a young heifer who has never yet been mated with, his weight is too much for her. She staggers and falls, and the bull sprawls on top of her. The young woman throws herself into the man's arms, weeping and shivering. The man urges her to be brave and wishes he could explain why she need not fear something like that happening to her.

### CLEMENT LEARNS MORE ABOUT THE FOXY GLEN

Therese Riordan and her girlfriend, whose name Clement still does not know, sit side-saddle on the lowest branch of the mulberry tree in an enclosed garden that is only one part of the confusing system of flower gardens and ferneries and shrubberies around Riordans' house. Therese accuses Clement Killeaton of always wanting to talk about rude things. She jumps down to the lawn, using both hands to keep her skirt pressed against her thighs, then walks towards the house. She calls out to the other girl that Clement is only allowed to come to Riordans' place because his father owes Mr Riordan hundreds of pounds and still wants to borrow more. When Therese has gone inside, the other girl asks Clement does he know any girls in his street who are the same age as her and Therese. He answers that Cynthia Glasscock is about their age. She asks has he noticed anything different about Cynthia's chest lately or seen anything new between her legs. He pretends to think hard before he answers no. As soon as he answers, the girl laughs and says – that proves you don't really see that girl without her clothes on because if you did you would have noticed how different she was after she turned thirteen. The girl then asks him has he discovered any more about Therese's Foxy Glen. He admits he hasn't and asks the girl to give him some clues about it. She asks what does he want to know about it. He asks how long has Therese had the thing. The girl says that Therese's mother or grandmother gave it to her when she was very young. He asks whether it has anything to do with religion or the Catholic Church. The girl hesitates, because she herself is not a Catholic, then answers that the Lord Jesus is able to look at it sometimes but that even He is not allowed to touch it. Clement asks how much Mr and Mrs Riordan know about it. She tells him that they have a Foxy Glen of their own to play with that they keep locked in their wardrobe. Mr Riordan would like to get Therese's out and play with it sometimes but Mrs Riordan helps Therese to keep it away from him. He asks will Therese ever forget about it or throw it away when she grows up. The girl says probably not because Therese will always want to have something that she can keep secret from boys and men and tease them about, and anyway she will want to keep it to remind herself of all the happy times she had when she was a girl. He asks whether the boy Silverstone ever saw it if it was such a secret. The girl laughs and says that Silverstone was her boyfriend for a while so she tricked Therese into letting him play with it. He asks where Silverstone went to live after he shifted from 42 Leslie Street. She answers that there's no hope of Clement finding out about the Foxy Glen from Silverstone because he went to some town away up north from Bassett but his father was always being shifted around and he could be anywhere by now. He asks what Therese would do if a boy like himself did unlock the tin and touch the Foxy Glen. The girl thinks a little, then says that nothing much would happen at first but a boy who discovered it could sneak into Therese's room whenever he wanted to afterwards and do what he liked there and Therese couldn't stop him because he knew her greatest secret. Clement asks whether Silverstone did that after he got at the Foxy Glen. The girl says he wouldn't do it straight away because he wanted to tease and frighten Therese and then suddenly he had to shift from Bassett but he could still come back to live there again one day and then Therese would be in trouble. Outside Riordans' front gate Augustine tells his son that he doesn't want to alarm the boy but it's just as well for him to know that things are going so badly at the moment that they might have to think of leaving Bassett and living somewhere far away. Clement looks out from the hill where Riordans' house stands, past the edge of Bassett towards the country where a boy might wander from house to house in search of a girl who would give in and let him into a side garden or a sleep-out, where the loudest noise all afternoon is the buzzing of a blowfly lost on the wrong side of a pane of glass, as soon as he boasts to her about the Foxy Glen that he saw and explored one day long ago in a shady place in a wide secretive city, hoping all the while that he will be able to explain what he saw in words that will make her turn away at once and go to unlock her own secret things.

## AUGUSTINE MIXES WITH CATHOLIC RACING MEN

On Sunday morning after Mass Augustine finds his racing friends talking and smoking in the shade of a date-palm near the path from the church to the presbytery. Clement knows that they may go on telling each other about yesterday's races and trots and dogs until long after the next Mass has started inside the church. He moves restlessly around and tries to catch his father's eye. Augustine tells the men that he'll be working as an amateur again next week and turning over his wages to the bookmakers. The man named Frank Hehir laughs and asks him why he didn't dip into the collection plate when it came past him during Mass. Augustine says that with his luck the way it is at present he would have been sure to pull out the dud penny that Frank Hehir had already slipped on to the plate. While everyone laughs, Augustine whispers to Therese Riordan's father that it's no joke because he's really in deep this time. Stan Riordan whispers to him not to worry because there's got to be a turn in the road soon. Clement leans his weight on his father's arm and asks will he go over the road and buy the Saturday Sporting Globe. Augustine makes a face that is meant to show the men that he is exasperated with his son but not able to refuse him. He says – yes I suppose you'd better let me read about all my past sins – it might just teach me a lesson. He pulls a ten-shilling note out of his pocket and hands it to his son. The boy then asks in a voice that is meant to sound innocent and girlish – can I buy myself a chocolate malted milk too please Dad? Augustine looks around at the men and says – why not – it's the bookmakers you're robbing – not me. Clement hurries to the shop across the road and asks for a chocolate malted milk and a Sporting Globe. While the young woman with her apron over her Sunday Mass clothes is mixing the malted milk, Clement asks her how much that will be. She tells him – a shilling. He answers that he'd better have a sixpenny cake of fruit-and-nut chocolate too. He chews the chocolate two squares at a time on his back teeth while he sucks the cold milk and the gritty sediment of malt through his straw. As he finishes the last of the chocolate his straw makes a roaring noise among the layers of sluggish bubbles at the bottom of the tall metal cup. He stabs the straw into the soft lump of ice-cream that still remains and lifts the blob to his mouth. When he has pricked the last bubble and captured the last droplets of milk from the can, he takes the Sporting Globe and the handful of change back to his father, dropping the chocolate wrapper in the gutter outside the shop. Augustine takes the coins from his son and drops them into a pocket without looking at them. Later, when no one is look-ing, he slips a finger into his fob pocket and verifies that it is empty of notes. While the others go on talking around him he reminds himself that he has already handed over the week's house-keeping money to his wife, who is a good manager, that he needs no money for drinking or smoking, that he can ride his bike to work instead of catching the bus and keep the silver in his pocket for a trunk call to Goodchild during the week, and that he will be paid on the coming Friday. A man that Augustine suspects of having a share of the Riordan brothers' bookmaking business asks Augustine can he look at his Globe for a minute. Augustine hands over the paper and then pulls his own shoulders back with pride to think that the man probably has a roll of tenners in his pocket but is still too mean to pay for his own Sporting Globe. Augustine sees a soft consoling light in the depths of the harsh sky. Something more awesome than the gaze of thousands of spectators focuses on the little bunch of racing men as God records in His infinite memory the value of their separate prayers in the Mass just ended, the sacrifices they made when they dropped their money into the collection plate, their willingness to buy little treats for their children or wives, the cleanliness of their bodies – whether their teeth and fingers are stained with nicotine or their kidneys poisoned with alcohol or their penises scabby from contact with hard-faced women on the nights after their greatest wins, and begins to decide which few of them will draw clear of the others and collect the reward that has long been due to them. Augustine moves a few feet back from the circle of men to let his own distinctive colours stand out even more clearly from those around him. He waits for that sudden insight that tells a rider even two furlongs from the post that his mount is going so well by comparison with the others that this will be his day. He jingles the few coins in his pocket and wishes his son would ask him for another malted milk or a large block of chocolate so that he could pour the handful of coins into the boy's palm and send him across the street to spend them all, and then go home with not a penny to his name to wait for the sudden reversal that will bring him all the money he deserves. The great jumble of words and thoughts and secret intentions and silent prayers that spill out across the white glare of St Boniface's churchyard is no more than a dozen or so patterns of colours sent out yet again by their owners in a last bid to get square, and the least movement forwards or backwards of the least-noticed pattern is only the result of some faint tremor in one of the long delicate strands that lead back from every man and every churchyard and every racecourse to God. The long reins grow taut around the Catholic racing men and tug at their most private thoughts and hopes. Augustine waits his turn to join in their conversation again. He checks himself from beating his fists against his chest, which is still radiant from his Holy Name communion, and crying out to them to let him through because he has only a few shillings left in his pocket to last him for five days and yet believes so firmly that all the rolls of notes in their pockets are only lumps of lead to handicap them that he wants to make his run now even this far from home, to dash clear of them all in his colours that announce to the world how badly he needs this victory, and to chase to the very end of the straight the slender thread that trails down towards him from God. Clement drags his feet through the gravel and pulls at his father's coat. The taste of the malted milk and chocolate is sour and sickly in his mouth. He asks his father when can they go home.

## AUGUSTINE TELLS WHY THE
## BARRETTS ARE UNFORTUNATE

On the way home from church Clement asks his father what is wrong with Mr Barrett. Augustine explains that all the men back in the churchyard are good practising Catholics. Some of them waste their money on the dirty habit of smoking and perhaps one or two of them are a bit too fond of their beer but they are all good husbands and fathers, although Pat Toohey is a bachelor of course, and not one of them has a dirty tongue or would ever be mixed up in anything that was the least bit unclean. It is a privilege for the boy to be allowed to hang around the men while they're talking and he must never blurt out to anyone else the things they talk about. Poor Mr Barrett was born and brought up a Catholic like all of them and went to school to the nuns but turned his back on his religion and got into bad company when he was young and silly and worst of all got married out of the church which isn't really a marriage at all as Clement ought to know from his Christian doctrine lessons because no matter what a man says or how much he tries to fool himself he can't fool God and he's still a Catholic for all eternity. Of course Mrs Barrett is not a bad sort of woman and their poor children go off to Shepherd's Reef State School every day and don't know any better but it's not their fault and Clement must never breathe a word to little Kelvin Barrett who's probably just as good a boy in his own way as Clement himself. But Mr Barrett is a wild sort of chap who suffers from gambling the way some people suffer from terrible diseases and can't help himself. He goes off to Melbourne every single Saturday and leaves his wife and children sometimes with not even enough money for house-keeping and forgets all about them while he's rushing round the betting ring all day and off to the two-up at night. If there's a dog meeting on the Monday night he's just as likely to stay in Melbourne for that too. Nobody knows how he keeps his job or pays his rent. He plays up his winnings and gets a big roll now and then but he never stays in front for long. He is the worst kind of gambler who chases his losses and can't let a race go without having a bet on it. Whenever Augustine sees him on a racecourse he keeps out of his sight, and Clement must never say anything about racing in front of little Kelvin Barrett.

## CLEMENT VISITS TAMARISK ROW ON A SUNDAY

Until the early hours of a Sunday afternoon after he has been to holy communion, Clement moves gingerly among the roads and farms in his backyard, aware all the time of the precious whiteness of the egg-shaped soul that floats inside him in the space between his stomach and his heart. He carries in the pocket of his shirt a few cards from his collection of holy pictures. When no one is watching, he kisses devoutly the picture on the front of a card, holds it obliquely in the sunlight to see the dull sheen of the circles of golden dust around the heads of the holy people, then turns the card over and whispers aloud the pious ejaculation – *Eucharistic heart of Jesus have mercy on us* – that is printed on the back. He puts the card back in his pocket, pressing it firmly against his heart, and stands waiting while the three hundred days' indulgence that the little prayer has earned him drifts downwards in a million-faceted cloud of jewelled dust and embeds itself in the yielding surface of his soul in the shape of the rim of a petal or the vein of a leaf that is still only half-formed at the outer edge of the arabesque that may take years more to complete. Through the unworthy streets of his city a boy carries little Jesus dressed in the ballooning silk sleeves and begemmed jacket of the Divine Infant of Prague. Clement knows that the great saints of olden times would lock themselves away from all sights of lawns and birds and coloured glass and rich cloths and pray alone in their rooms with such fervour that long before they died they could see within themselves far glittering landscapes whose inviting laneways led through groves of molten green towards iridescent courtyards where a person would never again need to search for those shapes and colours that he had once seen from each opposite end of the city where he was born but could never discover although he walked for years up and down its long footpaths. The most that a boy like Clement Killeaton can hope for, since he wakes each morning in a house whose doors fit so badly that the north wind brings in grains of dust that are all he ever sees of the towns he would have to pass through on a journey in search of cities where God once appeared to His holy people, and whose plaster walls are so worn that they let through strands of yellow hair that are all he ever sees of a girl he would like to take with him when he sets out for God's land, is that he might go on living quietly in a city whose yellowish soil and greyish grass-seeds cling to his skin and clothes while he repeats the prayers that are laden with indulgences from the Church's inexhaustible treasury of grace and goes to communion every Sunday to add a few more opalescent granules to the patterns forming slowly in his soul. But out among the tall ragged weeds of his backyard he keeps stumbling on the familiar roads that he has been forming for years with his own hands to lead back the owners of racehorses to the shaded houses where their wives wait during long hot afternoons, stripping off one piece after another of their clothes as the heat grows worse, and to make long and trying the journey of one man, the owner of a horse named Tamarisk Row, back to the property where his wife has waited so often during the years of their marriage but has still not yet heard late one evening that their horse has won the prize that they know he deserves. A faint grey film of grime settles all over Clement's soul. The hundreds of minute crevices between the chips and slivers of the semi-precious stones whose patterns he can still only guess at are slowly choked with a dark repulsive grease. On the wide expanses of tender white stuff that may one day be encrusted with glancing shards of holy communions and winking sequins of Masses and luminous crumbs of indulgenced prayers in a pattern more complex than any distant sight of silk-jacketed riders in some impossible race of a thousand tightly bunched horses that will show the long slow story of a boy's struggle to become a good Catholic and save his soul in the end, specks and blotches of sickly brown and dark-grey well up and spread outwards like weeping sores. Clement moves slowly through the tall marshmallow weeds, tracing the involved system of roads that a racehorse owner must follow homewards after one more unlucky race to where his wife's naked body is all he has to console him. The boy stands waiting while the owner leads the horse from the float to the loose-box and while he measures carefully the horse's evening feed. A scum-like coating obliterates the last details of the pattern that might have gone on forming all day in the boy's soul if only he had not remembered that man and his wife who never gave up hoping that one hot Sunday they could sit together reminding each other of how their own colours were fixed at last ahead of twenty other combinations in a pattern that could never be altered.

## THE FIELD LINES UP FOR THE GOLD CUP RACE

There is a city isolated by plains where on one day of every summer every man, woman and child and every priest and brother and nun finds a vantage point on a long slope of trampled grass beside the straight of a racecourse where the Gold Cup race will be run. Every person who watches the long line of horses walking out from the saddling paddock or cantering past on their way to the starting barrier has somewhere about him at least one betting ticket. Some people look up only briefly at the pastel-coloured sky on the morning of the great day and feel only a quick spasm of excitement to think that the afternoon will be hot and cloudless. These people wait until they arrive at the course before they each choose a horse and bet a small sum that they can afford to lose. Others keep glancing up at the sky all morning and feel a keen pleasure at the thought of the long fierce afternoon to come. These people have been trying to decide for weeks which horse they will finally call their own for the few minutes of the big race and how much money they dare to risk in the hope of winning what they have wanted for so long. Others, the owners and trainers of the horses entered in the Gold Cup, have felt on many mornings, while most of the people in the city were thinking of other things than racing, alternate waves of elation and fear as they moved quietly around their stables watering or grooming their horses or loading them into trucks or floats. They remember the successes or failures of their lives as glimpses of fields of horses rushing past slender winning posts in small towns of which the racecourses are all that they have ever seen. The horses that these people back in the Gold Cup are their own, the same ones that they have hauled home across miles of strange country and led back to their sheds late at night after races in which they failed by one thrust of their legs to earn their connections hundreds of pounds in stakes and bets. The bets that these people risk on their horses in the Gold Cup are far larger than those of the people who come to watch – not because the owners and trainers are wealthier than other people but because many of them depend on racing for their livelihood and must bet all the money they can spare whenever one of their horses has a chance of winning. Long before noon the people of the city begin to arrive at their racecourse. Lesser races are run. The sun grows still hotter. Seen from the crowded hill beside the straight the city is only a few towers and rooftops among confusing rows of trees. In the hottest hour of the afternoon the first starter in the Gold Cup appears on the track and the thousands of people standing with their backs to the city look down at their racebooks to check the colours and numbers of the field. As the voice of the course broadcaster announces each name the connections and supporters of that horse look up from the page to see the silk jacket of the rider, conspicuously alone against the waste of grass that fills the inside of the course. The sound of each name and the stately passage of each precisely coloured jacket past the stand remind the crowd that this day they have waited so long to enjoy is no ordinary holiday but a solemn occasion because despite all the ambitious claims of the resonant names and arresting colours only one horse will be famous for years afterwards while the followers of those that come within a few yards of winning will talk among themselves during those years of some trifling accident – a horse shifting ground for a few yards approaching the turn or a horse changing stride in the straight or a rider losing his balance near the post – that condemned them to remember only a victory that was almost theirs. Number one *Monastery Garden*, purple shade, solitudes of green, white sunlight, for the garden that Clement Killeaton suspects is just beyond the tall brick wall of his schoolyard – the garden where priests pray and meditate beneath the leaves on even the hottest afternoons. Number two *Infant of Prague*, alluring satin and embraceable cloth-of-gold, for the picture of the child Jesus that Clement tries to fix in his mind after holy communion. Number three *Mysteries of the Rosary*, incandescent depths of blue enclosing elusive jewelled points or stars, for the beads that Clement rolls delicately between his fingertips while he meditates on the joys and sorrows and glories of Our Lady. Number four *Silver Rowan*, a film of translucent rainy colour across the pure green of a country much older than Australia, for the horse that Augustine Killeaton still dreams of owning. Number five *Lost Streamlet*, a stripe of golden brown persisting through the grey-green of remote thickets, for the creek that might lead Clement to the secrets of Bassett if only he could follow it through a confusing maze of side streets where he sees only glimpses of it. Number six *Hare in the Hills*, the colour of lawns spotted with flowers in valleys where the birds and animals are almost tame, for the land of Little Jacky Hare – the land that no Australian boy has ever entered. Number seven *Passage of North Winds*, an orange-red colour that is best looked at from a certain angle and is continually threatened by a turbulent yellow whose true extent may be far greater than the colour it opposes, for the miles of plains to the north of Bassett which Augustine Killeaton once crossed and which Clement believes stretch unbroken to the heart of Australia. Number eight *Transylvanian*, grey or the colour of pale skin with seams or veins the colour of a precious stone from a far country, for the endless journey of the gypsies from Egypt through the gloomy valleys of Europe to the grassy back roads of northern Victoria and still further to places only they could discover because Australians all thought their country had been thoroughly explored. Number nine *Captured Riflebird*, a colour that wavers between green and purple enclosed with gold or bronze margins, for all the rare and gorgeous birds of Australia that Clement Killeaton only knows from books and may never observe except in some enormous aviary copied from the Australian landscape. Number ten *Hills of Idaho*, gold or buff the colour of endless distances edged with the faintest stripe or suggestion of mauve or pale-blue, for the most longed-for vista of America – the shimmering foothills that all hillbilly singers and film stars are trying to reach. Number eleven *Veils of Foliage*, a striking pattern of black and silver and gold overlaid with deep green, for the glimpses of sumptuous lounge-rooms behind flashing windows overhung with shrubbery that are all Clement has seen of the homes of the wealthy people of Melbourne who work as professional punters or illustrators of magazines or projectionists in picture theatres. Number twelve *Springtime in the Rockies*, all turquoise or peacock-blue or ame-thyst, for the sky over the mountains on the morning of the day when a man nears the end of his long journey back to the woman he has loved since he first peeped into her backyard as a schoolboy, and wonders whether she will have pity on him after all the miles he has travelled. Number thirteen *Den of Foxes*, a preponderance of black or dark-brown with only a hint of a smouldering colour like the flash of some rare treasure or the eye of a wild dingo in an inaccessible cave, for all the secrets that Therese Riordan and the girls of Bassett will never reveal. Number fourteen *Proud Stallion*, flamboyant scarlet per-versely opposed by a luxurious violet colour, for the furtive excitement that Clement enjoyed when he persuaded Kelvin Barrett to behave like a savage stallion and the mystery of what the Barrett family do in their house on hot afternoons. Number fifteen *Tamarisk Row*, green of a shade that has never been seen in Australia, orange of shadeless plains and pink of naked skin, for the hope of discovering something rare and enduring that sustains a man and his wife at the centre of what seem to be no more than stubborn plains where they spend long uneventful years waiting for the afternoon when they and the whole of a watching city see in the last few strides of a race what it was all for.

## CLEMENT HEARS THAT THE BARRETTS GO NAKED

Clement listens quietly from another room while his mother tells his father a story she heard from her friend Mrs Postlethwaite of how Mrs P went over to Mrs Barrett's for something or other and knocked on the front door because she doesn't really know Mrs Barrett well enough to go around the back and sing out and how Mrs P knocked a good few times and at last she heard someone coming down the passage and this woman's voice called out who is it and before Mrs P could get the words out of her mouth the door opened and there was Mrs Barrett poking her head and shoulders around but Blind Freddy could have seen she didn't have a stitch on and when she saw it was only Mrs Postlethwaite she opened the door wide and stood there as bold as brass in the nuddy and said she'd just been sitting in the bath with the kids to cool off because it was so hot and it never seemed to worry her whether someone might have been going past in the street just then. Poor Mrs P got such a shock she hopped inside so the woman could close the door and said what she had to say and got for her life but before she went this big lump of a Barrett boy as old as Clement at least strolled out of the bathroom as naked as an Indian to see who was there. Clement watches for Kelvin Barrett in the streets in the late afternoon. When he catches up with Barrett at last, Clement says – I wonder what it would be like if we played some of those stallion games again. Barrett says – I'm sick of all that stuff. He tells Clement that he has found out some much better games. A new boy at Shepherd's Reef school has been teaching him. The new boy has been shifting around all over the place and going to all sorts of schools. Clement says – I wonder if he ever knew the Silverstone boy. Barrett says – yes he's always talking about that boy. Clement asks – does your sister play the games and other girls too? Kelvin says – yes if they want to. Clement asks – does your mother ever watch you? The boy says – of course but she never tries to stop us. Clement asks how the Barrett family keeps cool on very hot days. Kelvin says – we go out on the back lawn under the hose or sometimes we have a cold bath. Clement hesitates, then asks could he come up to Kelvin's if his mother lets him one hot afternoon. The boy says – I suppose so. Clement does not dare ask his mother to let him visit the Barretts' until it is too late and he realises that the hottest days of summer are over. Late in March he watches closely a morning that seems likely to bring back the weather he wants, but something too subtle for him to see happens in the air and the day he has been waiting for disappears into the end of another summer.

## CLEMENT LEARNS OF THE DESPERATE
## JOURNEYS OF THE ARABS

Early on the first afternoon that Clement spends in grade three, the teacher Miss Callaghan makes the children join their hands in front of them on the desks. She tells them – now you're going to learn something about your new subject geography. She cleans a wide space on the blackboard then lifts out daintily between two fingers a stick of orange-yellow chalk from a new box. She rubs the chalk sideways across the board to make an unbroken plain then places the stick neatly back in its box, takes out a blue stick and makes a belt of sky above the horizon of sand or gravel. She tells the grade about the Arabs of Arabia or Egypt who have to spend their lives travelling across a cruel desert. She asks someone – what would you need if you lived in a desert instead of a city with trees all around? The child says – cool houses and lawns to play on. She asks other children until someone tells her – water. Miss Callaghan uses the blue chalk to make a neat round pool of water far out on the plain. With a few quick strokes of a stick of green chalk she puts three palm-trees, each with four identical drooping fronds, at regular intervals around the pool. She tells the children how the thirsty Arabs make for such places when they are hot and tired and still a long way from the end of their journey. Miss Callaghan says slowly and emphatically – oasis, and prints the word neatly beside the water. She tells the children it is an important word that they must not forget. Then they take out their geography exercise books and she shows them on which page to draw an oasis. Those children who have crayons are allowed to colour in the water, the leaves, the desert and the sky. Half-way through drawing his oasis Clement looks up across the furrowed orange-brown desk-top and sees on the wall a picture of a green lawn in England many years before. Two boys in flimsy summer clothes are trying to pour water from a watering can onto a dog. The dog struggles and barks but the girl with long fair hair cannot rescue her pet because the boys are too strong. She waits until one of the boys puts the can beside him on the grass. Before the boys can stop her she grabs the can and empties it over them, flinging the water through the wide hole at the top. While they stand shivering and howling, the girl's mother comes out from the house through the arbours of climbing roses. She orders them inside and makes them take off all their clothes to hang in front of the stove. The girl stands watching and smiling at their shrunken little cocks. Her mother tells her not to make fun of them, but does not send her away. When their clothes are dry the boys set off for home. Outside the house they whisper to the girl that they'll get even with her one day. Miss Callaghan says – who's that chattering and nattering down the back I'd like to know? Boys and girls each put a finger on their lips and shake the fingers of the other hand at a girl named Colleen Kirk. Miss Callaghan says – so you're the gossip Miss Kirk? The girl stands up and says – please Miss Callaghan it wasn't me at all. The children around her wag their fingers furiously and say in a chorus of shocked voices – ooer ooer. The girl says – Miss Callaghan they're picking on me. The teacher says – sit down for the moment but I'm keeping my eye on you. Two boys still wait their chance to tip water all over a girl when her mother is not watching from between the high walls of roses. They pretend that they are only interested in sprinkling the fluffy dog and never look past the rainbow that the sunlight makes in their drops of water towards a room where almost every week on some afternoon when the children have packed away their books ready for home their teacher says – we'll have a quick test in geography before we get out the door – first question what's the name of the place that the Arabs are always trying to get to on their travels across the desert in Egypt or Arabia? and still only half the class put up their hands to answer, and where the boy Killeaton begins to suspect that even on the last day of their year with Miss Callaghan no one, not even the teacher, will know any more of the story of the Arabs than that they set out to cross hundreds of miles of country and had to turn back from wherever they were heading for towards a place where in the comfortless shade of three unlikely trees they saw a shallow pool that hardly anyone believes would ever be found in such a barren place as they stand in the hottest hour of the afternoon chanting in loud strained voices their last prayers for the day – to thee do we cry poor banished children of Eve to thee do we send up our sighs mourning and weeping in this vale of tears, and a boy sees almost invisible droplets of water drifting downwards while children around him are thinking of other things that may never happen.

## CLEMENT WONDERS WHAT THE BASSETT CREEK CONCEALS

Long before the first hot days of summer, the water dries up in the creek that comes from somewhere among the stony hills where the Killeatons sometimes go out on Sundays to look for the rare Bassett waxflower and appears suddenly at the ends of streets that might otherwise have wandered for miles or runs for short distances beside the single railway track that leads northwards before it becomes a kind of drain and disappears beneath the main streets in the centre of Bassett after which Clement does not know what happens to it although his father has told him that a certain deep gully that he has seen on the other side of the city is probably the same old creek. But Clement still walks home from school on some afternoons in December beside the creek and even goes a few hundred yards out of his usual route in order to pass through a place where clumps of bulrushes hide from sight every sign of houses and streets towards Leslie Street and from which he can look in a different direction across a weedy paddock and see clearly the shapes of backyards up a few steep streets in a suburb named Diggers Hill that the people of Leslie Street think of as the opposite end of the city from their own. Clement returns home thinking again that a traveller who left the streets of Bassett and followed the creek for a whole afternoon could watch unnoticed from secure vantage places the simultaneous passing of people in parts of Bassett that no one else had ever watched at the same moment. The traveller along the creek might see suddenly thrust into view a network of streets that he had never realised could be disclosed so soon to someone who had just left behind him a view of quite a different place. One afternoon when Clement has even begun to believe that a person who followed the creek instead of his usual streets might be led unawares to a place from which he could see into a girl's backyard from the one quarter from which she never expected to be spied on and learn what she did when she thought she was completely hidden by hedges and shrubs, and is about to clamber up through tall bulrushes to leave the creek and reach home by the last of the streets that connect with Leslie Street, he meets a boy named Gerald Dillon from the Brothers' College. Dillon's house is just across the street from the creek. Clement explains to the boy that he has been trying to find a short cut home. When the older boy still looks at him suspiciously Clement asks – what do you look for when you go down the creek? Dillon says – I'm not that stupid that I go down where you've just been – that's where the Shepherd's Reef girls from my street have their hide-out where they go on Saturdays and sit for hours and do whatever girls do – the place where I go is somewhere else that I'm not telling you – some of the boys from the Brothers' have our own hide-out there – they've got a secret club and I'm a member. Clement asks – don't you ever try to visit the girls' place to see what they do there? Dillon says – not when the girls are there of course but the other Saturday after the tarts had gone we sneaked down and smashed their place to bits – now if they go down there they can only sit and stare at things or tell girls' secrets to each other or cry all the afternoon because they've lost the place they thought no one knew about.

## CLEMENT THINKS OF THE FIERCEST ANIMALS IN AUSTRALIA

As Clement stretches his body on the mat in the lounge-room and offers his chest and belly studded with bold pink titties to his pups for sucking, he decides that people like the girl who had to look for other hills than Palestine's deserve as a reward for never giving up searching the excitement of being the first to discover in the depths of an unexplored valley in the mysterious heartlands of Australia the cave where for centuries a dingo parent has lain with her young ones. As he arranges the lengths of smooth cream-coloured pine kindling wood at right angles to his old woollen jumper and remembers the day when his mother's friend Mrs Postlethwaite came suddenly into the room and his mother, who by then took no notice of the game although she sometimes said it was a stupid thing to play, explained that the pieces of wood were fox cubs or some sort of animal babies that her son was feeding and Mrs Postlethwaite kept peeping round the doorway and giggling and whispering that she'd never seen anything like it, Clement gently moves the piece of wood farthest from his face towards the shadowy hollow between his thighs but keeps a hand ready to snatch the wood back towards his belly at the first sound of his mother approaching. He knows that after all those years while the dingoes were groping and sucking at all kinds of hidden things in the dark and the full-grown dingo was always being surprised by the strange new games that the pups were learning and yet was still sure that there were still stranger places that they might tug at with their tough little gums because there was no one in all the blue-black creases of mountains that fell away on all sides from their valley who could teach them which places would never give milk no matter how hard they squeezed them, someone more powerful than the fiercest dingo may still burst through the opening of the cave and discover what has been going on there for thousands of years and go back to the coast and tell the people there that they can travel safely inland and clear the land for farms because there are no wild animals in Australia except a few dingoes who only want to keep out of sight in their lonely caves. But if, far inside the hills where the girl who nearly died at confession went at last to have a baby, there are still a few caves like those that were once at the heart of every system of hills, then the shadow that falls across the opening of the cave might only be that of a woman looking for an even quieter place to take her own child, and the dingo family will be safe for at least a few more years.

## BARRY LAUNDER AND HIS FEATHERED FRIENDS

During all his years at St Boniface's school, Clement Killeaton goes in fear of Barry Launder and his gang. No other grade but Clement's has a tyrant like Launder. Clement sometimes watches the boys in other grades. Fights break out between pairs of boys or sometimes between two mobs. Certain boys, roughly dressed and with uncombed hair, are acknowledged to be better fighters than the rest. But no one boy claims to be the ruler of a whole grade. When a fight breaks out in

Clement's grade it is usually between two weak or insignificant boys, and the winner never boasts of his victory or looks for someone else to challenge. Apart from these few private disputes, all fights are between Launder's gang and some outsider. And these are not really fights, because Launder's gang always wins. Barry Launder and his six closest friends (he calls them his fine-feathered friends after once hearing some teacher use those words) regularly punish other boys. It is a common sight to see two or three feathered friends dragging a whimpering pleading offender towards the quiet corner under the cypresses behind the boys' lavatory where Launder waits, blowing gently on his knuckles to cool them if the day is hot or holding them inside his pants against his balls if the weather is cold. The guilty one is brought before Launder. The feathered friends hold his arms until the last moment. Launder punches with all his strength once or twice into the victim's guts until he makes the hoarse gasping noise that means he is winded. Sometimes the noise of the victim as he rolls on the ground draws a small solemn crowd of watchers. If a teacher appears, one of the feathered friends steps forward and owns up. Usually the beaten boy and the feathered friend get one cut each from the strap. (The feathered friends are famous for never flinching under the strap and never having to nurse or wring or shake or blow on their hands afterwards.) Only rarely does a genuine fight break out between a feathered friend and a boy from outside Launder's gang. Perhaps twice a year some boy who has been goaded and tormented until he does not care what happens to him will throw himself howling and punching and even kicking at a feathered friend. Shocked watchers gather to see the end of this madness. They do not have to wait for long. Three or four feathered friends deal out the punishment. The most painful of the Chinese burns and rabbit killers and full Nelsons that they inflict are to teach the victim, so they explain, that he must always obey the rules of clean fighting. The feathered friends are hated and feared probably more than Launder himself. Barry Launder usually asks politely for what he wants – the cakes and fruit from a boy's lunch, or half of his lunch money – but the feathered friends will even bash a boy before asking him to run some simple errand for them. They devise ingenious schemes to collect funds for their gang. One day they give each boy in the grade a book of grubby numbered tickets. They instruct the boys to sell these tickets at a penny each to State-school boys on the pretext that a football is being raffled. Enterprising boys are expected to grab the Protestants' pennies and run away without even handing over the tickets. In this way a book of tickets may yield two or three shillings. Clement Killeaton throws his book of tickets over a fence in Cordwainer Street then steals sixpence from his mother's purse and tells the feathered friend who comes to collect his money that a Shepherd's Reef kid grabbed the last four of the ten tickets and pissed off with them. The feathered friend, named Michael Hannan, orders Clement to turn up on the next day with another fourpence or be bashed. But the gang is so pleased with the amount of money collected that Hannan forgets to ask Clement for the fourpence. The feathered friends' memories are not always so short. They remember and forget in unpredictable ways. A boy may be warned as he leaves the schoolground one afternoon that the gang will half-kill him next day. Yet if he arrives just before the bell next morning and plays inconspicuously he may well be ignored. Yet again he may be playing quietly with his own friends days later when he looks up to see two or three feathered friends sidling up to him. Their first words are a terrifying formula – remember that day son – that is meant to set the victim wondering what past crime he is about to pay for. Clement Killeaton hates and fears the feathered friends but cannot decide what to think of Launder himself. Launder sometimes shows more than a slight interest in Clement, and some of Launder's tricks for getting boys into trouble suggest to Clement that he and Launder could probably laugh at the same kinds of jokes if only the feathered friends would let him near their chief. By the time he is in grade three Clement has succeeded a little in winning Launder's favour. Launder lets him hold one of his enormous swollen bags of marbles as he swaggers from ring to ring, plundering dozens more in games whose rules he interprets to suit himself. When Launder mentions that he collects birds' eggs, Clement makes some little cards with coloured drawings of birds copied from Leach's Australian Bird Book and offers them to the chief. When Launder decides to collect milk-stones Clement searches for them all over the yard and hands some of his most lustrous pearly pebbles to the boy. He is disappointed when Launder chooses only one or two and distributes the rest among the feathered friends, but he goes on trying to discover some common interest that he and Launder might share. In his last year at St Boniface's Launder plays some of his best tricks. One day Michael Hannan, the feathered friend, brings to school a ten-shilling note that he has stolen from his father's desk. Launder first announces that he and his gang will spend the money on malted milks at lunchtime. Then one of the feathered friends suggests that they might be late back from the shops and it would be better if they took a few of the teachers' pets and the good kids with them so they could all get into trouble together. Clement tries to hide himself in the crowd but he and half a dozen other frightened boys are rounded up and marched down the street. They walk almost to the centre of Bassett before Hannan looks at his watch and says – it's almost bell time now – we'll stop and have a cool refreshing drink. They walk into a milk bar, all ten or twelve of them, and

Hannan and Launder order six chocolate malteds. The old lady behind the counter takes a long while to set out the six glasses brimming with milk and froth and the six cold metal pannikins each with at least another glassful inside. Launder and his gang drink slowly, pausing after each sip to breathe out slowly or belch loudly or lick the creamy coating from their top lips, knowing quite well how frightened their captives are of being late. When they have almost finished their pannikins they offer the other boys a guzzle each. Clement asks for a straw because his mother has taught him to be afraid of other children's germs, but he is not allowed to have one. The old lady says – hadn't you boys better run along to school now? Clement starts to tell her that they have a half-holiday, but Launder interrupts and says – we know we'll get the cuts when we get back but we don't care. The old lady looks shocked and stern and Clement tries to hide his face so that she will never recognise him afterwards. They stroll back to school. The yard is empty and silent. Launder orders them to stop at the gates to the tennis courts behind the Y.C.W. hall. The tennis courts are strictly out of bounds, and boys have been strapped merely for running onto them to retrieve their playthings. Launder lowers a tennis net until it sags in the middle. Then he orders the captive boys to run around in a circle and jump the net and to keep running and jumping until he comes back to get them. Then he and his feathered friends walk towards their classroom. After a few minutes the old nun who teaches the fifth grade sends a girl to see what is going on in the tennis courts. The girl stares amazed at the line of boys who are still trotting up to the net and jumping it. Then she hurries back to her room. She comes running back to say that Sister Hilary orders them all to march to Sister Tarsisius the head nun at once and tell her what they think they're doing. The boys walk slowly to the head nun's room. Clement tells her that Barry

Launder and some other boys took them prisoner and made them late and then made them run round and round the tennis courts. The nun says she doesn't want to hear any of that nonsense about boys making other boys do certain things because no boy can make another boy do anything. She gives them each two stinging cuts and sends them back to their class with instructions to stay in for the whole of every lunchtime for the next week. At afternoon playtime they are the centre of a crowd of boys who can scarcely believe what they have done. One hot afternoon when even Miss Callaghan, the third-grade teacher, stares out at the green fringes of the pepper trees, the children are told to write a composition on At the Picnic. No child shows any enthusiasm. Clement has not been on any picnic for a long time, but he finds it easy to write about a few families who travel all morning across clinking pebbles and between trees as hard as stone to a green embankment overhanging a pool where kingfishers skim the water. He writes *while the grown-ups rested on the soft grass my cousins and my friends and I went up the creek to explore.* While he wonders how much of what they discover at the head of the long valley that narrows into the sort of gully where foxes and dingoes and rare species of birds may have lived untroubled for years he might put down on his page, where already the sweat from his hands makes his pencil skid, one of the feathered friends comes up the aisle pretending to look for a pencil sharpener and whispers to Clement that Barry Launder has ordered every boy to write in his composition *at the picnic I let a breezer in my pants*, or else be bashed to smithereens after school. The feathered friend stands waiting for Clement to pass the message on. Miss Callaghan's head is bent over her desk. Clement whispers the message. Launder's boy says – now write it yourself. Clement's hand shakes with fear. He writes the first words slowly and awkwardly. He looks at the other boys in his seat.

They too are writing, with solemn frightened faces. Launder's messenger says I'll be back to see you later and make sure you've written it properly. He moves to the next row with his message. A hush falls over the boys' half of the room. Boys crook their arms around their books to hide them from their neighbours. Here and there a boy dares to ask his neighbour in a whisper whether he has written the words. A few who cannot decide what to do stop writing and bury their heads in their folded arms. Miss Callaghan says – you've all been busy workers this afternoon especially the boys – finish off your work now and leave your books open on the desk for two of my girls to take up when you've gone to play. Two of Launder's boys leave their seats to make a hurried inspection of books. Because Clement sits on the end of a seat he has to show his page. The words are written on the page. The feathered friend pats him kindly on the back. Then, because he would rather be bashed to death by Launder's gang than write impure words to a nun or a lady teacher, Clement uses a rubber and his pencil to change the sentence to *at the picnic I felt a breeze*. But there is still an odd-looking gap in the text. Miss Callaghan tells the boys to march out quietly. In the playground they form silent groups. Launder and his men stroll proudly around asking each boy did he write it. Not one boy answers no. The gang has never seemed so powerful. As they march inside for their last hour of school the boys stare at the pile of books on Miss Callaghan's desk. As soon as the prayer is over, one boy hurries to the front and says in a strained voice – Miss Callaghan can I have my composition back please because I made a mistake in it? The teacher looks oddly at him and says – you can trust me to find all your mistakes. The boy bursts out crying, and Miss Callaghan sends him outside to have a drink and calm down. Boys all round the room glance at Barry Launder. The chief nods his head slowly, and the watchers understand that that boy is done for. Miss Callaghan tells girls to give out pastels and pastel books. The grade has to draw a day at the beach. Then Miss Callaghan begins to correct the compositions. The boys watch her face. They do not have long to wait. She looks at the name on the cover of a book that she is marking and says – Henry Phelan come here at once please. The boy turns white and creeps out to her desk. Even the girls sense that something serious is happening. Miss Callaghan says – did you write this Mr Phelan? and points to a line in the boy's exercise book. The boy nods. She says – put away your pastels and prepare for a trip to Sister Tarsisius and heaven help you when you get there. The boy whispers – please Miss Callaghan Geoffrey Lunn wrote it too. She says – we don't need tell-tales in this grade thank you. But she looks eagerly through the stack for Lunn's book. Half-way through she pauses and stares at a page of writing. She looks at the cover of the book and says – Patrick Gilligan come here at once please – no stay in your place and you too Mr Phelan. She snaps at the grade – go on with what you've been told. It takes her about ten minutes to make a list of the boys who have written the words. Twelve boys out of the twenty-three in the grade are lined up at the front. Clement Killeaton is one of them. Miss Callaghan follows the line of boys out of the door. Behind her the class breaks into uproar. She leaves the boys standing outside Sister Tarsisius's room while she shows their compositions to the head nun. Sister Tarsisius comes rushing out to confront them. Her wooden rosary beads click furiously together. She says – what have you villains got to say for yourselves before I strap the devil out of you? Clement speaks up. He feels the wind seeping out of his bottom and the first hot oily trickles of poop following. His knee-caps begin to twitch. He says – Sister I didn't really write it. The teachers find his book and look at his composition. The nun says – what you're trying to tell us is that you wrote it and then tried to hide it which is just as bad if not worse. He cries like a baby and says – Sister Barry Launder and his gang made me do it. The nun avoids looking at Clement's face as she tells the others – I'm not going to listen to any excuse that some other boy made you do this wicked thing – no boy can make another boy do a thing as serious as this – in fact I'll give two extra straps to any boy who tries to tell me that story again. She makes the boys tear the offending pages neatly out of their books and carry them in line to the burner. When they return to her she gives them each four fierce cuts. Clement and a couple of other boys howl openly. Sister Tarsisius looks at Miss Callaghan as the nun tells the boys to buy new exercise books that night and report with them to her room every lunchtime for the next three weeks to copy out the whole Catechism in their best writing. When they get back to their own room Miss Callaghan makes them write a new composition while the others are drawing with their pastels. Clement cannot stop himself from sniffling. The whole grade soon realises that he howled when he was strapped. Long before home-time the news reaches Launder that Killeaton pimped on him to Tarsisius, and each time that Clement looks up he sees the clenched fist of a feathered friend being shaken at him. He starts to run as soon as he is out of the door. He gets almost to the school gate before they catch him. Perhaps because they are impatient to boast to each other about their greatest success in all their years at St Boniface's, the gang does not prolong Clement's punishment. Launder punches all the wind out of his guts, each of the feathered friends drives a fist as hard as he can into Clement's face, and Fat Cormack takes his shoes and socks and jumper and his school-bag and all his books and pencils and throws them one into each front yard along Fairbairn Street but does not stop him from trying to search for them.

## CLEMENT GIVES HIS FOOD TO LAUNDER'S GANG

Every afternoon when Clement reaches the back veranda and pushes open the fly-wire door, his mother calls out – did I give you enough for lunch today? and he answers – yes thanks. Every morning as he leaves for school she makes him put his hand into his school-bag to make sure he has not forgotten his two brown-paper bags – one for lunch and one for play-lunch. The lunch is always six little triangular sandwiches with at least two different kinds of fillings arranged so that as he eats his way through the stack he never finds the same filling in two successive sandwiches, a cake or a pair of sweet biscuits, and a piece of fruit. The play-lunch may be two fairy cakes or a slice of moist fruit-cake or two cheese cakes or a pair of biscuits with jam between them, but never the same as on the previous day. Sometimes his mother asks him – in all the years you've gone to St Boniface's have you ever had to buy your lunch once? He answers no, because even when there is no bread in the house on a Monday morning she sends him to school with just his play-lunch and waits at the school gate at lunchtime with sandwiches made from fresh bread. Sometimes she asks – have you ever had to take your lunch wrapped in newspaper? He answers no, because even his cakes and biscuits are always wrapped in clean lunch-wrap paper inside a brown-paper bag. And sometimes she asks – have you ever had to sit down to a whole pile of jam sandwiches with no butter? He answers no, because he always has such fillings as cheese and Vegemite, egg and lettuce, apple and raisins, dates and nutmeg, peanut butter, or Ovaltine mixed into a paste with the butter. His mother is always curious to hear about other boys' lunches and listens eagerly as he tells her how half of his grade run down to Keogh's Korner Shop with threepence for a pie or pastie or fourpence for a whole Boston bun which they eat without any butter or filling, and how some of the others have a stack of jam or Vegemite sandwiches without any butter and wrapped in nothing but newspaper. He never tells her how only a few days after he first started school a small crowd of the shabby poorer boys in his grade gathered round and stared as he unwrapped his dainty parcels of cakes and took out his piece of fruit, and how a few days later some boys that he knew, even without a trial of strength, were tougher than himself snatched away his bags and tossed pennies to see who would have Clement's fairy cakes or his apple or even the choicest of his sandwiches. In his very early days at school Clement believes that by allowing the rougher boys to plunder his lunch and play-lunch bags he is securing their friendship or at least making sure that he will be safe during the many lunch-hours when they go around looking for victims to bash or torture. But he soon finds that even though he reaches a perfect understanding with boys like Barry Launder or Michael Hannan or Fat Cormack, so that they only have to walk up to him before they go to Keogh's and say – what have you got for us today Killer? and he hands over everything but a few sandwiches to them to share among themselves, he is often one of the first to be hauled before Launder to be dealt with – sometimes only half an hour after he has given the gang all the tasty parts of his lunch. Eventually he tries such tricks as eating all his cakes and fruit on the way to school in the morning or hiding in the lavatory as soon as the grade is let out for lunch or eating his lunch as he walks only a few feet from the nun patrolling the shelter shed. None of these tricks works for more than a few days. In the end one of Launder's gang either bashes him or threatens to bash him until he agrees once more to hand over a fair share of each day's lunch. Then one day a big girl in Therese Riordan's grade, whose name he never discovers and whose face is not pretty enough to inspire or even to interest him, happens to see two of Launder's gang dipping into his lunch bag while he stands patiently by. The girl orders them to give the food back to Clement. When they tell her to bag her bloody head she slaps each of them hard across the face, takes the lunch from them, and sends them running away. For two weeks after that she meets Clement at the school gate each morning and takes his lunch into safe-keeping. Then at playtime and lunchtime she meets him and lets him sit beside her while he eats. Two or three times during those weeks Launder and his gang prowl around just out of her reach shaking their fists at Clement or holding their stomachs and groaning and crying that they are starving. But they never dare to bash him, even after the girl has left him. Then one day the girl tells Clement that he should know by now how to handle the boys if ever they bother him again, and leaves him to eat his lunch alone once more. About a week later she sees him in the yard and says – those little brats haven't been pestering you again have they? He says – no thank you very much, because he doesn't want to put her to any more trouble. But of course they have been ransacking his brown-paper bags since the first day after the girl left him. During the next few weeks he does not care how much they take from him so long as they do it quickly and out of sight of the girl who thinks she has saved him. As time passes and he and the gang move up through the grades they begin to trouble him less. Sometimes he tells his mother he doesn't feel like too many sweet things and she gives him only a tiny slice of cake. He shows this cake to the gang as proof that his mother doesn't allow him so much for lunch as she used to and so that when he eats his cake on the way to school a few days later they will believe that she has finally given him none at all. Some of the gang order him to tell his mother that he is dying for cakes and biscuits, but by then he is more skilled at deceiving them so he tells them that his mother says sweet things are ruining his teeth or that she is too sick to bake. Sometimes they forget about his cheesecakes on Monday and fairy cakes and fruit-cake on other days because they have more money to spend on their own lunches – enough for lollies or even a small bottle of soft drink. By the time they are all in grade three together the gang often finds it easier and more satisfying to steal money from their own mothers' purses than to grab a few cakes and sandwiches from Killeaton, and for days at a time they leave him alone. Then sometimes when he offers them something tasty to placate them, they refuse it or gulp it down and tell him it wasn't good enough to get him out of the trouble he is in with them. Several times during the grade-three year when he is threatened with a bashing from them he begs them to remember all the hundreds of good things from his lunches that they have eaten since the bubs' grade but they take no notice. One day towards the end of grade three when they are already wondering what it will be like next year at the Brothers' College, Miss Callaghan sends the boys out with their readers to the little wooden seats under the pepper trees. She tells them to sit six under each tree where she can see them from the windows and to go on read-ing to their monitors until she calls them back inside. Clement is monitor of a group that includes Barry Launder and one of the feathered friends, a boy named Reginald Pearce. As soon as someone has started reading, Launder and Pearce start talking to each other. Clement takes no notice of them until Miss Callaghan pokes her head out of the window and says – Clement Killeaton remember the names of all the talkers please and report them to me when you get back inside. Clement calls out – yes Miss Callaghan, as she goes away from the window. Barry Launder grins at Killeaton, sure that he is safe. Reginald Pearce, whose hair is always long and dirty, who wears his older brothers' patched trousers and their loose-hanging jumpers with unravelled cuffs where the sleeves have been cut down to shorten them, who lives in the shabbiest house that Clement has ever seen, with no curtains in the windows and a backyard heaped with scrap metal and empty beer bottles, who is so dirty himself that the girls make faces when they have to stand near him in line, and who is probably the least cruel of the feathered friends, looks Killeaton in the eye and says with no suggestion of a smile – don't pimp on me Killer please Killer and tomorrow I'll bring you a nice little piece of cheese from our place – tasty cheese – you like cheese don't you Killer? Clement thinks at first that Pearce is teasing him, but as he looks again at the boy he is not sure. When it is time to go back to the classroom Pearce walks close behind Clement and says softly – don't pimp today Killer – a nice little piece of cheese Clem. Inside the room Miss Callaghan is so busy that she says only – monitors send their talkers out to me please. Clement goes to his desk and says nothing. Pearce does not bring the cheese and never mentions it again. Whenever Clement sees the boy during the following weeks he shudders to think of a piece of cheese gripped between Pearce's dirty fingernails and wonders whether he ought to offer him some of his lunch because the boy might not get enough to eat in his shabby house.

### CLEMENT SEES WONDERFUL THINGS IN MARBLES

At night when Clement is adding to the entries in his book of marbles he sometimes urges his father to bring his book of chooks' pedigrees up to date. But while Clement will not be satisfied until every marble of the two hundred and more that he owns is safely written up under such headings as *Where It Came From, Who Might Have Owned It Before Me, Its Colours Seen From A Distance, The Colours Hidden Inside It, The Man It Stands For in Professional Foot Races,* and *The Horse It Stands For At Race-Meetings,* Augustine claims that he can keep most of his chooks' pedigrees in his head for the time being. One night to prove his claim he says – say we start for argument's sake with Green Ring the best of the clutch that Long-legged Granny hatched in the old barrel in the second woodshed – well she was the daughter of Long-legged Granny by the rooster I bought from Ryan Brothers at Wensleydale and Long-legged Granny was a daughter of Young Granny the hen that was chased and scruffed by that greyhound when she was grazing in the church-hall yard that night by Jim Senior the rooster I bred myself from a beautiful hen with a yellow ring who was never any good as a layer just the same and Young Granny was a daughter of Old Granny by the full brother to that rooster I was always sorry I killed for eating because his first lot of daughters had such miserable tails. Clement soon loses track of the pedigrees but he remembers many of the fowls that his father names because he used to peer at them as they sat brooding in tea-chests or barrels or petrol drums in out-of-the-way corners of the ramshackle sheds or crouching with their copper-coloured chickens safely huddled beneath them in cosy nooks under low clumps of the morning-glory that crept all over the heaps of rotting timber or in the deepest thickets of the bamboo, although their nests have long since disappeared because his father tidied up the sheds and the yard once in his holidays and the hens now search for nesting-places among the weeds or against the bare walls in the shadows of sheds. Among all the clutches of chickens that have scratched and pecked their way across the backyard, through the barley patch, around behind the horse's loose-box, past the tamarisks, under the lilac tree and down towards the square of lucerne and the front of the house, and all the pens of pullets that have been fed on mashes of the best bran and pollard and have grazed every evening in the church-hall yard next door and have had their first eggs identified by Mrs Killeaton, who had to run outside whenever she heard a certain kind of cackle in the mornings and bring in the new-laid egg and report to her husband that night that the pullet with such and such a ring left the nest cackling that day, and have been finally either killed and eaten or kept in the special layers' pen or allowed the run of the yard with the select breeding flock depending on the number of eggs that they laid in their first season and the size and shape and colour of their eggs, and the smaller pens of cockerels who have been killed and eaten for such slight faults as a lack of sparkle in their eyes or the wrong shade of yellow on their legs until only two or three remained who danced round each other and sparred with their beaks in tests of strength until one was finally chosen to be let loose with a mob of pullets to see what sort of chickens he would sire and whether he deserved to be kept as a replacement for the old rooster or as a second sire to keep some variety in the bloodlines, Augustine remembers the names and the main characteristics of a small ruling house whose generations have come and gone while he and his son have grown only a little older and the shrubs and sheds and fences that are such mighty landmarks for the poultry have scarcely changed. Sometimes at the dinner table on Sunday Augustine reminds his family that they are eating a daughter of Granny the third who was only four years old but had become too fat for laying and whose best daughter would carry on the bloodline anyway or a son of Jim Senior who was unlucky enough to be born with a crooked breastbone. He punches holes with red-hot wire in the toes of hundreds of chickens and slips rings on the legs of hundreds of pullets and cockerels and every weekend moves a few hens from one pen to another according to some obscure system of classification that he keeps in his head. Sometimes he nails up a small crate of birds to be collected by a man in an old truck and sold at the market in Bassett, but he admits that the money he gets for them does not even pay for a week's supply of wheat and pollard and bran. Sometimes a crate arrives from Bassett railway station with the label of a breeder of pedigreed Rhode Island Reds in some suburb of Melbourne and the notice PLEASE GIVE ME A DRINK with an arrow pointing to a jam-tin inside the crate. Augustine throws a hen from the crate over the fence into one of his pens. Before she can find her legs, a rooster runs with drooping wings and gaping beak and bounces up and down on her. Augustine hooks a long piece of fencing wire around a hen's leg and carries her squawking to the wood heap, where the axe leans against the chopping-block. Her friends and relations go on foraging in the yard where she will never be seen again. Augustine lifts out from under a hen the first of a new clutch of chickens. He wraps them tenderly in one of his old flannel singlets and packs the bundle into an old felt hat. He rests the hat on the hearth beside the kitchen stove so that the precious chickens will not be crushed by their mother while the late eggs are still hatching. Clement asks his father again to write it all down before he forgets it. Augustine says again that he will never forget the important bloodlines and that nobody wants to know what happens to all the hundreds or even thousands of birds that are only good for killing as soon as they are old enough. Instead of asking his father once more to try to preserve the story of the tribe of Rhode Island Reds whose ancestors came to Australia long ago from green hills on the opposite side of America from the hills of Idaho, but who have lived for longer than they can remember in a place around whose farthest edges all day are obscure sounds of other creatures whose tasks and journeys they never try to understand and within which are promises of plains that come to nothing and a dozen shrubs and creepers that are all they know of what a forest might be like, whose girl-friends and wives are chosen for them by a man whose wisdom they never question because he comes every morning and nearly every night to feed them, who forget their own relations so easily that they fight to the death with their brothers and fathers and mate greedily with their sisters and mothers, but who run up and down the wire fence at dusk to get back into the sheds where they have perched since they were small, stand solemnly calling out to some hen who has gone off to a secret place among the nettles behind a shed and comes back tossing scraps of grass over her shoulder to hide the trail to her nest from wild animals that (so Augustine says) used to prowl through the jungles of Assam thousands of years ago and calling to the others to tell her what part of the jungle they have wandered to while she has been laying, or stand up to fight a strange cat but allow the man and the boy that they know to walk freely among them so that Clement regrets that the true history of the long ages they have spent in this and other countries will never be recorded and, worse still, that the backyard where hundreds of them were born and discov-ered hide-outs and tunnels to secret places and great barriers between themselves and the ones that they wanted to be with and made long repetitive journeys across the same limited territory but never reached whatever lay beyond it will never be anything more than a backyard because no one sat down and wrote out their story, he sits down and writes about his marbles. He begins as a small boy in grade two making entries of a few words in each of a few columns. Before he has finished writing about half the marbles in his collection he gets from his father a much bigger ledger and starts a new system of entries with one whole page for each marble. Because his mother tries to stop him from wasting his time poring over pages of nonsense night after night, his list of entries grows very slowly. But all the while the number of his marbles increases steadily. Towards the end of his grade-three year he reviews what he has done and counts his marbles and calculates that it may still take him several more years and perhaps two or three more volumes to bring his work up to date. He writes of how he first came to own each marble, but he does not know where any of his marbles came from originally. When he asks his parents where marbles come from, they say that someone probably makes them in a big factory in England. There are sometimes a few marbles for sale in Coles or Woolworths in Bassett but these are brittle inferior kinds, and dozens of them have identical colours. True durable marbles are never seen in shops in Bassett. The few thousands of them that circulate among the boys of Bassett, wherever they may have come from originally, may never be replaced or added to, so that whenever a marble is lost it diminishes the total of marbles that a boy might collect in his lifetime, although years later another boy may find it again after a night of heavy rain has exposed it gleaming among the gravel and clay. One day Clement sees in a National Geographic magazine, in an article entitled *West Virginia: Treasure Chest of Industry*, a picture of a girl in a factory somewhere among steep forested hills almost as secretive as Idaho's packing thousands of coloured marbles into small bags. He looks closely at the marbles. Many of them seem to be the cheap almost wholly transparent kind that are sold in shops, but a few of them are very like some of the precious richly-coloured marbles that cannot be bought anywhere in Australia, so that he goes on hoping for a long time afterwards that someone in those dark treasure-laden hills will send across the sea some of the true marbles that are still being made after all and save them from dying out altogether in Australia. No one is even certain of the true names of the different kinds of marbles. Clement owns a few of each of the kinds that he calls peb, realie, dub, catseye, bullseye, bott, taw, rainbow, pearlie, glass-eye, and chinaman, but other boys often use these names to describe quite different kinds of marbles. And on the few occasions when his father takes an interest in the boy's marbles, Augustine uses familiar names wrongly or calls some marbles by names that Clement has never heard before. Augustine himself first made Clement interested in marbles when he took out of an old tobacco tin that he kept in his wardrobe about a dozen marbles that he said were older than himself because he had found them somewhere around the old house at Kurringbar when he was a little boy. Clement values these marbles so much that he never takes them out of the house and seldom shows them to another boy. The next most precious are the dozen or so that he has found in the backyard and that must have belonged to the boy Silverstone who lived at 42 Leslie Street before the Killeatons moved there. Some of the rest he gets by swapping cards from packets of breakfast foods or toys and scraps of timber or coloured paper that his father brings home from the mental asylum where the patients make gifts for children in orphanages, or by sitting up straight in school or knowing his work on days when his teacher tidies her desk and finds there marbles that she has taken weeks before from some boy who was fiddling with them, or from older boys who think marbles are only for babies, and one day Mrs Riordan gives him a bag of marbles because he is always so well behaved when he visits her house. He watches the boys at school playing ring games for keeps, but dares not join in. The only marbles that he takes to school are a few inferior kinds which he tries to swap for some that attract him in other boys' collections.

He wonders how some boys can lose half a dozen choice marbles during a single playtime and not seem worried about it. He goes home to spread out his own treasured ones on the mat and whisper their racing names to himself. For hours some evenings he dwells on the story of a single marble – how it might be older than the city of Bassett because it had been brought to Australia by early settlers from England or Ireland, how it might have lain hidden for years beneath the soil while boys who are now dead tramped over it without suspecting what colours lay deep under their feet, and how Clement Killeaton, the one boy in all Bassett who would take proper care of it, caught sight of one faint gleam from its misty depths, prised it up from the soil, washed and dried it and thought up a name for it. At night he sits looking up at the electric light globe with a marble held close to his eye trying to explore all the wine- or flame- or honey- or blood- or ocean- or lake- or stained-glass-coloured skies or plains where winds or clouds or ranges of hills or curls of smoke are trapped forever and to decide what secret tunnels or caves or valleys or walled cities or thickets or abandoned laneways might never be explored because they lie deep inside it close to its very essence where its truest colours would envelop any traveller who reached there trying to discover what has lain for so many years in the heart of the glass that people have carried without thinking from place to place and what it is to be inside a place that all other people see only from the outside. One night when all the marbles are spread out on the mat in the lounge-room, the amethyst- and white-streaked one named *Tupper* after a professional runner at a Bassett Easter Fair meeting and *Winterset* after a famous racehorse in Melbourne rolls away and disappears down a hole in the corner of the floorboards. Clement cries until his parents notice him. He asks will they lift up the boards or find a way under the house for him, but they tell him not to make such a fuss about one old marble. Clement does not forget *Tupper Winterset*. Often at night he thinks of the soft dust gradually sifting down onto his purplish lakes, whose depths no light now enters, and the white arcs of his shores that perhaps no one will ever hold up to his eyes and dream of crossing and of all the years when the house still rests solidly on its foundations and he, Clement, grows up and goes away and the new family living there never suspects that *Tupper Winterset* is somewhere beneath them and of a time when the house falls down at last and a new one is built and of a day, perhaps long after the second or even the third house has fallen when someone finds *Tupper Winterset* and makes up a story about him which is very different from the stories that Clement once told about him and discovers deep inside him colours quite different from those that Clement discovers and gives him a name very different from *Tupper Winterset*, which was not his real name anyway just as white and amethyst were probably not his true colours and the story that Clement believed of how and where he was first made was not the true story.

## CLEMENT SEES HOW AMERICAN FAMILIES LIVE

Clement has known for a long time that his father is very different from the fathers of other boys he knows. Augustine's telephone conversations with important men in Melbourne, the many Saturdays when he is away from early morning until late at night, the great wealth of racing knowledge that keeps him continually frowning into the distance during meals or sitting at his desk in the evening with a pencil in his hand scribbling rows and columns of figures in the margin of his racing paper, the hours that he spends carefully training the horse Sternie for the race that he might still win at good odds, and the creased racebooks that he brings back from distant race-meetings with their blank pages filled with details of bets and names of horses and men and will not allow Clement to play with for fear they might fall into the wrong hands – all these remind Clement that he must not expect his father to play cricket in the backyard as Mr Glasscock does or to take his wife and son out walking on Sunday afternoons or to have friends who might come to visit them on Sunday nights or to listen to the wireless for more than a few minutes without tapping a pencil against his teeth or crossing his legs and swinging his foot restlessly to and fro or reaching for a piece of paper to scribble on or going down the street to make a phone call. Clement understands that his father's racing business is the reason why Augustine has never been with his wife to the pictures since they were married, why he never learned to dance as a young man, and why he never brings home a bottle of beer or wastes his money on cigarettes or tobacco like ordinary men. But one evening in the summer holidays Mrs Killeaton finally persuades her husband that he can afford the time to take her and the boy to the Miami Theatre to see a film called The Sullivans that everyone in Bassett is talking about. Augustine has never heard of the film. He asks his wife whether it is for general exhibition. She shows him the newspaper advertisement to convince him, and he agrees to take them in on the special picture bus to Bassett. Clement is so pleased to have his father with him at the pictures that he keeps glancing sideways and nudging Augustine whenever the audience laughs during the newsreel and the cartoon, but Augustine does not seem to understand the jokes. The supporting film has so many adults in it and so much conversation that Clement gives up trying to understand what his mother calls the hang of it and simply watches a boy a little older than himself travelling all night in a luxurious railway train from New York to somewhere and when he first looks out in the morning in the heart of America seeing not desert as he had expected but smooth farms and inviting forests. The train stops at a tiny station, and the boy tries to get out and look among the great thick mats of cornfields and the massed tufts of plantations and the few lonely houses and deserted cross-roads where no signposts stand for his father, but the grown-ups who are looking after him, a woman that some of the men on the train have fallen in love with although her breasts are sharply pointed and cruel and her face is stiff with layers of powder and another older woman who keeps saying things that make the people in the Miami Theatre squeal with laughter, look meaningfully at each other behind the boy's back and the younger woman, his mother, tells him he mustn't keep worrying about his pa like that because he's gone to live in the most peaceful place of all. While the passengers go on chattering, Clement keeps his eyes on the edge of the screen where spikes of trees fling themselves at the train and roads appear at the windows offering access for an instant and no more to soft distant paddocks that may lie at the very centre of America and filmy bits of prairie float up and drift off again to wherever they belong until his eyes begin to water. Someone on the train says something about a gambler, and Clement watches to see whether the people are interested in racing, but a man takes out a pack of cards – something that Augustine has never touched in all his life – and Clement tries again to see the places where the boy wanted to go searching and beyond which his father has found a quiet town somewhere. Augustine whispers to his wife that he won't be long but he has just remembered a phone call that he has to make and he thinks he'd better save his eyes for The Sullivans because the film they're watching now is pretty dry. He climbs past the people's knees and walks out of the theatre. The film ends among tall buildings in a huge city, and the boy finds out that his father has died, probably in the war, and pretends that he loves the new father that his mother has decided to marry and never mentions again the great stretches of land that he saw all that morning from the train windows. The lights come on in the Miami Theatre, and Clement's mother shares a box of koolmints with him. The lights go out again and The Sullivans begins, but Augustine has still not yet returned. The Sullivans are a family of Catholic boys. Clement is shocked to see for the first time on the screen the inside of a Catholic church. When the smallest Sullivan boy only waves his hand in front of his face instead of making a proper sign of the cross because he is in a hurry to follow his big brothers out of the church, the audience roars with laughter and Clement suspects that most of them are Protestants making fun of the Catholic religion. The Sullivans' father belts his sons with a strap when they get into trouble, and the audience laughs loudly again. Clement realises that Mr Sullivan is only pretending to be angry with the boys and decides that the Killeaton family, whose quarrels last for days, leads a life so different from the true American life that it would be useless to to try to learn any lessons from the Sullivans. He notices the furniture and ornaments that clutter up the house although the Sullivans are supposed to be a poor family and the Sullivan boys' strange habit of throwing their arms around their mother and pressing their heads so hard against her tired old titties that she gasps for breath and giggles. Mr Sullivan works as a driver on an unlikely sort of train. Year after year he has to travel around the same route between the same drab backyards and factories. Clement's father climbs back into his seat just in time to see Mr Sullivan waving to his sons as he does every morning when his train passes the street where they walk to school. Augustine bumps Clement with his knee because the boys are so fond of their father. The boys are anxious to finish school so that they can find jobs on other railways that travel on fixed routes like their father's but through far wider districts of America where the sky is free of smoke and soot and people have more secrets in their houses and paddocks than the people of the crowded cities. Their mother explains to them that the war has started. She urges them to stay inside the steel-coloured gloomy corridors and cupboards of a battleship instead of looking for adventure all over America. But when they leave home to go to the war she throws her apron over her head and shakes her titties. Clement, who has never understood why his friends at school are so interested in war and the clashing together of machines whose names he does not even know or the plunging to earth of planes whose make and nationality he has never learned to distinguish among great surges of smoke that obscure what he would really like to see – the earth far below with its plains marked faintly by roads and towns – feels disappointed because he will see no more of the trains that the Sullivans might have driven all over America. Towards the end of the film, the submarines and torpedoes and bombs and the water pouring into ships' cabins and the men shouting orders at each other are so confusing that Clement has to ask his father whether the Americans or the Japs are winning. Only when a sudden tense silence settles over the Miami Theatre does Clement realise that the Sullivan boys have all been killed. Mr Sullivan still rides around the city on his toy-like train. Clement decides that Mr Sullivan is the real hero of the film because he has now become so used to the route that his train follows every day past the same back fences and grey streets that he will only be able to dream of going where his sons wanted to go out across strange plains where the railway line reveals little-known views of the rear ends of farms and forests. At the very end, when the old man looks out at the place where his sons used to wave to him, Augustine puts his arm around Clement and rests his hand on his wife's shoulder. Mrs Killeaton weeps into her handkerchief. Clement's throat and nose fill up with a great load of tears and snot for the sake of the tired old lonely man who still looks around the same old city for some place that he can stare at and believe that all his life he was driving his train towards a view of something marvellous that no one else had discovered. But as the curtains tumble across the screen, the Sullivan boys suddenly climb out of a great silvery explosion and stand on a shining cliff and point to something that may be more marvellous than any view from the most far-reaching railway line. Clement asks his father – didn't they die after all Dad? Augustine says – don't worry about them son – it was only a story that some Yanks made up. But someone in the seat behind them says angrily – no it wasn't – it's all true – I read where it said this story is based on actual fact.

## THE BOYS OF ST BONIFACE'S
## SUCK MILK FROM STONES

At lunchtime on a certain hot day the boys of St Boniface's school suddenly decide to search for milk-stones. After they have eaten their pies or sandwiches or Boston buns and been herded into the boys' yard, they crowd into corners and settle down on the gravel to spend the rest of the lunch-hour searching. Launder's gang occupy the choice spots – the corners near the taps and in the shade of a wing of a building. Other boys have to be content with the exposed parts of the yard where the gravel is hot to touch. Each boy sits flat on the ground, with his legs spread wide apart in front of him to enclose the area that is his own preserve, and scrabbles with his fingers in the dusty gravel. When he finds a small stone that is perfectly smooth and a flawless white he slips it under his tongue or into the space between his cheek and his gum. If his mouth becomes uncomfortably full of stones, he drops some into his shirt pocket or wraps them in a knotted corner of his handkerchief. The whitest stones, when they are sucked hard, yield a steady trickle of cool, sweet milk. Stones that are slightly chipped or marred with bluish streaks give only a thin, watery milk, or even plain water. If the flow of milk dries up it can be replenished by soaking the stone overnight in a jar of water or a glass of milk. Some boys store their stones in small jars of water as they collect them. When lunchtime ends they slip some of these stones into their mouths, hoping to have a continuous supply of liquid in the hot classroom, but the nun who has been watching the boys' yard usually whispers a message to the boys' teachers who then walk up and down the lines saying – out of your mouths with those silly dangerous pebbles, and sometimes even orders them to turn out their pockets and throw the milk-stones away. Clement Killeaton enjoys searching for milk-stones. He never admits to the others that he cannot suck milk from any of his stones. Sometimes he tastes cool water, but it never flows for more than a few seconds. He watches the other boys as they suck, and envies them the easy movements of their jaws and the contented looks in their faces. His father tells him that no stone could possibly give milk or water although the early Australian explorers sometimes put stones in their mouths to keep themselves from feeling thirsty in the desert, but Clement does not repeat this to any boy at school. One morning he hears some of the boys boasting that they know the secret of the stones. A boy has heard from his father or his uncle that the Bassett milk-stones are only inferior copies of precious stones that Arabs and travellers in the desert or Australian soldiers in Palestine or Egypt have found in places where a man could die of thirst after one afternoon without water. A man who finds a true milk-stone in those countries guards it with his life and when he has to cross the plains between two towns rests it under his tongue not only to keep his mouth filled with cool milk but to keep his mind clear so that when he sees between him and what looks like the horizon a tree-shaded city with fountains bubbling and trickling in every garden he will know at once whether it is one of those unreal cities that thirsty travellers often follow for miles until they die still as far away from their city as ever or the true city that they have set out to reach. The boys of St Boniface's school soon give up their search for stones and play some other game at lunchtime, but Clement sorts through his collection and keeps in a special tin those few that seem most like the true precious milk-stones found in far hot countries. He does not bother to soak them in water or milk, but for weeks he always carries one in his mouth while he is walking near Wallaces' end of Leslie Street or near the McCracken's Road bridge or in any slightly elevated place from which he can see a long swathe of street far-reaching enough to lead to a real or an unreal city. When he half-closes his eyes and strains with his tongue to force the juice from his stone he sees a boy who has already reached a city across a hot difficult landscape. Boys who might be his true friends and women with faces and arms brown from the sun but still beautiful and unwrinkled and their daughters only a little older than him pass close to the boy in the streets or look towards him from their front gardens as if they would welcome him into their homes but still cannot see him clearly.

Gerald Murnane

## A BOY FINDS A CITY THAT MAY BE A MIRAGE

When the boy who has reached a city but is still not sure whether the stone that he sucked on his journey was one of the true kind tries to follow the people into their yards and houses, no one bars his way or seems to notice that a stranger might be watching them. The people move from room to room as if to do something shameful, but even hours later, in dim rooms that no passer-by would expect the houses to contain behind their simple facades or in leafy corners of the gardens that a stranger might walk past without noticing, the boy sees only actions and gestures that people like the Killeatons and Glasscocks and Postlethwaites perform every day in the yards and streets of the city of Bassett many miles away. He follows one group of people who exchange looks suggesting that as soon as they are in some secret place together they will agree without fear or shame to do whatever they like with each other's body, but when he and they are sprawled on the grass behind branches so thick that in Bassett they would have compelled a boy to do behind them things that he thought only the people of a distant city would do without caring who saw them, the people still talk and smile politely and fiddle with the belts of their trousers or the hems of their skirts as the Wallaces or Riordans often do in Bassett, and as if they were afraid that someone from a city like Bassett might be spying on them all the time. The boy even makes signs that he has never made in front of anyone in Bassett, but the people still behave so cautiously and politely that he realises he may never know after all what they might do in secret or even whether he has really seen them in secret. In the hottest part of the afternoon, in the city that many people never reach because they have no precious stones to guide them, the boy sets out to find a place where one or two people could be hidden more cunningly and securely than anyone in Bassett has ever been concealed. He goes deeper into a backyard to a place where even the sunlight seldom penetrates. He sees a place like the form of a hare in some long grass under a bunch of low-hanging shrubbery. He lowers himself into the little enclosure of flattened grass and discovers that it has been made by the crouching body of a boy. He fits his arms and head and shoulders into the hollows that lie waiting for them and stares outwards through the leaves. He sees above the fences that enclose the yards there, just as in another city that he knows, the low ominous rim of the hills that even beyond that far town conceal some place farther out from which a person who looked back at the city on its plains might see no more than a dark smear on a surface like a white stone's and from which the secrets of the people in the city might seem as remote and elusive among all the lands around as the yellowish light that flickered occasionally in the vein of such a stone so that a boy who built a racecourse that remained for a few days in his backyard in Bassett never forgot that a stone of a certain colour stood for a landscape that for a few minutes during an important race stood for the unfathomable thoughts of a certain group of people as they once stared back at a certain town on a hot plain where no one might even know where the real town was unless he had a proper stone to tell him. And then for the first time since he has arrived at their town, some people, a woman, a man, a girl and a boy gather round the tree and stare towards his hiding-place as if they recognised him at last. He cannot even begin to tell them that all they might hope for after years of waiting patiently on their lonely plains might be decided far beyond the daunting glitter of their horizons when a child's hand pushes forward among a cluster of pebbles a lump of milk-coloured quartz distinguished by a streak of uncertain gold or that if the child whose hand is poised above that stone could only know that they, the people in a far town, were really as he hoped, then he would stay with them forever and let some other hand above some other racecourse decide what might happen to them all.

## THE MYSTERIOUS SILVERSTONE IS
## ENTERED IN THE GOLD CUP

Clement Killeaton, the owner of a collection of milk-stones long after the other boys at his school have lost interest in them, sorts through his jar of white pebbles, but because they are so alike in colour and shape, with only a slight bulge or a faint tinge of blue or gold to distinguish any one from another, and so much smaller than the stones that he first used for horses in racing games, decides that he cannot use them in any races that he might arrange. He visits again each hiding-place between the roots of shrubs, beneath forests of weeds, or in the shade of deserted sheds, and recalls again the long stories that he once composed about the people who live in such places, how each detail in each story was once represented by something in the colours of certain stones, much larger than his milk-stones, which he once found in his yard but later threw away because his parents said he was growing too fond of racing games. He walks past the place where his racecourse stood before it was torn down and goes inside to his room. He selects fifteen of the hundred or so marbles that he has kept apart from the others, because something in the colours of each of them reminds him of a stone that is now lost, but which he calls by the names of professional foot-runners when his mother is around. He closes his eyes and lets the marbles trickle out of his cupped hands to form a straggling field on the mat in front of him. He opens his eyes and enjoys the moment of surprise when he sees that one of the fifteen, one that he has not thought about for a long time, lies ahead of all the others. He looks forward to the hot day when his mother will leave him alone in the house with the blinds pulled down to make people think that no one is at home and he can run the Gold Cup with a pencil and some old exercise books on the rug beside him for recording the positions of the horses after each furlong, so that for weeks or months afterwards he may explore the thoughts of a few people during a few minutes of a certain hot afternoon when all the things they had hoped for and dreamed about for years appeared before them as part of an arrangement of patterns of colours whose changing positions would decide at last the worth of those hopes and dreams. Through a gap in his side fence he shows his jar of milk-stones to two of the Glasscock boys. The older Glasscock says that the kids of Shepherd's Reef State School never play with such stupid things, but when Killeaton boasts of how the Catholic boys can go all day without a drink of water when they have milk-stones in their mouths, Glasscock remembers that a few years ago the big boys at his school collected all the best milk-stones from the streets and yards in their part of Bassett so the Catholic kids would only find the smallest and driest stones. Clement remembers that he has never been able to find even one milk-stone in his own yard and suggests that the boy Silverstone probably collected the stones too. Glasscock says – yes he did all right – he had the best collection of all – some of his stones were as big at that. He makes a shape with his fingers that is as large as any of the stones that Killeaton uses for his racehorses. Clement goes away from the fence and scatters the milk-stones in his yard. Then he adds to the list of runners in the Gold Cup number sixteen *Silverstone*, a silvery whiteness, for the marvellous secrets of Bassett and its people that Clement will never discover for as long as he lives because someone before him has buried them out of sight more securely than any marble or stone hidden beneath the unyielding soil of the city.

## A WESTERN DISTRICT GRAZIER
## INSPECTS CLEMENT'S YARD

Late one afternoon while Augustine is out walking Sternie around the streets, a car stops outside the Killeatons' house. A well-dressed man comes to the front door and introduces himself to Mrs Killeaton. He is Con McCormack, one of Augustine's cousins from the Western District. Mrs Killeaton is embarrassed and says that the house is in a bit of a muddle as usual but Mr McCormack is welcome to wait inside for Augustine to come home. Mr McCormack sees Clement resting on his haunches beside a road that he has smoothed with his hands in the dirt, and says he'll stay outside and talk to the boy for a while. When Clement learns that the man is a relation of his father, he confides to him the true meaning of his system of roads and farms. He explains to the man how the network extends all along the least-used side of the backyard, how each of the dozens of properties forms a pattern of paddocks from any single one of which a man who stood there staring outwards might see a view, across fences and trees towards a stretch of road, different from any other that another man might see and so singular that even the boy who laid out the whole system can never properly appreciate it, even when he lies down on his belly and puts his face as near as he can to the place where the man might stand, and how each man who stood looking outwards across his own unique view of paddocks might believe all his life that somewhere, far out of sight, the great tracery of fences and roads came to an end and wonder what other country began there while the boy who arranged the whole pattern knows that if only he could break down the fences between fifty or a hundred of the yards in that one small part of Bassett that he knows he might lay out such a country that none of its inhabitants would discover in his lifetime any end to it. Mr McCormack asks how all those farmers earn a living. Clement explains that they all race their horses every week at the racecourse that lies at the heart of their district and live off the stake money and their winning bets. The man asks him how much his own father has won with his horse Sternie lately. Clement admits that Augustine has won nothing with Sternie yet, but he explains that Sternie has not been trying because he is waiting for an important race in a few weeks' time. Mr McCormack asks how can he be certain that Sternie will win the important race. Clement realises that he has been speaking of the one topic that his father has forbidden him to breathe a word about. He tells the man that in the district where he has built his racecourse, every owner wins his fair share of races in the end if only he has the patience to go on training his horse and backing him week after week until his great day arrives. Augustine walks into the yard, leading Sternie. He shakes hands cheerfully with his cousin, whom he has not seen for many years. McCormack smiles and says – young Clem here has been showing me over his farms – he even has a racecourse built somewhere in the bushes so all his farmers can flutter away their profits every Saturday. Augustine smiles weakly and says – of course his mother and I don't encourage him to take an interest in racing at his age but I suppose he can't help noticing all the work I put into training Sternie. Later, after Mr McCormack has gone down the yard to look at the poultry, Augustine grabs Clement by the shoulders and whispers harshly into his ear that Mr McCormack doesn't like people who waste their money at the races, that he is a very rich man with hundreds of acres of sheep country, and that Clement had better ask him some questions about sheep farming instead of blabbing to him for hours about horses and racing. But Con McCormack does not stay for long. He tells the Killeatons he is heading for Queensland to look up some distant relations who have done well on the land there. He says – of course you'd know who I'm talking about Gus – the McGuigans – they were your second cousins too I suppose. He drinks one cup of tea and drives away. Augustine tells his wife that he has always found it hard to talk to Con McCormack even though he is a cousin of his. He says that when he was a boy the McCormacks were even poorer than the Killeatons, the parents working like niggers and the little boys running round the cow-yard with nothing on but their shimmies even in winter, but that they finally paid off their farm and started to buy land round the district, that hardly any of them married, and that now they live in a house with about twenty rooms on a property that once belonged to some famous squatting family on the western plains. Mrs Killeaton says – and you're still living in this dump of a place up to your eyes in debt – I wonder what he thought of you. Augustine says – but I've got things that he'll never have – a beautiful wife and a lovely little boy – I can go to the races whenever I like – I've made dozens of wonderful friends in the racing game – I would have told him about Goodchild and some of the big wins we've had but I thought better of it because he mightn't have understood – he thinks all racing is a waste of time and money. Mrs Killeaton pulls an ugly face when her husband mentions his beautiful wife. Clement says to his father – racing properties are better than sheep farms aren't they Dad? Augustine jumps to his feet and says – I'm sick to death of hearing you talk about racing as though I'd never taught you anything else – come outside this minute and we'll cure you of racing. Mrs Killeaton says – he hasn't been racing those stones around the lilac bush again and calling them horses has he? I warned him weeks ago about that. They all go outside. Mrs Killeaton looks behind the lilac but sees no sign of rails or grandstand. Augustine takes his son's hand and says – we'll start with your biggest stud property – show me where it's hidden. Clement takes him to the place where one of the wealthiest owners, a man whose opulent colours have led home many a field, lives among tree-lined paddocks whose outer boundaries he cannot even see from the homestead. Augustine gets down on his haunches and shows the boy what to do. Clement has to tear up most of the dividing fences because sheep need broad acres. But he leaves the lines of trees standing so that the sheep will have shade in the summer. Augustine then explains that men like the McCormacks try to buy up their neighbours' properties. So Clement builds gates into the fence between the property and one next door. He and his father decide that the owner will live in the better of the two homesteads, leaving the other for his son, who will manage the huge property. Clement and Augustine work together until tea-time. The main shapes of the landscape are still the same, although Augustine orders a few low hills flattened and a few stands of forest cleared so that the country will look more like the rich plains of the Western District which he used to think of as a boy whenever he planned to be a wealthy grazier when he was older. All over the prosperous plains sheep graze contentedly. Augustine stands beside his son and looks at the places that they have built together. He says – don't throw away all your horses son – keep just a few of them – some of the wealthiest sheep men might keep a horse or two and race them as a hobby the way I've always wanted to – which is the way racing was meant to be enjoyed.

## THE GOLD CUP RACE BEGINS

Clement's mother tells him that she may be away in Bassett for most of the afternoon. She warns him to behave himself and not to answer any knocks at the door. When he hears the bus turn the corner into McCracken's Road, Clement feels the same kind of excitement that he once felt when he was alone in the house with Kelvin Barrett. He pours out the sixteen chosen marbles onto the mat and arranges them in a neat line. He lowers a length of timber into place behind the line of marbles and fixes his eyes on the wall at the far end of the room. Carefully, and without once lowering his eyes towards the marbles, he slides the timber back from the line then moves it forward again with enough force to send the sixteen rolling forward along the mat. Because he knows from experience that the marbles will have sprayed out a little, he feels for them gingerly with his hands, still keeping his eyes averted, and moves the outlying ones across towards the main group so that all sixteen form a loosely bunched mass with several already clearly ahead just as a field of horses appears at the end of the first furlong of a long race. Still without looking at the marbles, he touches them one by one and discovers with a thrill of pleasure that three of them are loosely spaced ahead of the main bunch while two others are clearly tailed off. Then he turns his back on the marbles and hugs his bare knees and grips his cock and balls to curb his excitement as he remembers how the dawn was chilly but the day promised to be the hottest of that summer when the owner-trainer of *Tamarisk Row* led his horse through the damp grass to where the tall-sided truck stood on the circular gravel drive, how the man's wife stood beneath the lavish green awnings of creepers that made a dark tunnel of the long veranda around the house holding in her faintly freckled arms their silken colours loosely folded

so that creases and ridges and pleats and knobs and indenta-
tions of fiery orange and soothing pale pink and astringent
green concealed the true pattern of the jacket and seemed to
comprise a design too intricate to be described by any words
in a racebook, how the man travelled with his wife beside him
for more than a hundred miles to the racecourse while the
drone of the truck's motor sounded like the ominous beginning of a piece of music, and how as the time for the race drew
near, the man and his wife, their best friend and their jockey
looked from one to another of the rival groups huddled together
and realised that all those others, like themselves, believed
that their day had arrived. The boy on the flattened pile of the
rug, where a golden or reddish pattern is now almost obscured
by stains and dust and the passage of feet across it, savours for
the last time the pleasure of knowing that soon a race will be
run which at each furlong of its journey will seem to promise
to a different contender a narrow victory but which will finally
prove that for months or years past fifteen groups of people
have gone on confidently devising schemes that would never
succeed while one group was planning for a day that when it
finally came would seem to those people to have been inevi-
table. He crawls around to the far side of the rug and lowers
himself onto the lino so that when he opens his eyes he will
see the field of horses across the bare space of the desert-
coloured rug. He peers between his eyelashes and sees the field
as if a cloud of dust had settled over the racecourse, but he
knows the sets of colours so well that he recognises almost at
once the flamboyant fuchsia-toned reds and blues of *Proud
Stallion* showing out boldly three lengths ahead of the field. At
once Clement shuts his eyes again and turns away from the
rug to comprehend what he has just seen. Defiantly, recklessly,
the rider gives *Proud Stallion* his head, and even at this early
stage of the race there are people in the crowd who begin to

wonder whether there will be after all not a final desperate struggle between a pack of evenly matched rivals but a strange homecoming before an almost silent crowd as *Proud Stallion* continues his astonishing run that allows no supporters of other horses even the least hope that their champion might overtake the leader. But then he guesses at the positions of the others in the field behind the leader and the unspent strength that their riders may be holding in check and shares with the supporters of *Proud Stallion* their fear of every other runner in the great bunch poised behind their horse and, whenever something makes a sudden movement forward, their sudden alarm and presentiment of defeat and even their resignation because it was too much to hope that their horse could lead all the way. He lies down again facing the field, and with his eyelashes just meeting turns his head slowly to the right, looking past *Proud Stallion* and across the space of three clear lengths behind that horse until he sees with a pleasant shock (which would have been just as great no matter which horse he had seen) colours in which the faded gold of long vistas predominates – the insignia of *Hills of Idaho*. Again he turns away, but not before he has glimpsed just behind the second horse a bunch in which many horses might be travelling with that easy loping stride that means they are only waiting to make a powerful run towards the lead. For a few minutes he enjoys the revelation that this one name among sixteen, *Hills of Idaho*, which people have spoken aloud so often with no special sonority may in future whenever it is spoken ring out like a battle cry reminding the hearers of the long story of how a little band of men never stopped believing that their day would come. Clement now looks towards the rear of the field where he knows there are several horses already being restrained well behind the main bunch. Sooner than he had expected, the shape of a horse comes into view and he cannot

wait to know which one is so far back so early in the race. He
stares at the pale aloof colours of *Transylvanian* and wonders
whether the sharp-faced secretive stable followers still do not
flinch or show the least concern as they see the fifteen rivals
that their horse must pass already so far ahead and still toss
their heads carelessly and scoff at the distance that most people
already believe is too great for *Transylvanian* to make up, whether
they will keep up that intimidating pose for long after they
have begun to realise that they were not the most cunning of
all that crowd after all their boastful posturing, and when if
ever they will admit quite simply that their schemes have
failed. He looks further to his left towards a horse whose rider
holds it almost as far behind as the conspicuous *Transylvanian*
and cries out with joy as he sees the ill-matched colours of
harsh desert and helpless skin enclosed by the tantalising
green of a country that no one has yet visited of *Tamarisk Row*.
He rolls forward onto the bare gritty surface of the rug. He
hunches his body so low that he feels with his thighs how his
cock has swollen with the hope of something too pleasurable
for words. He presses his fists tightly against his chest, trying
to restrain the horse that he has always known, whether he
was alone in the weeds of his backyard and trying, with nothing to guide him but a glimpse of a light so delicate that it
could irradiate even the blazing summer sunlight over Bassett,
to creep closer to the narrow but perfectly transparent window
through which he expected to see, more clearly than he ever
saw the shapes of racehorses in lumps of gravel or the histories
of their owners among the shadows cast by tall marshmallows,
long afternoons where another boy, if only he knew it, saw
the gravel and weeds so clearly on certain afternoons that he
never wondered whether there were others on other afternoons
so little distance away who saw their gravel and weeds more
or less clearly, or staring in the noon twilight inside his house

at a picture in a magazine of a village in the impenetrable hills of Romania towards sunset on a day that no one but himself now wondered about or a town on the incredible prairies of America at the beginning of a summer that no one but himself still persisted in searching for its unique essence and then peeping around the agitated golden membrane of the lounge-room blind in the hope of seeing the place that a person would recognise only if he had stared for years at the Carpathians or Nebraska or inland Australia and discovered what it was that was still missing from those lands because it was far away from each of them and yet on the way back from Bassett to all of them, would come from far behind and startle the thousands who had been looking anywhere but in his direction for the winner and oblige them to ask one another for long afterwards where he had come from and how it was that they had overlooked him for so long and never noticed his unwavering journey through the very thick of all those that had for long seemed certain to reach the coveted place before him. He thinks of the days when the husband and wife, the owners of *Tamarisk Row*, would promise each other some new pleasure – each undressing the other by daylight in their kitchen or lounge-room or watching while the other stood up in the bath and pissed, or tying the other up and tickling or torturing him or her between the legs and under the arms with feathers or hair brooms or chips of ice from the ice-chest, or painting the other between the legs with crayons or water paints or indelible pencils – that they would not enjoy until after the day when their little-known horse became famous and they knew that even though they were Catholics and had come to that country as strangers from somewhere else that they could remember little about, still the triumph of their horse before thousands of watching strangers and the rewards that it brought them meant that they need never wonder again what the people for miles around did in secret that made them smile so knowingly among their deceptively bare paddocks that their grandfathers had discovered for them and taught them what to do with. Before he has time to consider how the distant position of their horse in the early part of the race still reminds the owner and his wife of those other occasions when the same horse, or a few years earlier the unlucky Journey's End, would weave its way through crowded fields only to fail by cruelly narrow margins, Clement hears the bus from Bassett stopping at the corner of McCracken's Road. He picks up a pencil and writes down the order of the field and, as nearly as he can judge, the distances between the horses. As he writes he chants under his breath the words that the racing commentator cries out to the silent crowd at the course and the people beside wireless sets in towns where many of the crowd have never been and that sum up what a man would believe of the field who could see no more than a bunch of horses far out on an arena of dead grass with already a few dropping back so far that they seem unlikely to take any part in the finish – *Proud Stallion* striding out boldly three or four lengths clear of in second place *Hills of Idaho* settling down well on the inside of a bunch of horses with *Infant of Prague*, *Mysteries of the Rosary* and wider out to *Veils of Foliage* looking for a good position they're followed by *Passage of North Winds* going smoothly *Lost Streamlet* there too and then a gap to *Monastery Garden* followed by *Den of Foxes* a fair gap again to *Silverstone* but going nice and easily further back to *Captured Riflebird* and *Hare in the Hills* in a strung-out field dropping out towards the rear is *Springtime in the Rockies* and then comes *Silver Rowan* and further back still to *Tamarisk Row* and tailed off even this far from home is *Transylvanian*.

## CLEMENT THINKS OF THE PROTESTANTS'
## CITY AND HIS OWN

One Sunday morning Augustine takes Clement past St Boniface's and on through the main streets of Bassett towards St Thomas More's Cathedral to hear the eleven o'clock High Mass. In the very centre of the city they cross Trafalgar Square where a massive stone archway flanked with lions and unicorns and griffins reminds the people of Bassett that the men who did all the important work in the old days were Englishmen with manes like lions' and claws like griffins'. Augustine has now almost succeeded in teaching his son that the city with its porticoes and balustrades and columns and statues is not something to be proud of because, although the Catholic men of Ireland got to Australia as soon as they could, it was already too late and they found the same Protestant police and magistrates and landlords and wealthy shopkeepers who used to imprison and fine and rob them back in Ireland already in control of even the isolated inland places like Bassett. So Clement does not worry when he notices that the stone animals around the archway are disfigured with dirt, and only seldom wonders whether there is someone in Bassett who carries in his mind a map of all the tunnels and caves and cul-de-sacs and short cuts and arcades and passageways among the Protestants' city and appreciates its complexities as they deserve and as God might if He took an interest in non-Catholic places, or whether there are obscure angles and surprising convergences of far-reaching routes and secret intersections of almost-forgotten tunnels that no one now alive understands and enjoys and gloats over and each week or month a few more dusty alley-ways or mossy ledges behind parapets are forgotten by the last person who once knew even vaguely of them and form the beginnings of a mysterious district that ought to be explored all over again because now even a Catholic could find something stirring in its abandoned hollows or perhaps claim some neglected enclosure as his own. Augustine explains that the Irish who landed in Australia came too late to see the country as it had been for thousands of years when only scattered tribes of Aborigines wandered through it scarcely disturbing the parrots and dingoes in remote gullies where they did as they pleased, and too late to make Australia a Catholic country, so that now the lands of Australia would always be covered by roads and farms and suburbs of cities in patterns that bigoted Protestants and Masons had laid out. Now Australian Catholics can only gaze at the designs that have been impressed on their country in the hope that somewhere among the rows of squares and meshes of irregular shapes they might see corners that the Protestants had overlooked and which could still remind them of great mysteries just out of sight behind ordinary-looking things, or dream of plains far inland that are probably too harsh anyway but where perhaps a few Catholic families could live in a little community whose roads led only to properties within the settlement and nowhere else beyond it.

## BARRY LAUNDER DISCOVERS TAMARISK ROW

The Killeatons' backyard is narrow but deep. On one side of it is the picket fence of the Presbyterian church-hall yard. On the opposite side is the tumbledown fence that the Killeatons share with the Glasscocks. The back fence is a length of rusty ragged wire-netting. The yard beyond it belongs to people named Podger whose house faces McCracken's Road. Clement never sees anyone in the back part of the Podgers' yard, which is littered with rusted iron, car tyres, and broken machinery. Sometimes at night Clement hears shouting from the direction of the Podgers' house, but his father tells him it is only the big Podger boys coming home drunk and arguing back to their father. One afternoon Clement extends one of his outlying roads towards the Podgers' fence. As he moves slowly on his hands and knees beside the fence, he notices among the rubbish in the Podgers' yard a heap of broken china, some of it striped with a colour that might have been originally a striking orange-red. He pokes a stick through the wire, trying to scrape some of the china towards him, and disturbs a big boy Podger, about eighteen years old, who has been scratching around out of sight behind some old seats. The boy says – what are you after Snow? Clement says meekly – I thought if nobody wanted those old broken cups and saucers any more I could take a few little pieces for a game I was playing. The boy says – nick over the fence quick and snitch it if that's all you want. Clement makes sure that his mother is not watching, then scrambles over the sagging wire fence. He picks up only some of the china, leaving plenty in case the Podgers might still value it. He would like to ask what the stuff looked like before it was broken but he suspects that the Podger boy has already noticed something odd about him and is waiting for a chance to make fun of him. Just before Clement climbs back, the Podger boy says – I don't suppose you're the shitty bastard that pinched me magneto. Clement says – I've never been inside your yard before and I don't even know what a magneto is. The boy says – I had a fuckin magneto here somewhere and now it's gone. He tries to lift a pile of scrap metal with his toe. Clement stands timidly behind him, feeling that he ought to help. When the Podger boy sees him still standing there, he says – piss off now or I'll kick you where your mother never kissed you – and Christ help you if I find out it's someone from your place been fartin around our backyard. Clement goes back to his own yard. He spends the next few weeks rearranging the whole pattern of his farming country. He decides that he was wrong to think that as his backyard extended further out of sight of the front gate it became more secluded and remote and safe from disturbance. He realises that the further back a road might lead towards the quietest, least-visited reaches of a territory that a people have decided is theirs alone to explore, the nearer it might approach to the edges of a territory that is so familiar to another people that they have not yet noticed the strange country just outside its borders, although one of them might stumble on it at any time. He supposes that the reason why he has always been strangely affected by the sight of plains and flat grasslands viewed from a distance is that the most mysterious parts of those lands lie in the very midst of them, seemingly unconcealed and there for all to see but in fact made so minute by the hazy bewildering flatness all around them that for years they might remain unnoticed by travellers, and so determines to make the central districts of his yard the site of his most prized farms and park-like grazing lands. The property named Tamarisk Row cannot be moved from beneath the tamarisks, but he does shift it from the space between the trees and the church-hall yard around to the inland side so that it is protected on one side by the thick trunks and on the other by the level expanse of land between its boundaries and the flat heart of the backyard. When he has done all this he begins a scheme of scaling down the roads and fences and farms and towns and horses and people to a small fraction of their former size so that all of them will be concealed by the vastness and monotony of the backyard as if by the flatness and imprecise distances of a great plain and a person walking past them or even over them might see no more of the patterns of roads and farmlands than if he had glimpsed such things from a low hill many miles off. He has not quite finished this project when he hears beyond Podgers' fence a boy calling out – come and look – I can see Clem Killer down here – this must be little Killer's place. He looks up and sees Barry Launder, the leader of the gang that rules his grade at school, jumping down with his older brother from Podgers' fence and then walking across the yard to meet him. Clement is so shocked to see Launder, the boy who should have been kept out of his yard at all costs, strolling across the most secret part of it and to think that he entered the yard with one bound from the direction from which no other trespasser has ever come that he cannot invent answers to Launder's questions but answers timidly and truth-fully. When Launder asks him what he was playing in the yard by himself, he admits that he was building little farms. Launder demands to see the farms. Clement takes him to one that has not yet been made smaller. Launder understands at once that the rows of tiny chips of wood are fences. He crushes half a mile of fencing with his feet, not so much to annoy Clement as to discover in all seriousness whether the fence will sup-port his weight. He says – these fences aren't much are they? Clement himself kicks over a few hundred yards of posts and says – as a matter of fact I was going to pull all these fences out and make much better ones because they were the sort I made when I was only a little kid. Launder says – I think we'll have a good look around this yard. He and his brother stroll over to some of the poultry sheds. On the way they pass more farms. Although he seems not to notice them, Barry Launder man-ages to knock down almost every fence and to wipe out nearly every road that he walks across. Clement says politely – you'd better not open the doors of the chook sheds. Launder says – do you want to try and stop me? Mrs Killeaton calls out from behind the lilac bush – I'll stop you you brazen little brat. She hurries towards them, looking fierce. The Launder boys stand their ground. She says – you two whoever you are get away from that fowl shed and get back where you came from or I'll tan the hides off you. Very slowly the two boys turn towards the Podgers' fence. Barry Launder gives Clement a look full of meaning. Mrs Killeaton says – before they go Clement have they broken any of your toy farms – because if they have I'll make them get down there in the dirt and fix them all up again. Clement only wants his mother and the Launders to forget all about the farms. He says – it doesn't matter if they tripped over a few fences – I was pulling them down myself anyway. The Launders take a long while to reach the Podgers' fence and climb back over it. Clement's mother keeps him inside for the rest of the afternoon. She says – what nasty little bits of goods they were, and asks him who the boys were. Clement tells her their names and a little about them. He decides that after this the only farms and roads that he can safely build will be tiny lumps and faint roads so absurdly small that even he, their designer, will have to believe that he sees them from across an enormous distance, and even wonders whether he should make his backyard the country of a people like the Aborigines or even some earlier race of people who made no marks at all on the grasslands or in the forests so that he can follow their journeys without plucking out a single weed or altering the lie of the least patch of dust.

## FLOCKS OF UNSEEN BIRDS PASS THROUGH BASSETT

According to the Australian Bird Book in his father's bookcase, the few inconspicuous olive-green honeyeaters and elusive grey-brown fly-catchers that he sees retreating into the tree-tops at the rear of strangers' backyards and into the peninsulas of bush that still survive among the last scattered streets on the edge of Bassett are only a few of the more venturesome of a whole nation of native birds that lives out of sight among the coastal scrub and swamps and inland plains and savannahs and heathlands and rain forests and alpine valleys of Australia. Hardly anyone that Clement knows in Bassett, and certainly not his own father who has wandered for hundreds of miles across Australia nor his mother who grew up on the northern plains of Victoria nor his teachers who seem to know so much about places he has never seen nor the priests who when they close their eyes in prayer see at once a whole landscape that few ordinary people ever reach, knows the names of more than a few of all those birds or can tell him how far a boy might have to travel beyond Bassett to see them in their true homes. Only Mr Wallace the grocer, in the hours after his shop is closed and when Clement never sees him, goes on murmuring the names of strange species because there are still some that he has yet to capture for his aviary before he can walk in through the wire gate and not worry any more about the birds in all the miles of country outside because he can see them all as they are supposed to live among the swamps and heaths and jungles that he has prepared for them. In the front of the bird book is a map of Australia divided into zones. Over the place where Bassett would be if it were important enough to be marked, a dense flight of tiny arrows shows that a great belt of open forest country occupies northern Victoria. In all the pages describing individual species of birds there are dozens of wrens and fly-catchers and honeyeaters and diurnal birds of prey and water-birds and parrots and cockatoos common alone or in pairs or in small or large flocks in open forests. Hundreds of complex patterns of plumage, green and blue and slate-grey and orange and crimson and rufous and buff and lemon-yellow and chestnut and turquoise, persist all round the outlying suburbs of Bassett and perhaps even pass along secret pathways in the tree-tops of its parks and gardens and wastelands on their way from one part of their territory to another. While Clement is confined for season after season among crowds of people, none of whom has yet been able to show him into that bright system of hidden roads that they surely must have discovered in all the years they have spent in Bassett, the small or large flocks move freely all over their zone of open forests. Each spring and summer the males of every species flaunt their gorgeous colours from prominent perches all over the country that coincides with Bassett but has seldom been seen by anyone in that city. Cup- or saucer- or dome- or platform-shaped nests of twigs or bark or other coarse fibres lined with dried grass or moss or cobwebs and camouflaged with lichens or mistletoe or dead twigs, with one or two or from three to six eggs pure white or pale creamy-brown or reddish-white sprinkled with rich red and a few underlying markings of lilac-grey more pronounced at the larger end, hang in every tree and low shrub of the forests that no one can point out to him but which are somehow superimposed on the already intricate red and grey and orange patterns of Bassett. Some pairs stay together faithfully for life and remember at last a grove or a thicket that only they know of in the forests that no people know of as the place where they first mated and then no longer wanted to mate with any other, while other kinds that form new pairs each year go searching through the country that belongs to them, although the people who claim to own it have never heard of them, for the sunlit clearing where a sudden flash of unexpected vermilion or discordant yellow decides which of all the mates that they might have chosen will be theirs for a season of north winds and afterwards only someone that they remember dimly among other mazes of leaves and branches when other mates plunge beaks deep into the feathers of their necks and then go with them to look for nesting-places. At the end of a week when Clement has spent every night reading the bird book and wondering about the flecked and striated and variegated populations that pass to and fro along green tunnels beneath the surface of Bassett, Augustine invites the boy to the racecourse to watch Sternie in a trial gallop against two other horses. They reach the track long before breakfast, but the summer sun is already high in the sky. Augustine sees a woman leaning against a long dazzling car. He whispers to Clement that the boy will have to meet Mrs Moy the jockey's wife and tells him to think of something sensible to say to her but not to mention Sternie or racing. The boy stares hard at Mrs Moy but sees no trace of Chinese colouring in her skin. She is easily the most beautiful woman he has seen. Out on the track Harold Moy warms up Sternie for his trial. Clement is sorry to see the jockeys wearing only plain shirts instead of racing colours. When he shakes hands with Mrs Moy he sees in the glossy black circles of her sun-glasses the white-railed arcs of racecourses where a solitary horse looms up and dwindles again, far from its rivals in some mysterious race. When she turns her head to watch her husband doing battle against the small field of strange riders and their horses, Clement glimpses in the smoky glass, where only a few months or years before a gaudy array of wind-creased jackets veered upwards on a long crazy course that reached far back into the depths of the black glass pressing against her expressionless face until one mass of colours more splendid than all the others flared up for a moment like a rare flame and overflowed the round dark mirrors and she decided that her next mate must be Harold Moy who thrust his arms and twitched his legs like a madman absurdly far ahead of the field and wore like fluttering plumage his colours of molten jewel, burnished crossed sashes and sleeves, iridescent armbands and cap, strange shifting vistas of a tiny racecourse set among symmetrical groves of trees far different from any in Bassett. Mrs Moy goes on staring into the sunlight, and Clement wonders what kind of racecourse, what sequence of horses and assortment of colours she sees as she looks out from the other side of her private sky towards the landscape that he scarcely recognises in the light of the usual sun. After a long silence he forces himself to ask her politely whether she lives somewhere near the racecourse and not far from the edge of Bassett. She says – yes, that's right Clement – you could almost see our house from here if it wasn't for those trees over there. She points to the stand of timber at the far side of the track. Without stopping to think, Clement asks – do you ever see many parrots or kingfishers in the bush around your house? Mrs Moy looks deliberately down at him so that he sees only bush unmarked by any sign of a racecourse in the dark screen between her eyes and his. She says – that's a funny question to ask – no we're too busy to stop and look for birds I suppose but I'm sure there are plenty around if you only knew where to look.

### THE GOLD CUP RACE CONTINUES

While Clement waits for his mother to leave him alone in the house for long enough to guide the field a little further on its long circuitous journey, he turns the pages of the bundle of exercise books that he brought home for the last time from school a few weeks earlier, just before the start of the Christmas holidays that promised so many idle afternoons that he planned to spend one day in January looking through the rows and rows of his own handwriting and gloating over the remoteness of the hours when he struggled to keep the sweat on his hands from staining the pages and traced faintly from time to time with his pencil on the marbled cover of his book a journey as arduous as the struggle of the afternoon to reach the hour when he could escape from the dusty room and gulp down

water at the taps. On almost every page he sees some project –
a set of sums, a passage of transcription, a composition on At
the Baths or A Thunderstorm or An Adventure With a Snake,
a page of geography about the Eskimos or of history about the
Crossing of the Red Sea or a test of ten words from the spelling
list – that began when he wrote with slow unfaltering strokes
the letters J. M. J. (for the names of the Holy Family) at the top
of the page and then watched anxiously as the first letters of
the first words appeared from beneath his pencil because he
wanted no mark of his rubber and no altered stroke of his
pencil to mar his page. As he kept on with what he and the
teacher called his work, he looked forward to the time when
the whole of the smooth double page would be filled with
words or figures or neat pencil drawings not of his choosing
but ordained by his teacher, who knew that when it reached
from edge to edge of the white sheets it would show a boy as
much as he was permitted to know of the intricate systems of
learning that adults so often saw in books that were too difficult
for children. But looking through the discarded exercise books,
Clement sees how the uniform slant of his letters gradually
lapsed on so many pages into a jumble of tottering summits
and distorted slopes and how the light and shade in his pencil
strokes soon became an unvarying dark-grey and the projects
themselves, which were originally meant to spread themselves
across two pages and to remain for long afterwards as evidence
of his perseverance and industriousness, petered out long
before the end of the second page in a sentence that was never
finished or a sketch that was left with its mysterious shapes
unlabelled. He remembers the rewards that his teacher once
promised and the punishments she threatened to urge him
and his forty or fifty classmates to finish every word of their
work and to pay close attention to neatness and wonders
whether these are all now utterly meaningless because, sooner

than any of them had expected, the bell rang outside and the grade shuffled out into the hot afternoon and next day there was some new piece of work to begin and in no time at all it was the Christmas holidays, or whether the uneasiness he feels whenever he glances through the unfinished pages means that his punishment is still to come. In one of the books he finds a bare white space which, if his teacher had found it, might have cost him an hour of pastels or free reading because he knew as well as anyone in the grade that every space had to be filled, but which now, so soon after the days when he had to keep it hidden in his desk, he can stare at openly for as long as he pleases. Under a few sentences from the story in his reader, The Race – *The winning post was now not far off. The prince threw his last apple, hoping and hoping that once more Atalanta would stop. She saw the gleaming fruit roll across the sand and felt that she must have it. For just one second she bent and caught it up. That was the prince's chance. Darting past her, he reached the winning post just,* are some words that he wrote in the early days of the holidays telling the story of a race a few months earlier than the Gold Cup race. He cups his hands over his mouth and his left ear, and prepares to describe softly to himself in the phrases of a racing commentator the race whose story is written as only a list of horses' names with a series of numerals beside each name to show the position of that horse at the half-mile post, then at the turn into the straight, and finally at the finish, and illustrated by a sketch of a sprawling racecourse of an irregular oval shape that fills all the remaining space between the stories of a prince, who had to succeed in an almost impossible race before he could marry Atalanta, and of the horse *Tamarisk Row* whose owners never gave up hoping for a great win and the end of the second page. He tells how the field, with the best gallopers striding comfortably and well within themselves, travels around the long gradual curve at the far side of the course where a boy might have felt the point of his pencil flowing smoothly across the paper and heard the voice of Miss Callaghan as she went on with what she called her urgent private work at her desk saying – there'll be something special for anyone whose writing can stand the test of a magnifying glass, and still the little-known horse *Tamarisk Row* waits patiently near the rear for the moment when his rider asks him for an effort. His whispering voice grows a little harsher as the leaders begin the slow turn towards the top of the straight across the faint lines from which a boy may once have mopped a few tiny puddles of sweat because he heard his teacher saying as she looked hurriedly towards the front desks – pity help anyone who can't show me two pages of beautiful work at bell time and that means no marks from grubby sticky fingers, and the horse that he relies on to enact something heroic in a space that has so far been marked only by timid journeys and predictable homecomings seems likely to be thwarted in its run by the wall of horses ahead of it. And he allows the air rushing from his throat to obscure his words as the noise of the crowd might drown the words of the course broadcaster while the field struggles up the long straight across the space that was still unfilled when Miss Callaghan said – I've changed my mind – because it's such a hot afternoon I'm going to let everyone go home on time but mark my words I'll be taking up all those books tomorrow and woe betide any person whose writing isn't their best or anyone with spaces or gaps in their pages, and he realises that *Tamarisk Row* will finish on the heels of the winner after a desperate but unlucky finishing run that perhaps only his owners will see and appreciate. The boy's mother comes to tell him to be good while she is away in Bassett just as he notices that the names of horses, the numerals, and the sketch of the racecourse have been made so carelessly that there are still many gaps between them and the edges of the pages, so that even though no teacher may ever point to the spaces and ask him accusingly what does he mean by them, he should still find room there for more names and numbers telling of great races to finish the task that he began so seriously and fearfully on a hot afternoon in a room where he will probably never sit again and perhaps to see spread out across the page the sort of pattern that his teacher believed possible and that once seemed to promise such satisfaction. Even before he hears the bus pull away he is writing in a space near the edge of the page the names of the runners in the Gold Cup and arranging the sixteen marbles in the positions that they reached soon after the start. He kneels beside them and, with his eyes tightly closed, pushes each runner forward. After each push he waits, listening for the click of glass against glass that tells him a runner has been checked by another in front of it. If he hears no click he hugs himself with excitement to think that a horse whose name he can only guess at is making a long run through the field and perhaps passing a whole bunch in one sudden burst. When the last runner has been pushed he gropes for the absurdly wide runners and moves them closer to the rails. Then he opens his eyes and gloats over the many changes in the field. He enters the runners' positions in the exercise book, closes his eyes again, and pushes them all forward once more. He intends to bring them as far as the turn into the straight and then to enjoy the sketches and figures describing their positions for perhaps a week or even longer until he is left alone for the whole afternoon that he needs to lie beside the field as they make their last runs in the straight, to keep his eyes closed until he can no longer bear not to see which horse has run last after all, then to close them again and wonder about the second-last horse and then all the others in turn. When the field finally reaches the turn he describes the race again in the words of the course broadcaster – as they start the run around the big sweeping turn about three furlongs from home and the field begins to bunch up all but this leader *Lost Streamlet* who's slipped away a couple of lengths clear from *Veils of Foliage* and *Hare in the Hills* still continuing that long run right around the field from near last they're followed by *Springtime in the Rockies* waiting for the last run *Hills of Idaho* there too and *Proud Stallion* who looks beaten *Passage of North Winds* close enough if he's good enough and *Infant of Prague* under the whip making no impression then *Captured Riflebird* and *Den of Foxes* with a big job in front of them then a gap to *Monastery Garden* followed by *Mysteries of the Rosary* dropping out about to be passed by *Silverstone* and *Tamarisk Row* together a long way back and then *Transylvanian* who couldn't get up from there and last of all *Silver Rowan* about twenty lengths from the leader. When the positions are safely entered in his book, he sits waiting for the sound of the bus outside and enjoying what he will dwell on in secret every day until the race is finally decided – that moment when the supporters of almost every horse can still believe that their fancy will still justify their hopes even if it has to finish with a run that even they will marvel at for long afterwards. He holds his breath for the sake of *Lost Streamlet* whose rider has dared to make his run so far from home and fears at every stride the arrival close behind him of a whole bunch of determined challengers but who may yet cling to his narrow advantage all the way up the straight. He clenches his fists for *Hare in the Hills* who was among the tail-enders early and has steadily improved his position ever since, but wide on the track, so that he may have used up already too much of his precious stamina. He gets to his feet and walks all around the room in his anxiety for *Tamarisk Row* who has only two horses behind him and must now wait until the field has entered the straight before he makes his run because there is no way through the pack ahead of him. From different points around the room he tries to estimate the distance between *Tamarisk Row* and the leaders, and realises that no matter how strongly the horse finishes he will not catch the eye of the course broadcaster until near the post, so that many even of his supporters might have given up hope and looked instead at the leaders before they first hear his name *Tamarisk Row* roared at them like a battle cry above the confused noise of the crowd and perhaps only a handful of faithful friends will know that almost unbearable elation that gradually rises as a forgotten horse passes one after another on his long weaving run through the field and still the crowd has not noticed him bearing down on the leaders.

## THE PEOPLE OF TAMARISK ROW LOOK OUT OF THEIR WINDOWS

Whenever Augustine returns from taking Sternie to gallop at the Bassett racecourse, Clement listens eagerly to his father's conversation for news of Mrs Moy, the jockey's wife. But Augustine mentions her so rarely that Clement sometimes has to ask in his most innocent voice – did Mr Moy ride Sternie this morning Dad? and when Augustine says – yes of course he did, to ask – did he come in his big Studebaker? and when Augustine says – how else would he come? to ask – did Mrs Moy come with him to watch him ride? The answer to this is usually – no she did not. Clement, who is always alert to such things, notices the hint of embarrassment in his father's voice and guesses that there is something about Mrs Moy that he (the boy) is not meant to discover. He guesses that on some summer morning when the sun was already blazing and the wind had set in from the north, Augustine went to the Moys' modern brick house that sprawls among trees tall and leafy enough for a dozen birds' nests and saw through the fly-wire door at the front (because the frosted glass door had been left open all night because of the heat) that the Moys when they are alone together do the things that Clement himself, soon after he had first glimpsed in Mrs Moy's dark glasses a racecourse shaped differently from any that he knew and wondered what shapes she herself saw from her side of the sultry glass, discovered the man and his wife doing in the isolated homestead of Tamarisk Row. That place is still so remote among plains and the view of those plains that the people there see when they look through windows darkened by vines and creepers towards places dissolving in sunlight is still so changeable that the only likeness to it that Clement knows is the landscape that alternately expands and contracts in the polished panels of a woman's sun-glasses. During the days when Clement does not disturb them, the man and the woman behind the glass see a great flat expanse of paddocks run together into one white molten globule no bigger than the pupil of an eye, or a road that leads on like the straight of a racecourse deflected so that it sweeps boldly towards but never reaches some distant landmark. Sometimes, when the man points out to his wife through the shaded glass the big pink pizzle dangling beneath the horse *Tamarisk Row*, a monstrous glowing column of fleshy pink appears above their lawn and gardens. Sometimes even on their own side of the glass they see sudden freaks of light – the margin of an inch or so between the horse *Journey's End* and the winner of the Gold Cup in the photograph in the lounge-room is magnified until it looms like a broad shadowy gulf that can never be crossed but before which they must stand every day of their lives, and when they walk through the house naked on the hottest days some obscure corner of the woman's body now and then floats in the troubled glass as if it would merge there with the focused essence of the throbbing plains outside.

At last Clement hears his father telling his mother that he isn't keen to take the boy to the racecourse of a morning because the woman often turns up and Clem seems to have taken a silly fancy to her and he's bound to be blurting out and calling her Mrs Moy and although that's apparently what she wants to be called he (Augustine) feels a bit of a fool knowing as he does now that she's someone else's wife. Augustine says – it makes me feel very disappointed in Harold but I couldn't bring myself to sack him after all the years we've known each other on the racecourse. Clement is sorry that he may not see Mrs Moy again but pleased to learn that the Moys turned out after all to have a secret behind their glass.

## CLEMENT LEARNS A GIRL'S SECRETS AT LAST

A man steps out of a car at the Killeatons' front gate, and Augustine hurries to meet him before he can come inside. The man goes back to his car and sits waiting. Augustine tells his wife that the man's name is Ray Mendoza, that he owns a lot of horses, and that a while ago when Augustine was going well at the races Mendoza tried to talk him into leasing one of his good three-year-olds, that of course Augustine cannot possibly afford to lease another horse as well as Sternie but that he'd like to visit Mendoza's place and at least have a look at his horses before he tells him politely there's nothing doing. Mrs Killeaton tells him to take Clement along for the ride. Mr Mendoza drives Augustine and Clement out to a suburb named Franklin's Flat near the racecourse. The Mendozas' brick house and their front garden are about five times as big as the Killeatons', but the huge lawn and the wide driveway are almost bare of trees and shrubs. Behind the house, too, is a smooth bare lawn with only one tree set in it, so that any boy or girl who lived there could never do anything around the yard without being seen by people going past or by parents peering out of the tall windows. Mr Mendoza takes Augustine straight to the stables. Augustine starts to say that circumstances have changed quite a bit since he first hinted he might be interested in leasing a horse, but Mr Mendoza puts an arm around Augustine's shoulders and says – just wait till you see the horse Gus – just wait till you see him. While the men move towards the horses' stalls, Clement pushes open the door of a feed room and steps inside. A pair of hot sweating hands reaches out of the darkness and covers his eyes. A girl's voice says – guess who it is and I'll give you three wishes. Clement says – I give up. The girl grabs him by the shoulders and wrenches him around to face her. In the half-light of the shed he sees the girl who is Therese Riordan's best friend, the same girl that he has met several times at Riordans' place. She closes the door of the feed room and leans her head on one side to listen. Clement decides that if only her face was not so ugly he would have her for his girlfriend. The girl says – you can have your three wishes anyway because it wasn't fair to make you guess like that – wait on – I know what you're going to wish before you even start – first of all you want to know what my name is – well it's the same as Therese's middle name – second you want to see Therese's Foxy Glen – well the next time we're up at Riordans' together I'll probably get it and let you look at it – and I bet the third wish is you want to see me with my pants off. Clement says – there's something else I want to ask you too – what did you used to do with that big boy Silverstone who used to live in Leslie Street – and did you do it in his backyard or at Riordans'? She laughs and says – I used to do it right where you're standing now and it wasn't just with the boy from Leslie Street either but dozens of other boys too. Clement says – but what sort of things? The girl says – the same things that you told me you're always doing with the big girls next door to your place. She thinks for a moment, then says – that means you've already had three wishes but just because you're one of Therese's boyfriends I'll let you have your other wish. Clement says – did Therese Riordan really tell you I'm one of her boyfriends? – The girl says – hurry up do you want your wish or don't you? Clement says – yes please – and I'll take my thing out too for you to look at. She says – you needn't be bothered – I've seen so many boys' things I'm sick of them – just tell me are you circumcised or not. Clement says – I think so. She says – that means you must have a little pink knob on the end the colour of a baby mouse with no fur on – you'd better give me a quick look just to make sure I'm right. Clement takes out his cock. She looks at it and says – yes I was right again. She tugs at it gently and teases it with her fingertips until it grows bigger and more rigid than Clement has ever seen it. Then she tells him abruptly to put it away out of her sight before she belts it with a stick or a stock-whip. Clement pokes it back awkwardly into his trousers and says – you still haven't taken your pants down yet. The girl says – I'll let you look at me if you tell me first what I look like. Clement says – your cock isn't much like a boy's because it's flatter and half stuck in to your skin between your legs and your balls are tiny and hardly wrinkled at all and they're pressed up close to your skin too. The girl looks hard at him for a moment and then grins. She says – hang on a minute and I'll show you how stupid you are. She turns her back on him, pulls her white silk pants down around her knees, crosses her legs tightly, looks down at herself, does something with her fingers between her thighs, and then, still with her legs crossed, turns around to face Clement. He looks eagerly between her legs but sees only the white skin of her belly disappearing between her thighs, which are pressed tightly together. She says – there you are you were wrong after all – I've got nothing there at all. He says – I know you're hiding it between your legs. She turns away from him and says – I am hiding something – look. When she turns back to face him, he sees two long fine golden-brown hairs growing out of the otherwise bare white skin at the very lowest part of her belly. She says – tell the truth have you ever seen anything like that before? He says – no never – but isn't there something for you to do piss with? She says – only a stupid little hole that you wouldn't be interested in. He reaches out a finger to touch one of her hairs and is startled to find her skin warm, when he had thought it would be cold like silk or marble. She jumps up and pulls her pants on and says – now I know you never really did play with those big girls next door and pull their pants down did you? He feels so grateful to her that he says trustingly – no I didn't really. She says – when I tell Therese how stupid you are she probably won't even bother to talk to you again. He says – please don't tell her – anyway you promised you'd help me find out about her Foxy Glen. He stops suddenly and says – do you think Therese would pull her pants down for me if you told her you'd already done it with me? She says – get out and find your old man or I'll go and tell him what you've just been doing. She opens the door, and the two of them walk along the passageway towards the two men. Augustine says – hullo where have you been son? He looks so keenly at Clement that the boy blushes. The girl steps forward and says sweetly – I was just showing him a lovely little nest of baby mice in the feed room – all pink and soft and cuddly – would you like to come in and see them Mr Killeaton? Augustine smiles and says – some other time thanks. As the men walk towards the car, Mr Mendoza says – look Gus there's still time for you to change your mind and come inside right now and sign the lease papers and this very afternoon I'll send the horse over to your place in a float. In the car on the way back to Leslie Street Mr Mendoza says – now Gus the minute you decide on something give me a ring and I'll call round in the car and drive you back to my place again and you can take as long as you like to look around. In the back seat the girl Mendoza pinches Clement hard on the thigh near the edge of his trouser leg.

## CLEMENT HAS DOUBTS ABOUT BARBARA KEENAN

Augustine and Mr Mendoza stand for a long time near the Killeatons' front gate, still talking. The girl Mendoza asks Clement – who's your little girlfriend at St Boniface's? He says – I've got one but I'm not telling you her name. Then although the girl pleads with him he refuses to reveal the name Barbara Keenan which stands for a face as aloof as the marble above an altar but in whose serene pallor a few oddly placed, delicately tinted freckles never fail to surprise him and to suggest that the girl may be pleasantly unpredictable in her ways and may even agree one day to be the wife of a racehorse owner on condition that he leads in the winner of the most famous race in a land of mighty plains and, while the lustful owners of a dozen beaten horses are clutching and kneading their wives' bodies and trying to forget their defeat, may allow her husband just once, as a reward for a great win, to undress her and mate with her before she becomes again the reserved unsmiling unapproachable woman that he cheerfully woos for months with stories of great races yet to be won. The girl Mendoza says – it doesn't matter because I can ask Therese to find out the girl's name or I might even stand outside St Boniface's gate myself one afternoon and see for myself which girl looks like the sort of girlfriend you'd pick because don't forget I know a lot about you now and the sort of girls you're after. Clement is not worried by this threat because he knows that God or Our Lady or Barbara Keenan's patron saint or guardian angel makes sure that no one but himself, who would not dare to lay a finger on her body until long after he had married her, ever notices how beautiful she is. He remembers a day when Barry Launder and some of his feathered friends were gathered round a photograph of their grade trying to bag the prettiest girls for themselves and Launder said – I bag Pauline Duffy – she's the best-looking tart there is, and Michael Hannan said – you bugger Launder I wanted Duffy for myself, and Clement began to fear for Barbara Keenan because the girl Duffy had such a sweet innocent face that he had never suspected that Launder and his gang would want to get her pants down or fall in love with her or might even have seen between her legs already or touched her there, but even though some of Launder's gang started bagging more than one girl for themselves not one of them mentioned Barbara Keenan and Clement knew that she would be safe until the end of the year when all the boys in the grade would leave St Boniface's school for the Brothers' College and she would almost forget about boys and concentrate on keeping the pages of her school-books neat and earning holy pictures for good work. The girl Mendoza says – well have you told the girl you love her or passed notes to her desk or tried to kiss her on the way home from school? Clement wonders whether he should tell Barbara Keenan by just one sign that she is his girlfriend before he leaves St Boniface's, where the only sports are the few confused races that he himself struggles to organise among the mobs of heedless boys and which few girls ever stop to look at, for the college where every Wednesday every boy wears a coloured sash and plays for his House in a football or cricket team or in November runs in sprints or distance races but at sports grounds where no girls ever come to watch, so that a girl whose face inspires a boy to come from fifty yards behind in a mile race might hear, a few months later, only a vague story about a race in which some little-known runner appeared suddenly wide out at the top of the straight and made the watchers gasp, but no more. The girl Mendoza says – why don't you tell the little girl what you want to do with her and see what she says? Clement remembers an afternoon in grade three when Michael Hannan, who was always talking about boys and their cocks and balls and girls and their holes, who often tried to persuade Launder's gang to tell stories about girls they had chased or even to chase them on the way home from school, and who came to school one day with the story that Clement laughed at but was not quite sure he understood – there was this little kid and he came home from school one day and said Mum what's a cock and his mum said don't worry son a cock's just a hat so he came home the next day and said Mum what's a shit and his mum said well son a shit's just when you sit down and have a rest so he came home the next day and said Mum what's a fuck and his mum said a fuck's when a man and lady have a talk together so the next day the minister came and knocked on the front door and the little kid went and answered it and said come in and hang your cock on the wall and have a shit in the front room Mum won't be long she's out the back having a fuck with the baker, told all the boys he was going to write a note and pass it across to Pauline Duffy and her girlfriends in school because he wanted to see which would be the best one to take down the creek on the way home one night and Clement himself read the words in Hannan's best writing on a whole clean sheet ripped from the back of one of his exercise books – what is a fuck a fuck is when you take a girl into the bushes and take her pants down and get on top of her, and trembled with embarrassment as he passed it on its way because it had to travel across the desks of Barbara Keenan and some of her friends who were shy and innocent like herself before it reached Pauline Duffy and her friends. He still does not know for certain whether or not Barbara Keenan opened the note and read it because he buried his face in his hands and prayed that Miss Callaghan would come back into the room and that Hannan would get scared and grab the note before the girls could read it, but outside in the yard afterwards he stood listening while Hannan told everyone how all the girls enjoyed his little message and giggled over it, and for days afterwards he was on the point of deciding that he would have to find a new girlfriend from one of the junior grades – a girl who had not been spoiled by boys like Hannan because Barbara Keenan had probably giggled when she read about girls having their pants pulled down and would not be satisfied until she found out from boys like Hannan what it was really like in the bushes beside the creek. The girl Mendoza says – if you've never kissed your girlfriend or told her you love her she's sure to find someone else for her boyfriend – I bet she's already found a place in her backyard like that feed room in my old man's stables and you know what she'll be doing there any day now with her new boyfriend. Clement is pleased to see Mr Mendoza getting into his car and beckoning to his daughter. When the Mendozas have gone he walks past all his farms and looks into all the homes of the people that he has known for years, but nothing that he sees there helps him to decide whether Barbara Keenan really does think often about her pants and would giggle if a boy talked or wrote to her as Michael Hannan wrote to Pauline Duffy, in which case he ought to forget about her and try to learn as much as possible about girls from the girl Mendoza in the feed room and then ask Mendoza herself to find him a girlfriend who likes doing the things that she does or even ask Mendoza herself to be his girlfriend until he can find someone whose face is not so ugly, or whether the girl Mendoza is lying because she wants him for her own boyfriend who will go into the feed room whenever she asks him and let her do what she likes to him, in which case he might let Mendoza have her way and then one day a long time afterwards, perhaps when he is making his last desperate run in some great race and looking up at the crowd he sees a pale beautiful face watching him, Barbara Keenan will show him what she thinks of a boy who lets an ugly non-Catholic girl with warts on her fingers twist and tug at his cock day after day in a dirty room in a stable and turn her face away and walk off with some Catholic boy who really did believe that she was pure and innocent and leave him to make his run with only Mendoza, who would never understand such a subtle thing as racing, to watch him, or whether Barbara Keenan is not only not as Mendoza has described her but is so spotlessly pure and free from sin that she would not have understood a word of Hannan's note and even if Mendoza herself told her exactly what she and Clement did in the feed room would not know what the non-Catholic girl was talking about or believe that Clement could have done anything that made him unfit to be her boyfriend, and, best of all, so utterly different from the ugly, sniggering Mendoza girl that when Killeaton, perhaps years afterwards after he and his horse have proved themselves and he has earned the right to undress her in some comfortable homestead, finally does take down her pants he will see between her legs something very different from the uninteresting skin that Mendoza was once so coy about and begin all over again with Barbara Keenan to discover the things that a pure Catholic girl has kept hidden for so long and forget all about the girl who once tried to trick him by sticking two hairs from a chestnut horse between her legs and pretending that they were all she had to show.

## AUGUSTINE BACKS STERNIE IN A MALLEE HANDICAP

Sternie, the horse named after a Melbourne Jew who has never seen the northern country where the big chestnut was finally sent after years of failure around the city, runs his first two races just as Augustine has planned. In a weak maiden race at Peechunga, a town on the Murray, Sternie finishes fourth out of six, and Harold Moy reports that the horse was anxious to go much faster in the straight. In a stronger field at Wensleydale, where many Melbourne horses race, Sternie runs nearly last, but Harold is pleased with him again because at the turn he was going strongly just behind the main bunch. That night Augustine whispers to his wife that the time has come for him to have a go with Sternie. The race that he chooses is a novice handicap of seven furlongs at a place named Jerram more than a hundred miles north-west of Bassett on the edge of the Mallee. Sternie is eligible to run in maiden races, but most maidens are run over five or six furlongs, and Augustine believes that the horse needs a longer distance. He knows too that the bookmakers will give a better price about Sternie in a novice than in a maiden. Augustine visits Stan Riordan, but without taking Clement. He persuades Stan to risk thirty pounds as a bet on Sternie at Jerram. When Stan has handed over the money to Augustine he offers to do what Augustine has not dared to ask him – to forget all about the couple of hundred that Augustine owes him if Sternie wins and the bet comes off. Stan then asks Augustine has he got enough cash himself for a decent bet on Sternie. Augustine is so grateful for the chance to wipe out all his debts to Riordan that he insists he has all the money he needs to back the horse. That night Augustine telephones Len Goodchild and tells him that the horse named after a mysterious friend of theirs in Melbourne is ready to win and that a very smart bookmaker in Bassett is sending a good-sized bet to the course. He urges Goodchild to send a money order to Leslie Street so that he (Augustine) can get him the best odds on the course and pay him back for some of the many good turns he has done him in the past. Goodchild says that he'll see about sending something. Each afternoon of the last week before the race Augustine takes Sternie for long walks among the least-travelled streets and the rough grassy lanes through scrub where old pensioners sitting at the doors of their humpies wave briefly and stare gravely after him. On the Friday before the race, Goodchild's money has still not arrived. Augustine does not like to bother Goodchild by phoning him again, and decides that the Master is probably so busy with all his Melbourne business that Sternie and the race at Jerram have slipped his mind. Augustine tells his wife that he is entitled to a cut from Stan Riordan's winnings, that supposing he has Stan's thirty pounds on at seven to one he would only be expected to give Stan odds of six to one according to an unwritten gentleman's agreement of racing. He does not tell her how much of his own money he intends to put on, but she agrees to give him four pounds from a store of two-shilling pieces that she keeps somewhere in her dressing-table. He leaves early on Saturday morning, riding his bike, with Sternie trotting slowly behind him, towards the stables of a man who has offered Augustine and his horse a place in his truck. The Jerram races are not broadcast on Station 3BT Bassett, but at six o'clock in the evening Clement's mother switches on the sporting results program and stands waiting with her rosary beads entwined in her fingers. Towards the end of the program the announcer reads in a cheerful voice the results of the meeting at Jerram. Each time that he names a race he pauses before announcing the winner's name as if to tease the women waiting for news of their husbands' horses. He says – the Novice Handicap of seven furlongs, pretends to be peering hard at the list of names in front of him, then blurts out as happily as if he himself had backed the winner – this was won by Docile J. O'Mullane starting at five to two – second placing went to My Heliotrope K. Bennett starting at seven to one and third money went to Sternie H. Moy starting at four to one. Mrs Killeaton turns off the wireless at once. She tells Clement not to mention a word about racing again as long as he lives and warns him that if she ever catches him looking at a Sporting Globe or the back pages of a newspaper or trying to listen to a race on the wireless she will take to him with his father's razor strap until he has to stay in bed for a month. Clement lies awake in the dark until he hears a truck pulling up at the front gate. He listens at the open window while his father backs Sternie out of the truck and says – goodnight and thanks again for everything, to the driver. While Augustine is putting Sternie into his loose-box and giving him his feed and water for the night, Clement creeps out of bed and stands near the door of his room. He hears his father tell his mother that if he wasn't so badly in debt he would be feeling quite pleased with Sternie's run because he made up half a dozen lengths on the leaders in the straight and was going as well as the winner when they passed the post. He hears that Sternie was beaten by less than two lengths and that if only there was a mile maiden somewhere in the next few weeks Sternie would be a certainty in it. Jean Killeaton says – I would have thought you'd be trying to think of a place where we could all go and get away from all your cursed damn bookmakers and debts and there wouldn't be a racecourse for hundreds of miles around – somewhere like the Western District you're always skiting about. Augustine says cheerfully – don't worry I've been thinking the same thing myself a few times lately – of course there's plenty of racecourses in the Western District too – but there's nothing wrong with racing if only a man would only bet what he could afford to lose. She asks him how much he lost at Jerram, but he says he can't think about it now and asks whether she or Clement remembered to feed the chooks and bring in the eggs.

### AUGUSTINE CONFIDES IN A BOOKMAKER

Augustine waits for a few days after Sternie's third placing in the novice at Jerram, then telephones Goodchild in Melbourne. Neither man mentions the money that Goodchild was supposed to have sent to Augustine before the race. Goodchild reminds Augustine that Sternie is not the kind of horse that you try to win money on, that he nearly broke his previous owner's heart by always running a promising race but never winning, and that he (Goodchild) explained to Augustine when he handed the horse over to him that he was only supposed to race Sternie at northern meetings purely as a hobby. He laughs as he tells Augustine not to forget that a certain Hebrew gentleman once put a curse on the horse. Augustine says that his wife has been wondering a few times lately whether they wouldn't be better off going onto a farm somewhere in the Western District because they just can't seem to make ends meet on his wages and he has a few troublesome debts that are starting to bother him. Goodchild says – break it down now Gus – things can't surely be as bad as all that – anyway if you can wait a few more weeks all your worries will be over because our men are planning something that will earn us all enough to retire on. Goodchild cannot reveal any more for the time being, but he urges Augustine to keep in touch with him and get a big bank ready because the Master and all his faithful followers are going to get their reward at last. Augustine takes Clement up the hill once more to Riordans' place. He leaves the boy to play in the garden and goes into Stan's office. He tells the story of Sternie's run at Jerram and apologises several times to Riordan for causing him to lose thirty pounds on Sternie. The bookmaker says – think nothing of it Gus – but what's more important are you going to give Sternie away now? Augustine says – I suppose I'll have to Stan – but there's something else I want to tell you – before I tell you I want to say that it's something I've never done before in all the years I've been connected with the racing game so you'll realise how desperate I am at the moment – and what's more I'm telling you because I know I can trust you as a Catholic gentleman and the best friend I've made in Bassett. Stan Riordan looks out of the window. Augustine says – Stan the smartest men in racing – the bunch of men I've cultivated and kept in touch with for years are getting ready to have a really big lash at something in town soon – I never dreamed I'd be telling a bookmaker this sort of thing but as I said before I've come to think of you as a friend I can trust more than a bookmaker – well Stan to cut a long story short I can't tell you the name of this horse yet because I don't even know it myself – well when the big day comes and I get the word from them they'll be wanting me to have a fair bit of money on for them with the biggest bookmakers in Bassett – I know I'm telling you nothing new when I say that I've just about exhausted my credit with all the decent-sized men in this town – what I'm suggesting is that you'll do the betting for me – you can ring up Horrie Attrill or Eric Hooper a few minutes before the race and have on all the Melbourne money plus as much as you want for yourself – if you leave the bet until the last few minutes before the race Horrie or Eric or whoever you bet with won't have time to ring any of the big bookmakers in Melbourne and lay the bet off – that's something my men are always afraid of as you'd know – the worst thing that can happen is for one of the big smart Melbourne

S.P. bookmakers to phone money to the course and ruin the horse's price – well if we guard against that happening none of my men in Melbourne will be any the wiser. Stan Riordan sits thinking. Augustine says – as you can see it's a desperate thing I'm doing – risking the confidence of some of the toughest men in the game – chaps who've been very good to me over the years – but still there's nothing really dishonest in what I'm suggesting – they'll get their money just the same and you'll win enough to cover the money I still owe you – as far as I'm concerned I don't want any more than that – if I can clear up what I owe you it's as good as having a big win. Stan Riordan says – I understand exactly the position you're in Gus and I don't think any the worse of you for trying to work something like this – the only thing that bothers me is whether your friends might have some other agent besides yourself in a place as big as Bassett – because if they do and I ring up my bet at the last minute it's more than likely the chap I ring will be so loaded already with money for the good thing that I won't get set – what with your friends' money and the money I'd need to put on to wipe your slate clean it might amount to a decent sort of bet I'd be wanting to get on – and we'd look lovely wouldn't we holding all that money ourselves when the barrier went down. Augustine says – I see what you mean and I want to make things as easy as possible for you Stan – I can only say that the man in charge has told me repeatedly that I'm his Bassett agent but I'll make doubly sure of where I stand before we go any further in this business – suppose we say nothing more just for the moment and I promise to have another chat with you well before the big day. While the men are inside the house, Clement finds Therese Riordan and her friend the girl Mendoza waiting in the shade of a grapevine whose leaves have long since hidden from sight the trellis supporting them, so that they hang like the abundant folds of some carelessly draped green tent. The girl Mendoza tells him that they are waiting for her father to come in his car and take them to the baths because it is so hot. She tells Therese Riordan that she gave Clem three wishes at her place the other day and there are still a couple left that she owes him. Anything to do with wishes and secrets appeals to Therese, and for the first time in months she looks at Clement with interest. She says – ooh tell us what they were Pat. Clement says – ha ha you've just granted one of them right now hasn't she Pat? While Therese looks at the girl and then at him for an explanation, he decides that at last Therese Riordan, who is prettier than even Barbara Keenan who after all has never allowed him to explore her garden or watch her playing with treasures like the Foxy Glen, is about to relent towards him and even perhaps to confide to him the kinds of secrets that the plain-faced Pat Mendoza has already confided because she knows that he can be trusted and means no harm but only wants to have with them such an understanding that he could sit with them in shady places in hot weather and stretch out his legs for cool-ness on mossy flagstones so that one of his balls might be clearly visible lying limp and sweating just inside the leg of his shorts and each girl would see it but would not laugh or scream or tease him about it but would simply stretch her own legs further out along the comfortable stones and not care how much of her pants he saw or even how much of her white skin was showing under the edges of the pants as she loosened them to cool herself, and talk of his most secret games and treasures with no fear that they might smile at their strange-ness. Out of gratitude to Pat Mendoza for all that she has done for him, and to show Therese Riordan that he and she need not have any more secrets between them, he makes a slight noise and clutches himself between the legs. He walks a few paces away from them and stands facing a bed of ferns. His back is to the girls. He hears Pat Mendoza saying – well one of the wishes was he wanted to see me without my pants on and I wouldn't let him of course but now that we've got our bathers on under our dresses we could pull our dresses up a little way for him couldn't we? He takes out his cock and aims it at the ferns but cannot make any water come. Therese says – that's silly Pat and I don't want to talk about it. The other girl says yes we could – well I will anyway there's nothing wrong with it look at me Killeaton I've got no pants on under my dress – go on Therese it might teach the little kid a lesson. Clement shakes his cock vigorously up and down as he has seen his father shaking the last drops of water out. He tries to turn around to face the girls with the thing still in his hands, but at the last moment he falters and pushes it into his trousers for fear of Therese Riordan. As he turns towards them his fly is still undone and he is fumbling with the buttons. Therese almost screams – look what he's been doing in our ferns the dirty little bugger – it's your fault Pat for talking like that – I'm never going to speak to you again Clement Killeaton you filthy little sneak. Clement dares not look at her. He goes home convinced that neither of the girls will ever speak to him again.

## AUGUSTINE SEES THE CITY OF BOOKMAKERS AND GRAZIERS

Whenever Augustine comes away from Riordans' place he remembers the profusion of things in their house – the massive walnut-varnished wireless set and radiogram, the stainless-steel-and-glass revolving ash trays, the gilt-framed pictures of kingfishers swooping over a lonely bay of a misty lake and of 'Evening Light in the Gippsland Forest', the electric fire with its replica of a heap of glowing coals, the slender-legged wooden pedestals holding brass jardinières filled with crimson-leaved coleus plants, the statues of birds and animals on every window-ledge and mantelpiece, the fragile, painted-glass tulips drooping from their bowl in the centre of the wide, dark, mirror-like dining table, the towering china cabinet with diamond-shaped glass panes in its doors, and inside on every shelf an array of crystal-ware set close together like the domes and turrets of an intricate narrow-laned glass city – and can hardly believe that all these have been bought with money left after the Riordans have paid for their imposing house, their Buick car, their wardrobes full of clothes, the meals that they eat and the whisky that Stan likes to sip after tea, and the money that Stan gives without a murmur to St Boniface's parish, the nuns at the convent, the brothers at the College, St Roch's Orphanage, the St Vincent de Paul Society, and half a dozen other Catholic charities. Augustine has always owned one expensive suit, one soft grey hat with carefully composed dents and creases and a fiery-green peacock feather in its band, and one pair of shoes with gleaming uppers, so that in the crush of the betting ring or in the open spaces of the mounting yard he appears the equal of any Goodchild or Riordan. He has never bet with anything smaller than a pound note on a racecourse or five pounds in a credit bet by telephone. He has travelled long distances in taxis rather than admit to some of his racing acquaintances that he has no car. And whenever a group of his friends stand fumbling in their pockets for the price of a racebook or entry to the saddling paddock, it is nearly always Gus Killeaton who pulls out a ten-shilling note and pays for everyone and waves away the coins that they find at last and hold out to him. Because he sometimes talks vaguely about his family's property in the Western District, some of the men that he mixes with on Melbourne racecourses believe that he comes from a wealthy family of graziers, and those who have noticed that he is sometimes able to go to midweek meetings suspect that he does not work for wages but lives on the income from his share of the family estate, but when he swings open the rusted iron gate in Leslie Street and picks his way along the vague track through the gravel and weeds to the back door and walks into the tiny kitchen and sees the wooden table covered with blue linoleum frayed at the edges, the four unsteady wooden chairs bound around their legs with fencing wire, the pea-green wooden ice-chest with its legs resting in jar-lids full of water to keep out the ants, and the cupboard of varnished plywood where his wife keeps the remains of the only dinner-set that they have ever owned and the assortment of odd cups and saucers and plates that she buys at Coles as replacements, Augustine wonders at the boldness that has enabled him for so many years to pass himself off as a prosperous racing man. His wife has a savings account which never amounts to more than a few pounds but he himself has rarely been inside a bank. When he has a good win, which happens every three or four months, he keeps the roll of notes in his fob pocket by day and under his pillow by night. He peels off two or three ten-pound notes and gives them to his wife to buy some clothes for herself and Clement and something for the house. He uses most of the remaining money to pay the most pressing of his accounts with the starting-price bookmakers of Bassett. The money still remaining becomes his bank for the next few weeks. When he is desperate for cash, he sometimes borrows from some wealthy Catholic bookmaker or racehorse-owner and usually manages at last to pay the man back. None of his racing friends, not even Stan Riordan, has ever seen inside his house. They welcome him as an equal into their homes because they know from his dress and the way that he carries himself with his shoulders squared and the fluency of his speech that by rights he ought to have been born the owner of a thousand acres of Victoria.

Augustine has never even considered whether he ought to live from just his wages as assistant farm manager at the Bassett Mental Asylum. He has never thought of renting a little shop and gradually amassing capital as Mr Wallace does. He believes that there is only one place where a man with little money behind him but with more than average brains and cunning can hope to win for himself his rightful share of the wealth that he sees every day in the possession of men much less able that himself. For nearly twenty years on racecourses all over Victoria, Augustine Killeaton, with only his native shrewdness and his neatly pressed suit to help him, has gone on trying to wrest from graziers and factory-owners and bookmakers just a little of the wealth that allows them to sit in cool houses and watch the late afternoon in their Gippsland forests or the bewildering twilight among their crystal palaces.

## CLEMENT PEEPS INTO THE FOXY GLEN

One morning at the Bassett racecourse Augustine sends Sternie on a mile gallop against a horse that has lately won an open handicap at a small town in the Mallee. Sternie lopes along two or three lengths behind the other horse. Near the end of the gallop both riders urge their mounts with hands and heels. Sternie gains slowly and then draws level with his rival. Harold Moy tells Augustine afterwards that he could hardly hold the old horse at the end of the mile and that it looks like they have found out the distance that suits him best at last. He urges Augustine to enter the horse for a nine furlongs open handicap and to forget all about him being only a maiden because he can stay all day and still come home strongly at the finish. Augustine says – I might as well tell you Harold not that you probably haven't guessed it anyway but things aren't

going too well for me at the moment and I can hardly afford
to keep Sternie in training let alone find the cash to back him
next start. Harold says – don't let that worry you Gus – there's
a good mate of mine who'd be only too happy to put plenty of
his own money on and give you the odds to a fiver – I would
have mentioned him to you long ago only I thought you were
happy just having a small bet on Sternie and not needing a
punter. Augustine realises that Harold's friend, whoever he is,
is the kind of regular punter that every jockey uses secretly to
back the horses that he rides, that the man probably sneaked
around the betting ring at Jerram having his own thirty or
forty pounds on Sternie and that now when he, Augustine, has
admitted he is broke the punter will come out into the open
and have the best of the market for himself. He guesses that
the reason why Harold has stuck with him over the years is not
that Harold feels loyal to the owner-trainer of Clementia but
simply that the jockey and his secret punter have been waiting
to collect for themselves on any winner that he, Augustine,
might manage to train. He says to Harold – tell your man he
can come with us when Sternie has his next start but there's
no need for him to sling me anything – I'm sure I can raise
the money for a good-sized bet of my own. A few days later
Augustine takes Clement up the hill to Riordans' once again.
Even before he sees the high dark-green ramparts of cypress and
the complex ridges and valleys of roof, Augustine knows that
he will not dare to ask Stan to back Sternie once more. When
he reaches the front gate he sees Mendoza's car parked outside,
and is relieved to think that Stan will not be able to talk about
debts and loans in front of the third man. Augustine leaves
Clement walking on the low wall around the sunken garden
and fishpond. The boy goes looking for Therese Riordan and Pat
Mendoza but finds only the Mendoza girl. She is alone in the
fernery arranging groups of small white stones or pearls from

a broken necklace to represent the eggs of birds in well-hidden nests. She tells Clement that Therese will not be back from her music lesson until lunchtime. He asks her is she interested in birds and their nests, and she tells him she wouldn't mind being a bird because then she could live with her husband in a shady tree outside someone's house and watch the people in their bathroom or bedroom but no one could see what she did in her nest. Clement tells her that he has always been very interested in birds because they take no notice of roads and fences and travel wherever they please and make their own roads as they go until they find safe places to hide where people pass to and fro every day but never guess who lives just out of their sight. She says – I never knew you were so interested in girls' games – the only other boy I know like you is someone you've probably never seen. Clement says – Silverstone. She says – that's right – his favourite game was hiding some of his treasures and saying that nobody could find them except the person he loved – sometimes he said he could turn himself invisible and find all the treasures that the person he loved had hidden – and by the way I still haven't granted you all of your three wishes yet have I? if you promise to keep your trap shut I'll sneak inside and get that tin of Therese's you keep calling the Foxy Glen. She goes inside Riordans' house and comes back with the tin hidden under her dress and says – I'll count up to a hundred while you look in it – and see that you put everything back in the proper place or Therese will find out and never speak to me again. He opens the tin easily and finds first a holy picture of a little girl or boy climbing up onto the altar to reach the tabernacle and talk to baby Jesus in the Blessed Sacrament. On the back of the picture in small neat writing is the message *A happy and a holy Christmas little Therese from Sister M. Philomena.* He looks briefly into an envelope filled with holy cards. Beneath the envelope is a set of broken rosary beads with the Hail Mary beads of translucent blue stuff and the Our Fathers like polished chips of a pearly white stone. Lying in the corners of the tin are tiny pebbles of different colours, some of them a little like milk-stones. In a glass tube that once held junket tablets are a few grains of pure gold, probably from some of the abandoned diggings around Bassett. Folded between sheets of tissue paper are a few brown fragile petals from some flower that Clement does not recognise. A piece of yellowed newspaper reads *Do You Know? The hoop and the ball, those popular modern toys, are known to have been used by children in ancient Egypt. Judith Kennedy aged 9 years of Sheehan Street Bassett earns a Blue Certificate.* Clement is about to open a small blue-covered notebook with a label in a child's handwriting *My True Secrets*, when Patricia Mendoza comes up behind him and says – your time's up hand it over and make sure everything's stacked in the right place. He puts the things back in what he believes is their proper order and hands the tin to the girl Mendoza. She says – it's your job to put the tin back in Therese's room – I've got to go and talk to Mrs Riordan and a grown-up lady who's just come to visit the Riordans. Clement holds the tin behind his back and goes alone into the house. He reaches Therese's door without being seen, but dares not go inside. He pushes the tin a few feet into the room and leaves it there. He knows that Therese will never speak to him again if she discovers that he has seen inside her Foxy Glen, but he suspects that Patricia Mendoza may have tricked him and put some worthless odds and ends in the tin before she brought it to him and that the real secrets of the Foxy Glen are hidden where he will never find them in a place like a silk-curtained tabernacle towards which pure children who have never felt someone else's sticky hands groping and kneading and pinching between their legs may clamber over an altar as white as the rarest milk-stones that reveal to those on whose innocent tongues they nestle a pathway, paved with the pictures that nuns and mothers and aunties give year after year to their favourite children to keep their thoughts on holy things, that leads past a trellis in which the latticework is dark-green like the few gardens that are all they want to remember of their journeys through an arid city while the field of gold that it bars is all that remains of the streets that they have never had to walk from end to end wondering what comfort or revelation could lie beyond the pattern that they formed. He waits near Riordans' front gate for his father and wonders whether it is worth his effort to begin all over again the search for the true Foxy Glen or the thing like it that some other girl than Therese Riordan keeps hidden. Augustine strides down the path, takes the boy by the hand, and says – well we didn't get what we came for but perhaps it was best in the long run because now we're all on our own for the last battle of all.

## AUGUSTINE PUTS HIS LAST THREE POUNDS ON STERNIE

Augustine enters Sternie in the Publicans' Handicap at St Andrews. He asks Harold Moy to make sure that his punting friend comes to St Andrews with as much cash as he can lay his hands on because the stable commission might be only a handful of small change. A few nights before the St Andrews meeting, Augustine spreads out on the kitchen table a map of Victoria. He discovers that the trip to St Andrews will be the longest journey that he has ever made from Bassett to a race-meeting in the north. Augustine and Harold Moy and Sternie are driven from Bassett to St Andrews by a man named Ivan McCaskill. The man has with him his friend Rita. Several times during the long journey between paddocks so wide that whole systems of low hills rise up and fall away again within their far-reaching fences, Augustine looks sideways at Rita, who is plump and no longer young but still what he would call attractive. He sees a wedding ring on her finger and wonders whose wife she is or was once. He sees on her chest above the top of her dress an arc of pale freckles that he guesses must reach right to the tops of her breasts. He remembers that he has prayed for two weeks to Our Lady asking that Sternie might win the Publicans' Handicap at St Andrews and regrets that McCaskill will probably spend most of his winnings on beer and spirits and cigarettes to dope himself before he nuzzles nearer and nearer to the edge of the freckles. In the main street of St Andrews McCaskill stops the car, and Augustine goes to look at Sternie in the float behind. The other three walk towards the veranda of the hotel. McCaskill laughs and says – couldn't face up to a race day without something strong and wet inside me. Augustine follows them inside. The lounge where they sit is almost dark. The woman Rita catches Augustine looking at her. She smiles kindly and says – I suppose you must get nervous on a day like this with so much at stake. Augustine shifts in his chair and looks at Harold and says – ah when you've been at it as long as I have you lose all your nerves, and wonders whether he sounds uncivil. McCaskill says – what'll you have gents? Harold says – better make mine a shandy Ivan I can celebrate with the hard stuff when I've done my day's work. Augustine says – make mine a lemon squash mate, and wonders whether the woman admires him for being a non-drinker. Rita says nothing, but McCaskill brings back a glass of beer for her. McCaskill drains half his glass at once and says quietly to Augustine – you're the boss Gus – what's your instructions for the betting? Augustine glances at the woman and says – will Rita be helping us too? McCaskill laughs and says – what a question – she's the brains behind us – we work as a team. The woman smiles again at Augustine. Augustine says – well as Harold probably told you I'm not having much on for myself – I'm saving my cash for a big bet in Melbourne soon. He realises that they don't believe him. He says – you please yourselves what you have on but my experience tells me you'll probably get eight or even ten to one if there's more than half a dozen runners in the field – you realise the horse is still a maiden? McCaskill says – we know enough about him to be confident and we won't forget you after the race either Gus. Augustine supposes that Harold Moy has kept them informed for months about Sternie and his ability. Harold gets up to buy another round of drinks. Augustine says – I'll sit on my squash thanks Harold. McCaskill says – we'll separate as soon as we get to the course – you and Harold can look as if you don't belong with us. Augustine says – yes that's only sensible. The woman says – is your wife interested in racing too Gus? Augustine says – not really – she's got so much to interest her at home she never bothers to come very often. He gets up to buy a third round of drinks. As he passes behind the woman she puts her hand to her face so that her arm covers the front of her dress, which has fallen away from her body. While Augustine stands at the hotel bar he wonders what Len Goodchild would think if he saw him on the morning of a race day when there was important business to be done drinking in a pub with such poor types as McCaskill and his girlfriend after all the years when he kept himself aloof from the riff-raff of racing. For most of the afternoon Augustine stays with Sternie in the horse's stall. When the betting begins for Sternie's race he leaves the horse and has thirty pounds to three on Sternie, ashamed of his miserable bet and hoping that no one in the ring recognises him as the owner-trainer. When he meets Harold Moy in the mounting yard he says – your friends are no fools Harold – they waited and got twelves and backed him down to fours and fives and I think they're still putting more on. Harold says – they know what they're doing Gus – anyway they've got plenty to play with – and they'll have plenty more in a few minutes. Augustine stands staring after Harold and Sternie as they go out into the straight. As he walks back towards the crowd he thinks briefly of the horse Silver Rowan that he always dreamed of training but has never saddled up on any racecourse. He knows that if Sternie is beaten he might never load another horse into a float in the early morning and travel with him to some town where all the mystery and uncertainty of far northern distances gathers for one afternoon at the far side of a racecourse. Harold Moy will go on riding other men's horses, and men like McCaskill and their girlfriends will cheer home winners that land them bets of hundreds of pounds, but Killeaton might never again send his colours out towards an imprecise horizon and watch them being shifted about by forces that he has no control over and wait to see swept back towards him a great jumble of colours and signs and patterns with one arm of an emerald-green jacket, far out to one side of the rest and just ahead of them, rising and falling in a rhythm that starts something alternately soaring up and plunging down inside him. Harold Moy, with the smooth face and sinewy arms of the Chinese who once jogged overland a hundred miles and more to the Bassett goldfields, goes out into the haze on the horse that was discarded as worthless by Mr Sternberg, the soft-fleshed Melbourne Jew. A sleeve the colour of lawns around a mansion in Ireland rises high above jackets and caps and other sleeves coloured after the dreams and fancies of a few farmers and small businessmen and publicans in the dusty north-western corner of Victoria. The flimsy strip of green that once fluttered above the horses Silver Rowan and Clementia flaps and falters and threatens to break clear of the interleaved reds and yellows of the northern plains but goes on fluttering to the end against a background of those commonplace colours. The course broadcaster calls it a blanket finish and says he cannot separate Red River on the inside and Sternie on the outside. The judge awards the race to the horse named Red River. While Augustine is sitting alone in McCaskill's car outside the St Andrews hotel, he wonders whether Harold Moy and McCaskill might have been planning all along to outwit him, whether Harold might have known that Sternie was good enough to win an open handicap and deliberately brought him home too late in the novice at Jerram so that McCaskill could get ten to one for his money at St Andrews, and whether after all it was the Chinese that he knew and trusted and not the Jew that he had never met who had ruined him. When the others have come back to the car and McCaskill is driving them towards Bassett, Harold Moy says – I've said it a dozen times and I'll say it again – if the race had been twenty yards further we'd have won – but come to think of it Gus I said the same after the race at Jerram didn't I? he might be one of those horses that's always going to win a race and ends up breaking your heart. When Harold and Ivan and Rita have come back from spending half an hour in a hotel in a town along the road, Ivan McCaskill says – I hope you'll excuse me for this Gus but Harold tells me you're not going so well – I wonder whether you'd consider selling the horse to me tonight if you like for cash on the spot and I'll fix up the papers and things later in the week – I'm sure if he can't win a race on the flat we could make a good hurdler out of him. Augustine says – how much will you give me for him? McCaskill says – well he's seven years old and he's still a maiden – what about twenty-five quid? Before Augustine can answer, the woman says – Ivan he's worth more than that. McCaskill says – I'm sorry – I only pulled a figure out of the air – say thirty quid then. Augustine says – he's yours mate and I hope you get your money back on him – he's brought me nothing but trouble but I still think he'll win something before he's too old – you know one of the smartest men in Melbourne picked him out at the yearling sales and paid a good few hundred quid for him. When they reach Bassett McCaskill drives to a big house near the racecourse. Augustine sees the name Tiberius Lodge on the gate and realises that the place belongs to one of Bassett's leading trainers. He wonders how much of the money that McCaskill bet on Sternie at St Andrews belonged to the trainer and for how long the man had been quietly watching Sternie and waiting to back him. Augustine stays in the car while they lead Sternie away. McCaskill comes back and hands Augustine the horse's bridle and says – this belongs to you of course Gus. They drive Killeaton home to Leslie Street. McCaskill hands him three tenners from a small roll of notes and shakes hands with him. Augustine goes inside with the bridle still in his hand. He says to his wife – a chap just bought Sternie from me and I'm damned if I know whether to laugh or cry – wasn't there one of those American songs that Clem used to hear on the wireless There's a Bridle Hanging on the Wall?

## AUGUSTINE THINKS OF HIS HOME
## IN THE WESTERN DISTRICT

Augustine finds on the mantelpiece a letter from Kurringbar. He reads it through quickly then says to his wife – a man's mad. He waits for her to ask him what he means but she goes on rummaging in a cupboard. He says – a man's mad to go on wasting his life here when by rights I've got a fifth share in 250 acres of good dairy country and the price of land's gone up every year since the war. His wife says – haven't I been telling you that for months only you're scared of what your father might say if you turned up on his doorstep with nothing to show for all the years you've been working except the seat out of your pants? Augustine says – don't talk to me about being afraid when I've heard you say a dozen times you'd never live near my sisters with rosary beads draped over their bedsteads and holy pictures on their dressing-tables and asking you questions to see how much you know about your faith. She says – you know damn well I'll live anywhere if it means we can get away from your stinking rotten cursed debts. Augustine says – it so happens that my brother Phonse is getting married in a few months and starting out on a farm of his own – that leaves only Dan and my father to work the home farm and reading between the lines in Dan's letter I reckon they'd be happy to have me home again as a working partner even after all these years I've been away – we needn't live on the property with my sisters still there – there's bound to be a neat little cottage to rent somewhere in the district and I could ride the bike backwards and forwards each day until we could afford an old car. Augustine writes a long letter to his father. He reads it aloud to his wife before he seals it. Clement is puzzled by the opening words – my dear father a lot of water has flowed under the old bridge. When the answer to the letter arrives Augustine reads it silently in front of his wife and son. Then he opens the door of the stove and pokes the letter and its envelope into the fire. He tells his wife – if you must know the old chap says he's put up every spare penny he can find to start Phonse off on his farm and all the profits from the home place will be needed for years to come to pay off another mortgage – he says he and Dan can handle all the work on the home place and they can't see why I want to descend on them when I've got a good safe government job. During the next few days Clement hears his father deciding aloud to look for a position as a share farmer in the Kurringbar district. Augustine explains that a share farmer does all the milking and certain other jobs around the farm for a third share of the milk cheque. He does not explain how even the poorest farmer struggling to pay off his own farm and wading knee-deep in mud in his cow-yard looks down on a share farmer as a kind of low-caste labourer. Clement, who knows that his father is planning to sneak out of Bassett without paying his debts, is secretly glad that Augustine will not be living on his father's farm where the bookmakers or their men might find him at last after following his trail all the way across the western plains asking where people named Killeaton lived and trap him in one of the treeless paddocks beside the ocean so that he can only lie down like a hare in the long grass and try to hide from them until the sea wind blows his scent their way.

## CLEMENT SEES NO MYSTERY IN
## THE WESTERN DISTRICT

When Clement arrives home from school on hot afternoons his mother allows him to have a glass of water from the jug that she keeps in the ice-chest. While he sips the water he goes behind the kitchen door to look at the calendar. He knows by now that the streets and footpaths and waterless vistas of Bassett may be no more than a plain of yellowish stuff that happens to be marked with patterns of squares that give some meaning to the continual journeying of children or men or horses to and from buildings or groves of trees that the people thereabouts call old but which are no more than a few golden grains scarcely more prominent than thousands of others on a plain of countless dusty specks across which the inhabitants of a landscape of quite a different colour might trace far longer and more challenging journeys than those of the people who think that each journey is about to bring them to some place where they may rest and be satisfied that they understand a little of what all that untrodden yellow around them means. As he looks more often at the squares and learns how insignificant are his own travels across the bright stuff, he tries to remember the stories that his father has sometimes told him of how he, Augustine, first set out from the Western District, a country of grey-green grass that leans before the wind, and only came across this place of dull golden gravel on his way back from a much wider expanse of reddish-gold dust farther north. As page after page of the calendar does no more than tempt the boy Clement to discover, with nothing to help him except his pink stubby fingers and his cock, which he might poke into the teasing dust and lay bare some path leading like a great broad glorious stripe towards a flaw on a distant horizon that will prove to be the first sign of a land not yet pictured on any calendar, the colour whose unyellowness must shine across places much wider than calendars, he wonders more often about one last journey that the whole family might make away from the inland place, where they had given up the hopeless struggle to find some dome or mound or hill whose hundreds of closely packed layers they could peel back like pages to see what other countries they might possess without setting out on any journeys again, towards the plains that Augustine had once known for longer than any others. If the Killeatons should turn back towards the place that Augustine sometimes calls his true home, Clement will know before they set out that ahead of them is not the search that he had once hoped to make among unexpected prospects of yellow with barely perceptible boundaries for a far-reaching square in which people like themselves could see in certain directions as far as any of the saints and holy people saw within their remote borders, but a journey across a great grid of perfectly regular angles and interstices whose only mystery was that they seemed to stretch back so far in a uniform sequence beyond the place that Augustine called the true end of it all, with still only the overhanging scenes of holy people in dim countries to distinguish any row of rows from any other, or the wonder that nowhere on all those routes of lifetimes paved with stages of journeys was there any gap through which a traveller might wander into the other squares that surely lay somewhere only a little apart from the yellow squares and the sheer blessed wall to one side of them.

## CLEMENT AND HIS CLASS REFUSE
## TO LEARN FROM MR COTTER

Clement Killeaton and all the other boys in grade four stand quietly outside their room on the morning of their first day at the Brothers' College. The Head Brother walks across the yard towards them. Beside the brother is a frail young man with a foolish grin fixed on his face. The brother tells them to say good morning to their teacher Mr Cotter. The boys are shocked. Every other grade has a brother for their teacher, but they have a young man looking unseemly and effeminate in a light-grey suit instead of a brother's manly black skirts. The Head Brother says – they're all yours Mr Cotter, and strides away. Mr Cotter says – well chaps let's get inside and get to know each other. A murmur of resentment travels down the rows of boys as they shuffle into their room. From the very first day the boys exchange rumours to explain who Mr Cotter is and why he is teaching at the college. They say that he wants to join the brothers but has to prove first that he can teach, that he has recently been expelled from the brothers but has to work for them for years to pay them back for all the food that he ate while he was one of them, that he was in love with a Protestant woman but his parents sent him far away to stop him from making a mixed marriage. Mr Cotter himself tells them that he comes from the New England district. A boy asks him why doesn't he talk like a Pommie, and the teacher realises that his class has barely heard about New South Wales, let alone the New England Ranges. He gives them a geography lesson about New South Wales and makes jokes about the rivalry between Sydney and Melbourne which none of the boys understands. Before lunchtime on the first day, Mr Cotter has lost control of his class. After lunch he reads them poems that he says he keeps by his bedside every night, but the boys can make no sense of them. He tells them that every single blessing and success in his life he owes to Our Blessed Lady under her title of the Immaculate Conception, but they are embarrassed to hear from an ordinary man things that should be mentioned only by priests and brothers and nuns. He sings them a song that he says will make them tap their fingers, and cannot deliver the last verses above the thumping of fists on the desks. He allows them to put on a little play about St Francis taming a wolf, and has to run in and save St Francis after the wolf has felled him and begun to savage him on the classroom floor. Not long before home-time Mr Cotter calls a boy to the front and says that he is very sorry but he will have to give him a taste of the stick. The class falls silent at once. For years at the nuns' school they have told stories of the canes as sharp as knives that slashed through the trousers of boys at the Brothers' College. During his last week at St Boniface's, Clement Killeaton talked for hours about the brothers' canes that were so much more painful than the nuns' straps, in the hope that Barbara Keenan would overhear him and wonder sometimes during her year in grade four whether the boy who loved her was bending over touching his toes and waiting for the cruel stick to fall on his trousers. Mr Cotter takes out of his desk a common black leather strap no different from Sister Tarsisius's or Miss Callaghan's and tells the boy to hold out his hand and bear up like a man. The class murmurs. The boy at the front explains to Mr Cotter that boys at the Brothers' are always caned on the pants. Mr Cotter hesitates, then tells the boy to bend over. He brings the strap down with an awkward over-arm stroke. Afterwards the boys are uncertain whether to call this strapping or caning. They watch closely as they pass the windows of other rooms to verify the stories that they have told for so long about the brothers and their canes. Sometimes they hear noises like the swishing of canes, but nobody actually sees a cane. Being the youngest boys in the school they know better than to make fools of themselves by asking older boys. While the question is still being argued, Mr Cotter one morning sees a boy grinning at the class after being strapped on the trousers. Mr Cotter orders the boy to hold out his hand and straps him just as the nuns used to strap boys. After this even the more polite and tractable boys are reckless of what they do to annoy Mr Cotter. Each day as he struggles to teach them they misbehave more outrageously. The only time when he holds their attention for more than a few minutes is around ten o'clock in the morning. The autumn frosts have come early to Bassett, and Mr Cotter tells the boys that they need exercise for the body as well as food for the mind. Half-way through the morning arithmetic lesson he stops suddenly and says – down to Fairbairn Street and back. Forty boys leap from their seats and rush for the narrow door, grunting and squealing and dragging at the clothes of those ahead. Some who sit in distant corners of the room spring like deer across the tops of desks, scattering exercise books and pens as they go. A struggling pack forms in the narrow doorway. Boys kick and punch to force a way through. Every morning two or three tumble down the steep steps to the gravel, but they pick themselves up and join in the race to the Fairbairn Street fence at the opposite end of the playground. Clement Killeaton, who feels sorry for his teacher and only misbehaves when he finds himself in danger of being called Sir Cotter's pet, sits half-way across the room from the door and tries every day to win the long race to Fairbairn Street and back. Day after day he makes a long run from the middle of the field but the finishing line is too close, and he is never better than fourth or fifth. One morning Mr Cotter warns the grade to prepare for their term tests. The boys squawk and yelp and pretend to be terrified. Some boys boo softly. Someone else says – we'll report you to the Head Brother sir. Clement is no more interested in the tests than the other boys. After the first day of tests Mr Cotter pins to the notice board a list showing every boy's name and his marks in every subject tested so far. Beside it is another list showing each boy's total marks to date. The second list is arranged in order of merit. It shows that Killeaton C. lies in second place, five marks behind the leader. The other boys take no notice of the marks, but Clement draws on the back cover of an exercise book diagrams showing the positions of the boys after every test, as if each test was a furlong post in a long race. He is fifth after Arithmetic, third after Spelling and Dictation, and second after Composition. He sees himself coming from behind to threaten the leaders as the field enters the back straight. Next day the boys have tests in Reading, Poetry, and Grammar, and that afternoon Killeaton takes a narrow lead. On the third day there are tests in History and Art. Clement deliberately does not answer several questions in History because he wants to drop back behind the leaders as the field enters the home straight and then to come again with a late run near the post when the last test, Geography, is given. For the test in Art Mr Cotter tells the boys to draw in pastels Our Lady, Star of the Sea. Clement has never been able to draw realistic human figures. He draws Our Lady standing on the mast of a ship with stars in her hands and rays of light shining from her robes. Some of the boys around him catch sight of the absurd squat figure like a stuffed bird with a doll's face perched on a mast like a telegraph pole, and begin to laugh. Killeaton smiles too because he is ashamed of not being able to draw. Mr Cotter comes down to Killeaton's desk to see what the trouble is. He turns white with anger and says – I hope you little devils know who it is you're laughing at. He snatches the pastel book from Clement and says – I'll mark your art as it is now Killeaton. Next morning Clement finds himself in third place, twelve marks behind the leader. He checks every answer on his Geography paper, crouched stiffly like a jockey in his desk. He takes heart from the fact that Geography is his best subject, and that he can recall the name of nearly every capital city and river and mountain range that he has ever learned about or looked at in his atlas. That afternoon Mr Cotter pins on the board the marks for Geography. He points out that Killeaton's mark of 100 is the only hundred that any boy has scored in all the subjects tested. Then Mr Cotter sits down to add up the total marks. The boys chatter and laugh among themselves. Killeaton sits waiting for the numbers to be hauled up over the judge's box on a crowded racecourse. Mr Cotter says – Michael Maggs is your dux chaps, and walks briskly down to Maggs's desk to shake the embarrassed boy by the hand. Then the teacher says – Maggs won by only two marks from Killeaton who almost caught him at the finish. Clement realises that no one but himself will know the true story of his great finish and decides that perhaps the best way to run a race is to lead all the way and go further ahead the further the race goes on.

## BROTHER COSMAS TAKES AN INTEREST IN CLEMENT

Each morning after play Mr Cotter leaves the room, and Brother Cosmas comes in to take the Christian Doctrine period in grade four. The brother's dimpled girlish face and his gentle voice convince Killeaton that he has never taken enough interest in his religion. Listening to the brother talking about grace and holiness and prayers and Mass and the sacraments, Clement feels sure that he alone of all the boys in the class understands the true meaning of Christian Doctrine. He wonders whether he will ever have the chance to describe to Brother Cosmas the intricate patterns and compelling colours that come to his mind during Christian Doctrine lessons and for hours afterwards (an incandescent scarlet for the Sacred Heart, a green waterfall divided into three veil-like streams for the Blessed Trinity, a fierce orange for the Holy Ghost), his own private notion that every virtue corresponds to the colour of some precious stone and that its presence in the soul sets its special colour glowing against a background of sheer white, or the task that he has imposed on himself of laying out in his mind an elaborate garden, such as he once believed might lie behind the tall galvanised iron fence around the brothers' own house until he started at the College and discovered behind the fence nothing more than an untidy circular lawn where a white plaster statue of Our Lady with indistinct features stared out at the grass and gravel around her, into whose concealed islands of lawn and remote trickling grottoes he might walk a little further whenever he said a silent prayer on the way to school or alone in his backyard. He soon becomes one of the brother's favourites by answering questions correctly in a sweet girlish voice and by asking at the end of nearly every lesson the meaning of some ritual or Latin word in the Mass or of some strange phrase that he has read in his father's missal. He begins to dislike a boy named Billy Malady who can produce a voice even more effeminate than his own and whose questions are so involved that Brother Cosmas often invites the boy to come around and ring the bell at the side of the brothers' house after school and have an answer explained to him in detail. One day Brother Cosmas asks the class to tell him all the swear words that they know, so that he can warn them which are sinful and which are just plain vulgar. While other boys stand up and say bloody and bugger and bastard and try not to blush or laugh as they hear themselves actually swearing in the classroom in front of a religious brother, Clement waits with his hand meekly raised. Brother Cosmas says – tell us the worst Clem. Clement says sweetly – what about barmaid Brother? knowing that the word is almost certainly not sinful but trying to appear worried about it so that the brother will be struck by his innocence. Brother Cosmas smiles and says – I don't suppose it's a very nice word but it's certainly not a swear word. Clement is satisfied until Billie Malady stands up and says – please brother there's a little boy in our street and he's always saying fuckin, and sits down looking deeply troubled. The brother says – boys that word is a nasty horrible word that no Catholic boy should ever say. Billy Malady's eyes open wide. Brother Cosmas says – don't be worried now Bill – remember before we started I said you wouldn't be committing any sin if you told me a word just to find out how bad it was – I'm very pleased you told me about it Billie. Clement wishes that he could have thought of the word before Malady. The brother says – and now boys I want to ask you if ever you hear a boy at this school using that word to come quietly to me and tell me about it and I'll say something myself in private to the boy and he'll never know who told me. The boy named Reginald Pearce puts up his hand and says – please Brother when my big brothers get drunk they go around the house and shout that word. Brother Cosmas looks sadly at Pearce and says – you poor little chap – I'll pray for you and your brothers every night from now on, and Clement envies even Reginald Pearce. One day Brother Cosmas urges the boys to persuade their parents to say the family rosary every night. He draws in a special panel of the blackboard a huge rosary with each of the beads only a faint white outline. As each boy reports that his family has begun to say the family rosary every night or has always said it, that boy is allowed to choose a bead, to go over its outline with blue chalk, and to write his initials inside. Clement cautiously asks his father whether they might start saying the family rosary. Augustine says – it's all very well for families whose fathers come home from work with nothing better to do than put their feet up over the fireplace to be falling down on their knees for half an hour – in my position with hours of racing work to do on top of my ordinary job God doesn't expect us to be droning out long prayers like Pharisees and Bible-bashers. Clement whispers a decade to himself each night while he lies in bed. He reports to Brother Cosmas that the rosary is now being said in the Killeatons' house, and writes C.K. in blue in one of the beads. When Brother Cosmas spends a week talking about vocations, Clement asks such questions as whether every brothers' house has a chapel somewhere inside and whether the brothers have special prayers like a priest's office that they say every day walking up and down the paths in their garden. He mentions to his father that he would love to see inside the brothers' house and find out where their chapel is hidden. Augustine warns him not to start talking like that in front of the brothers or the next thing he knows they'll be signing him up to join them. One day Clement complains of feeling sick during Brother Cosmas's period. At the end of the period the brother tells him to come over to the brothers' house and have a cup of hot cocoa. Brother Cosmas leads him down a long bare corridor into a big steamy kitchen. An ugly grey-haired woman grudgingly prepares a cup of cocoa and hands it to the boy without a spoon so that he has to drink it with a sheet of scum clinging to his top lip. He wishes that he could ask the brother to show him the chapel that is some-where among the long corridors. When he tells his parents about his visit to the brothers' house, his father says – now I suppose the brothers will think we don't look after you properly at home. A few days later Clement goes to bed with chicken-pox. After he has been away from school for a week, Brother Cosmas knocks on the door on Saturday afternoon with a bag of oranges and a stack of comics. Mrs Killeaton is embarrassed because the house is untidy and Clement is ashamed that the house is so simply designed that merely by walking into the front passage Brother Cosmas can see where all the rooms are and could not suspect that other rooms might lie hidden from his sight. That night Augustine tells his wife that she should have refused to accept the oranges and told the brother they were perfectly capable of feeding their boy properly. He says that he'd better check the comics to make sure they're fit for a boy to read.

## CLEMENT FINGERS HIS PRECIOUS ROSARY

Each night when Clement says his decade of the rosary he uses an old set of wooden beads that his father has given him. One Saturday morning he asks his father for three shillings to spend and has to admit that he wants to buy a new set of beads. Augustine hands over the money reluctantly and says – it's no use trying to shame us into saying the family rosary just to please some brother at school – I'm sure God would be much more pleased with you if you were a better boy to your parents instead of buying fancy beads and tricking your bedroom out with altars. Clement looks at his mother, but she hides her head behind a newspaper, ashamed of having told her husband about the sprays of cassia and tamarisk in glasses of water and the picture of Our Lady that Clement sometimes arranges on his dressing-table. Clement goes to Mrs Linahan's shop and chooses one of a sheaf of rustling sets of beads all labelled *Genuine Irish Horn Made in Eire.* His beads have a crucifix of a dark amber stuff with a few motionless bubbles trapped inside, Hail Mary beads that are a greenish-blue but each of which is a different shade and even a slightly different shape from the others so that as he passes them through his fingers he is continually surprised to discover faint protuberances or minute caves where the tunnels through the beads have been imperfectly formed or even a jagged edge where a whole corner of a hemisphere is missing, each of which turns his thoughts in a new direction and reassures him that the rosary is not a monotonous prayer, that if he keeps his mind alert and moves his fingers forward regularly after each Hail Mary he will surely feel between his fingertips unexpected shapes continually challenging him to imagine still more abstruse glories of Our Lady. Better still, when he says his decade with the bedroom light turned on and watches the beads being hauled by fractions of inches into the grasp of his index finger and thumb and sees how the green in one lapses into a sugges-tion of golden-orange just beneath its surface, or in another competes against a knotty core of blue whose influence spreads far and wide, or in another is so thick with strange bubbles and granules that it maintains its true colour only against the strongest light, he begins to appreciate what a profusion of things – tears trickling endlessly down noble affronted faces, golden aureoles with long spears of light reaching upwards a thousand miles and more to some dazzling window on the plains of heaven, and long cruel journeys lying ahead of the most devoted families – must lie behind the Mysteries of the Rosary. Often, instead of saying the prescribed number of Hail Marys and Our Fathers, Clement says his own version of the Rosary, reciting in order the names of the fifteen mysteries – Annunciation, Visitation, Nativity, Presentation, Finding in the Temple, Agony, Scourging, Crowning with Thorns, Carrying of the Cross, Crucifixion, Resurrection, Ascension, Descent of the Holy Ghost, Assumption, and Coronation – starting at some bead chosen at random and moving forward one bead for each mystery so that whenever he pauses and holds a bead between his fingers like a marble against the light, its colour always takes him by surprise and forces him to search for some correspondence between something in the mystery that it stands for and the cool minute fire within the blue-green horn. He becomes so skilled at this that in only a few seconds he can relate the subtlest shade from an almost impenetrable bottle-green to an elusive fragmented lime-yellow to some landscape that Our Lord once passed through or some sunlit leaves that Our Lady once waited beneath and can see the name of any mystery as no more than a frail wall, like the outer quivering skin of a globular jelly, barely containing the luminous unstable mass behind it. When some of the metal links of his rosary break, Clement goes to Brother Cosmas, who once announced to his class that he could mend broken rosaries. The brother takes Clement to a workshop for senior boys. He repairs the beads with a pair of pliers in a few minutes. Clement sees that the room is almost deserted and says in his most fetching voice – I love my rosary Brother. Brother Cosmas puts his arm around the boy and whispers – you must be Our Lady's little baby.

Gerald Murnane

## CLEMENT ENJOYS DEVIL DOONE COMICS

Clement's parents never allow him to waste money on buying comics. If he borrows some old comics from the Postlethwaite boys his mother glances through them first to make sure that they are fit for him to read. While Clement lies on the couch recovering from chicken-pox and reading the comics that Brother Cosmas has brought him, Augustine says – I'm surprised that a religious brother approves of his pupils wasting their time with such trash. When his parents are out of the room Clement turns his face towards the back of the couch and reads again his Devil Doone comics. A man with dark hair brushed smooth and flat and a thin moustache travels wherever he pleases in an unnamed land of deserts and prairies and towering cities that can only be America. Clement discovers that, just as he had suspected, there are secluded places in cities like New York where a man can keep the woman he loves safe from any mischance and hidden from the eyes of other men. He studies every line in the drawings of Devil Doone and a beautiful woman in a penthouse and even tries with a pencil to embellish the meagre, faintly disappointing, outlines and unfinished pen-strokes to help him visualise more clearly the dazzling sheets of plate-glass that keep out the least breeze from the roof garden, the elongated couches set among thickets of greenery from potted plants and piled absurdly high with satiny cushions, and the ornate cages of exotic birds and tanks of brilliant fish. He is pleased to learn that when a man is sure that the woman he loves will never again be tempted to admire other men he can find places called night clubs where he and she can sit for hours in private corners behind pillars faced with mirrors and look out between gigantic palm fronds to where the shining windows of skyscrapers outnumber the stars. Clement reads aloud the words that float above Devil

Doone's rigid moustache in the last panel of a comic as he clasps his arms gently around the woman that he has had to travel hundreds of miles to find at last and rescue at the risk of his life – so my kitten has learned not to play with fire – now there's one more lesson I want to teach her. He stares hard at the few lines in the background that suggest that the place where the man and woman have found each other at last is in the heart of the flat countryside of America far from any penthouse or night club. He tries to draw the scenes that follow but cannot make a landscape or a woman's naked body that is any more than a few unsatisfying black strokes on a grey-white background. He turns to the next in the series of Devil Doone's adventures. Like the mysteries of the rosary, the Devil Doone comics offer different scenes and different kinds of struggles towards triumphant conclusions that can be meditated on to reveal many kinds of truths. But even after a whole afternoon spent pondering on the Devil's mysteries, Clement realises that there is still some secret hidden from him which, if only he could discover it, would make Devil Doone and the woman he loves and the countryside all around them as real as the people and the landscape around Tamarisk Row and might even teach him how to build in the country around the racecourse a city like New York or St Louis where people could do as Devil did. Devil Doone in his last and greatest adventure stands on a mountain that ought to have been in the Rockies and tells a woman who has been the most evasive of all his girlfriends that she must come and look at his etchings. Clement asks his mother what etchings are. She claims she does not know. He asks his father, and Augustine wants to know where he read the word. Clement has to show him the Devil Doone comic. Augustine burns all the stories of the Devil in the stove and tells the boy to stop reading American trash and to find something worthwhile in his own bookshelf. The only book there that appeals to Clement is Man-Shy by Frank Dalby Davison. He glances again at its pages and cannot wait to build in a corner of his backyard some timbered ranges where a herd of wild cattle can breed and wander unchecked by fences, easily avoiding the men who are slowly working their way towards them. But when he puts Man-Shy back on the shelf he notices a dictionary there, and looks up the word etchings. He decides that his parents and the adults who produced the Devil Doone comics must be aware of things that he has still not yet discovered. He builds his timbered ranges, but sets them in mountains even further away than America so that the people who advance slowly towards the wild cattle may come from cities where, in stranger places than penthouses and night clubs, men and women do things together that cannot be described in words or pictures.

## CLEMENT DRAWS WONDERFUL
## PICTURES WITH CRAYONS

In the first week of the year Brother Cosmas tells the boys to cover their Religion exercise books with brown paper and then to choose a holy picture and paste it on the cover. He advises them to spend a lot of time choosing the picture because it is meant to inspire them with devotion all through the year and for years afterwards. He strongly recommends that they choose a picture of Our Lady, who is the best patron that a boy could ever have. Clement persuades his mother to pay twopence in Mrs Linahan's devotional shop for a card that shows Our Lady so close up that the texture of her skin and the shape of her face compel him to run his fingers gently over her perfect features. Around the edge of her blue mantle is a row of stars of a gold so delicate that it fades from his sight when he holds the picture at a certain angle in strong light and suggests to him a motif for the next inch or so of the pattern of grace that he is trying to embroider on the white stuff of his soul. Once each week Brother Cosmas allows the boys to fill a page in their books with a few sentences that he prints on the blackboard and a picture that they may draw to please themselves. Only a few boys can afford coloured pencils. Clement, like most of his class, has a small box of cheap crayons. He uses all his time in class to print his sentences neatly, then takes the book and his crayons home at night to finish the page. After tea he tells his mother that he has a lot of hard homework in Religion and works on his page for an hour at the kitchen table. He chooses two colours that he knows are not often used together by other boys (dark-blue and green, purple and orange, pink and black) and adds rays or aureoles or ghostly outlines to all the words of his sentences – one colour for capital letters, the other for small letters. Around evocative words like sacrament, sanctifying grace, rosary, extreme unction, he makes a special border of the two colours. Because he has never been able to draw anything better than childish stick figures, he searches through his collection of holy cards and the religious books (Little Brother Jesus, My Lord and My God – A Child Assists at Mass, Our Lady's Bouquet) that his aunts have sent him as presents and traces the outlines of holy people onto tissue paper, then copies them into his Religion book. After this he only has to colour in the outlines and add trees or hills or stars or rays of splendour or clusters of flowers or clouds with spears of light thrusting through to complete his illustration. Sometimes his father glances at his Religion book and tells him what a pity it is that he doesn't spend more time making himself a saint around the house instead of titivating a book to curry favour with the brothers. But Clement is confident that he and Brother Cosmas know the truest kind of religion, which has nothing to do with drying dishes or answering parents cheerfully but is meant to make a person aware of the shadowy trees and shrubs in the background of holy pictures and of what might be behind them, or to show him pictures of incredibly smooth skin and garments coloured like the sky or the sea and altars glowing like jewels in labyrinthine churches which will inspire him to make his own heart and soul a maze of naves and tunnels and crypts and fiery altars draped with strangely coloured cloths so that Our Lady and little Jesus and the saints may delight in discovering at odd corners places after their own hearts, which they have prepared in heaven so that those who love them can wander off out of sight of the throngs of ordinary Catholics who have only just managed to save their souls and compare inch by inch each pathway that leads to further pathways and each alley-way that seems to end in a blaze of light from no apparent source with the miles of pathways and alley-ways there. Every Monday is Gospel Day, when Brother Cosmas tells the class a story from the New Testament about Jesus. This is the day that Clement likes least because there is nothing in the story of Jesus as a grown man that seems suitable for the pages of his Religion book. On every day but Monday Clement listens closely to Brother Cosmas, waiting for words and phrases that he can enshrine in coloured crayons in his book at the end of the week. One day the brother holds up in front of the class the Religion book belonging to Billie Malady and says – this page is probably the most beautiful that any boy in this grade has ever done and yet if it was a thousand times more beautiful it wouldn't even give us the faintest idea of the beautiful places that are waiting for us if we listen to Jesus.

## CLEMENT'S PARENTS ENCOURAGE HIM TO READ

When the first-term tests are over, Clement takes home his report and tells his father proudly how he gave the dux of the class Michael Maggs a long start from the turn into the straight and only just failed to catch him. Augustine says – I'm very disappointed to hear that my son couldn't even beat a field of weak Bassett hacks. He tells Clement to find out what Maggs's father does for a living, and supposes that he is a meek little man behind the counter of a shop with nothing better to do at night than stand over his son and drill his homework into him. Augustine takes Clement to the corner of the lounge-room and stands him in front of the bookcase, resting his hand on the boy's shoulder. He says – I'm sorry to say I've never really had the time or money to build up a proper collection of books – but now that you're at a college you should be ready to read some of these and get some benefit from them – there's even a few books here that I'll bet you wouldn't find in your precious Maggs's house – when I was a boy I used to sit up till all hours in the kitchen at Kurringbar by the light of a kerosene lamp with my nose stuck in any book I could lay my hands on – you can pick out anything here and read it provided you show it to me first to make sure it's suitable. Clement knows the titles of his father's books almost without looking – Leach's Australian Birds, Man-Shy, Dusty – the Story of a Dog, Lasseter's Last Ride, The Complete Poetical Works of Robert Burns, Fair Girls and Grey Horses – Ballads by Will Ogilvie, The Arabian Nights Entertainment, Chambers' Etymological Dictionary, On Our Selection, Our New Selection, Three Plays by Sir Arthur Pinero, The Children of the Pool and other stories by Arthur Machen, Victorian Government Handbook of Meat Inspection (with pictures inside of cows and bullocks marked with dotted lines), Mendelism (with coloured pictures of white, black and

golden rabbits, sweet peas, and human hands with chubby
fingers), a book with the cover missing and with pages of diagrams of different kinds of Japanese and German bombs and
instructions for digging air-raid shelters, The Path to Rome by
Hilaire Belloc, J. J. Miller's Sporting Annual 1947, Coast to Coast
an Anthology of Australian Short Stories 1946, half a dozen
National Geographic magazines, several dozen Walkabout
magazines, more than a hundred consecutive issues of the
Australian Journal. Augustine takes down Man-Shy and says –
this is probably the best book for a boy to start with – you're a bit
young for some of it perhaps but there's a good dictionary there
for looking up any words you don't understand. Clement does
not remind his father that he has already read the book only a
few weeks before. He remembers how he wept all through the
last chapter, and sits down to read Man-Shy again. Before he
goes to bed he asks his father may he join the junior library in
the Town Hall buildings. Augustine asks suspiciously whether
any Catholic boys from the Brothers' College are members of
the library. Clement says that he has seen some of the bigger
boys changing books there. Augustine says that he can join on
condition that he shows every book to his mother or himself
before he starts it. The first book that Clement brings home
is called Manco the Peruvian Chief. When he has almost finished reading it and is planning to convert his backyard into
the landscape of Peru crossed by secret pathways known only
to the Incas whose treasure lies concealed at the end of the
most formidable of them all, his mother tells his father – I
was looking through Clement's book today and I don't think
it's suitable for a Catholic – he'd better take it back tomorrow
and borrow a Geographic magazine or something harmless.
She reads aloud to Augustine – the Indians of that part of the
country had been converted by the Spanish priests and were
nominally Roman Catholic. But in secret they scoffed at the

creed of the priests and went on celebrating the rites of their forefathers. Augustine says – yes I see what you mean, and tells Clement to take the book back the next day.

## MR GLASSCOCK AND AUGUSTINE
## GIVE UP BEER AND BETTING

All Saturday morning Augustine stays in his backyard. He catches and handles every young pullet from a pen of about twenty and puts purple rings on the legs of a select few. He explains to his son that he is culling. Clement pretends to be interested, but whenever his father turns his back the boy watches the roosters in the pens where the pullets are being thrown for the first time. As soon as a pullet falls fluttering to the ground a rooster pounces on her and bounces up and down with his beak gripping her neck feathers and his pink bottom pressed against hers. When Mrs Killeaton goes into Bassett Clement wanders through the house wondering whether he will ever have another chance to be alone with another boy or girl now that his father is going to give up going to the races. At lunchtime Clement finds it strange to see a cloth spread over the old blue lino on the table and his father sitting with the paper propped against the tomato sauce bottle. Augustine reads the racing page. He tells his wife that he has marked down five good bets just to see how he would have gone if he had travelled to Melbourne or taken the house-keeping money to the Clare Castle just around the corner where a small S.P. bookmaker bets all day in the bar. Clement wanders outside to the Glasscocks' fence. Mr Glasscock is hard at work scything the long grass that has grown unchecked in the corners of the Glasscocks' yard for as long as Clement can remember. Clement goes inside and tells his mother. She warns him not to say anything to the Glasscock boys about their father being home on a Saturday afternoon for the first time for months instead of out drinking. Clement listens with his father to the first race in Melbourne. His mother says she doesn't see any harm in the boy taking an occasional interest in racing now that his father has been cured of it for good. Augustine's selection wins the first race. Augustine says – of course it was favourite but it's a good healthy way to build up your bank early in the day backing the favourite in the two-year-old race – I'll put myself down for six pounds to four – I'm winning six pounds already and the next race is the hurdle – I'll go off under a shady tree somewhere and have a sandwich and a yarn with a mate – a man's mad to touch the jumping races because the jumping riders all belong to a ring that works out whose turn it is to win. He goes back to his chooks. Clement peeps through the Glasscocks' fence. A game of cricket has started, with Mr Glasscock and little Nigel versus Gordon and his older brother. Mr Glasscock has opened the batting for his side. Clement leaves the fence and goes on with a game that he has started a few days earlier after bringing home the first book that he has borrowed from the junior library in the Bassett Town Hall. He builds a monastery for a community of monks who do not suspect that as they retreat farther back into the mountains away from the fierce Spanish soldiers, their own countrymen, they are drawing nearer to the secret lost city where the last of the Incas still rules his faithful band of soldiers and his palace filled with wives. Mr Glasscock's score mounts up. Sometimes he slogs a six into the Killeatons' backyard and Clement has to toss the ball back. For years the Glasscock boys have had a rule that over the fence is six and out, but today they ignore the rule for fear of annoying their father. Augustine calls Clement inside to tell him that his each-way special in the third race has run a close third at about eight to one so that he has made a profit of two pounds and is now eight pounds ahead on paper. The monks chant their office and enjoy the peace of their garden and the serene ridges of green hills stretching for as far as they can see in every direction. A cry goes up from the Glasscocks. Mr Glasscock has been clean bowled for 128. The boys sympathise with him and point to the rough patch on the pitch that caused the ball to keep unfairly low. They offer to declare a no-ball and to let their father continue his innings, but Mr Glasscock insists on going out and hands the bat to Nigel, who gets a soft easy delivery and lifts it over into the Killeatons' bamboo patch for six. One of the holiest of the monks builds a little hermitage of his own over the brow of the hill beyond the monastery with a grotto where he plants rose bushes so that Our Lady may rest her feet among the petals. Augustine's third bet wins at about seven to two, making him twenty-two pounds ahead. He decides to play up his winnings and have a good lash at his last two bets. Nigel is finally caught out by his own captain, Mr Glasscock, who has been invited to field by the opposing captain. Mr Glasscock opens the bowling for his side. The monk can hardly believe his eyes when he sees across the valley the golden walls of the lost city. He sits down out of sight among the trees and tries to decide whether to return to his monastery and help the monks to go away again on another weary search for a spot that is truly remote and secure, or to stay and help the Incas to guard their treasures and their wives during the last few years before the Spanish soldiers finally discover them, which may be even sooner than they expect. Mr Glasscock bowls both boys with fast round-arm yorkers for a total of seventeen runs, then sends them in to bat again, trying for an outright win. Augustine paces up and down the kitchen with his hands to his head because his second-last bet has come home at about five to one. He decides to have twenty pounds each way on his special in the last, and says that he has a good mind to go around to the Clare Castle after all and have at least something on it. His wife says – so that's how long your promises last. Mr Glasscock's side wins by an innings and 118 runs. He tells his wife that he's so hot and thirsty from playing cricket that he'll just nick around to the Clare Castle for a few bottles. Augustine's horse runs second in the last race. He listens to the starting prices and works out that he would have won nearly a hundred pounds on the day. He sits for a long time with a pencil and a notebook and the racing page, then says that he honestly doesn't know how he can live with himself for the rest of the night. Mr Glasscock surprises his family by arriving home before dark. He sits on the back veranda drinking from a bottle and tossing tennis balls at the stumps still standing in the backyard. His sons run to retrieve each ball. Shadows fill the valleys of the Andes. The monk finally goes to plead with the Incas to let him live as one of them for the years that remain before the Spaniards find them. They give him cold lumpy porridge for his evening meal and a wife with scabs in the corners of her mouth and a red rash all down her chest. The monks in the monastery decide that he is lost in the jungle, and do not go searching for him.

## THE MASTER SUMMONS AUGUSTINE

After weeks of weather so hot that even Mrs Killeaton, who has spent all her life in northern Victoria, goes around muttering – I'm fed up to the back teeth with this stinking rotten heat, huge black clouds arrive over Bassett from some unlikely quarter further inland. When the first lightning strikes at the town, Clement watches his mother running from room to room hanging clothes over the mirrors and the glass-fronted pictures in the way that her own mother once taught her to keep the bolts of lightning from getting into the house. The boy is still just as frightened of storms as he was when he was little, but his mother no longer lifts him onto her knee and tells him about little children waiting in their shabby leaking houses for parents who will never come home because they have been struck by lightning while they tried to shelter under trees or recites poems until he cries. Now he stays as far away from the windows as possible and asks God to keep the Killeatons' house safe from the lightning and its walls and roof secure against the rain. His mother reminds him that his father is still not home from work and may be pushing his bike through the storm outside. Clement kneels down in front of the altar in his bedroom and prays – dear God please keep Dad safe and bring him home so we can all go away together to the Western District. The storm passes, and a strange colour spreads across the northern sky. Clement sees it as a kind of orange-red and suggests to his mother that a great fire might have broken out on the far side of Bassett. His mother says that she can't see anything to make a fuss about. She claims that the colour is the reddish-pink of the soil in the northern country and that it comes from a dust-storm just like hundreds of others that she has seen since she was a little girl in a town north of Bassett. She thinks that she has read somewhere lately that a bad drought has struck up north and that farmers have to stand and watch their land blowing away. Augustine comes home and laughs at Clement for worrying about his father during the storm. Clement makes him look up at the sky. Augustine says that it looks more like an orange-golden colour, that sometimes the light plays funny tricks after a storm, and that the thing in the sky could be the miles of paddocks of wheat away to the north-west, in that part of the Mallee which is the only district of Victoria that he has never really explored, reflected or mixed up somehow in the sunset. After tea the rain starts again and hammers on the Killeatons' iron roof. Someone knocks at the front door. Augustine walks up the passage, whistling the vague tune that he always uses to hide his uneasiness. The visitor is Stan Riordan, who has never before called at the Killeatons' house. Stan refuses to come in and says that he has a message for Augustine. Someone has just phoned the Riordans from Melbourne. Augustine has to ring a Melbourne number at nine o'clock on the dot. Augustine looks at the number in Riordan's notebook and says – I don't have to write that number down mate – I ought to know it by heart after all these years – it's the old Master sending for me urgently – there's something terribly important in the air. Stan offers to drive Augustine back to his house to use the Riordans' phone. Augustine leaves him standing at the door while he puts on his hat and coat and takes out of his wardrobe his best propelling pencil with the silver cap and the notebook that his wife is not supposed to look into because it contains a record of his bets. Clement is in bed when his father arrives back from the Riordans' place. The boy sits up in bed and listens through the wall. Augustine reminds his wife that this is the first time in all his years at Bassett that the Master has phoned him, but she does not seem impressed. He says it has cheered him up no end after all his troubles to think that Goodchild is keen to use him as his agent in Bassett. Mrs Killeaton asks him how does he know that Goodchild hasn't phoned other men in Bassett and told them the same story. Augustine says he has no idea what the name of the horse is and he won't know until late on Friday night when he phones Melbourne and Goodchild talks to him in code and tells him the name and how much money to put on it. His wife asks him where on earth he can find any money to bet with when he owes every bookmaker in Bassett. He tells her not to worry because he'll be happy just to square his account with Stan Riordan and let the others whistle for their money. She says she can't understand all the mumbo-jumbo that goes on over a single race and why Goodchild doesn't just take all his money to the races and plonk it on the horse and be done with it instead of worrying the life out of men like her husband all over Victoria. Augustine cheerfully explains to her the idea behind S.P. betting. He explains that if Goodchild was stupid enough to take say two thousand pounds to the races and try to put it on a horse, every sticky-beak and gig in the crowd would back the horse too, so that if Goodchild wasn't killed in the rush he would probably average something like two to one for his money, but if he spreads his two thousand around with his agents and each of them has say a hundred on the horse two minutes before the race starts, and if, while all this is going on, Goodchild is at the racecourse standing under a tree where everyone can see him eating a pie or picking his nose and not taking any interest in the betting or better still throwing away twenty pounds on some other horse in the race, then the price of the horse he really wants to win might drift out to sixes or eights which means of course that his two thousand at starting price odds will return him twelve or even sixteen thousand pounds, provided of course that some agent doesn't let the team down and phone his bet too early and give some S.P. bookmaker time to ring Melbourne and warn the big S.P. men there who have men waiting outside the course ready to rush inside with big money and lower a horse's price before the race starts. Mrs Killeaton says she thinks she understands what big betting is all about for the first time in her life and realises why her husband has always kept so quiet about his bets. Augustine does not tell his wife that before leaving Riordans' that night he told Stan that the best bet of all time would be coming up in a few days and that his boss in town might want two hundred pounds on it, or that Stan Riordan agreed to place the bet himself with another bookmaker and add perhaps another two hundred of his own, and certainly not that he (Augustine) will lie awake for hours every night until the day of the race hoping that Stan will not make his bet too soon and ruin everything.

## CLEMENT SAYS A PRAYER THAT HAS NEVER FAILED

One day at school Mr Cotter tells the boys that although they learn their religion from Brother Cosmas it will do them no harm to learn something extra from him. He tells them what they have already heard many times from him – that he has a special devotion to the Immaculate Conception – and that they can forget all he ever teaches them so long as they remember to pray to Our Lady whenever they really need something. He stretches his arms out towards the pale statue of Our Lady on the altar in the corner of the room and says – there she is boys – and I tell you from the bottom of my heart that she'll never refuse you anything you ask her. The boys are silent. Some faces even show the beginnings of a genuine interest in the strange young man and his special devotion. Then Mr Cotter adds, in his normal teacher's voice – so long as it's for the good of your soul of course. The boys relax again, and their faces fall back into their usual slackness. Clement Killeaton believes that he is the only boy still interested when Mr Cotter begins to write on the blackboard the words of the Memorare, the one prayer that will always be answered, and tells the boys to copy it into their books and learn it by heart. As Clement writes – *Remember O Most Loving Virgin Mary that never was it known in any age that anyone who fled to thy protection, implored thy help, or sought thy intercession was abandoned. Inspired with confidence therefore I fly to thee O Virgin of Virgins my mother. To thee do I come, before thee I stand sinful and sorrowful. Do not O Mother of the Word Incarnate despise my prayers but graciously hear and grant them. Amen*, he recites them under his breath as though they were the last words of a race-broadcast shouted hoarsely into a microphone as a bunched field passes the post and rippling outwards in unseen waves across miles of somnolent farmland where women on shady verandas and men alone in bright treeless paddocks and children beneath great solitary pepper trees never suspect what a story of victory won against tremendous odds is passing silently above their heads towards houses perhaps a hundred miles away where people who have placed their trust in horses will hear the end of it all. Before the end of the period Clement has learned the words of the prayer by heart. Lying in bed that night, he whispers certain words and phrases aloud until they suggest the vague movement of indistinctly coloured jackets wheeling aimlessly on the far side of a racecourse before the start of a decisive race. He focuses clearly in his mind first the streets of Bassett in some year to come when Clement Killeaton, the champion long-distance runner of the Brothers' College, sees again for the first time in many years the girl he once loved at St Boniface's school and realises that she has heard of his great finishes in mile races and is willing now to let him take her to any quiet shady spot and do whatever he wants to her, then the cold coastal plains of the Western District in the same year when Clement Killeaton, whose father allows him to run his own cattle in the farthest paddocks of his farm, stands watching his own young bull mating with his favourite heifer in a sheltered hollow and realises that he will soon have enough money from the sale of his calves and yearlings to look around for a wife of his own although there are so few Catholics in the district that he may have to choose some Protestant girl who, since she was a small child, has watched bulls and cows mating and played animal games with the boys at the State school and who will want to copy the animals when she and her husband are alone together, and trusts that Our Lady will decide which of the two places will be better for the soul of Clement Killeaton. Until he falls asleep he recites the Memorare with all the fervour he can muster. He does the same every night for a week. Then he learns that his father is planning to have one last bet to get out of the worst of his debts. That night as he prays the prayer that has never yet failed he sees in the last hundred yards of the straight of a racecourse a desperate struggle between two evenly-matched horses and, as first one and then the other head shows in front, alternate glimpses of two landscapes, one a cluster of low hills glinting with quartz in the western sun and marked with intricate patterns of gardens and streets that might yet reveal something that has so far escaped the people who came first to look for gold beneath the soil and stayed to sit behind drawn blinds during long silent afternoons when anything might have happened but nothing did, and the other a sweep of thickly grassed plains, marked only by distant stands of dark-green cypresses and exposed farmhouses and relieved only by a few hollows near the cliffs of an abrupt coastline, that promised so little to the people who settled there that their only hope was to remember in some room overlooking a tract of plain that few others crossed another land where great deeds were done on every hill until something in all that windy expanse told them that even there one day a man might discover why the land where he had lived all his life mattered after all, or of two young women, one who might have kept all her life a face as pure and aloof as any saint's on a holy picture but was persuaded at last to learn a little of what pagans did alone together, and the other who might have spent all her life playing games that she learned from animals until her husband persuaded her that some games were too wicked for him to enjoy, and leaves the result to Our Lady.

## SOMEONE STILL WATCHES THE
## CREATURES IN THE GLASS

On the Friday evening before the most important race of his life, Clement finds the front passage filled with a dull yellowish glow. The sun as it sets on the far side of Bassett lies directly opposite the narrow gap in the cypress hedge in front of the Killeatons' house, so that even the obscurest corners of the panel of green or gold glass in the front door are as brightly lit and as plain to see as the most exposed streets and hillsides of Bassett in the hottest part of the day. Standing inside the passage Clement presses his face against the glass until he sees the country of the creatures from the same direction as when he first discovered it separated from Bassett by a misty plain of uncertain width and texture and lying at such an absurd angle to the sun that he cannot guess what, if anything, the creatures might see if ever they looked in his direction. He is surprised to find no creatures crossing the airy distances between their towns and what seem to be towns farther out. He looks for signs that all the travellers may have crossed at last into the vaguely tinted depths that surround their land on all sides, but there is no trace of any creature there. He looks again at the settled regions where a few creatures used to spend whole lifetimes trying to retrace some journey or to re-enact an old story of some shape or creature, the least-favoured of many, that came from an unexpected quarter and passed before thousands of watchers on its way to a famous place ahead, and discovers this time that the creatures, which were once so distinctively shaped or marked that he could follow the movements of each one across populous valleys and through mazes of streets, are now no more than wavering indefinable outlines each enclosing a drifting unstable mass of the same nameless stuff that forms the landscapes and clouds and roofs in that world. But as the very last of the sunset reaches across Bassett to the places where he once hoped to mark the progress of journeys greater than he would ever be expected to make, it seems to Clement Killeaton that somewhere in all that translucent continent there must be still a few creatures who could recall a time when someone, not the God who was supposed to have given them all their shapes and who would probably inspect their colours again one day, but some other huge watchful figure, looked at them in a certain light as if he yearned for them to begin the most perilous, far-reaching journeys so that he could delight for ages afterwards in all the complex patterns that their lives would represent and the strange intricate creases and lines that their journeys would stamp on them, and still hoped that he still remembered that once on a certain afternoon in his own country he did see them all in their separate shapes and tried to comprehend their thousands of overlapping and interwoven journeys and the stories of their lives and might be still waiting for a time to come when he would hold his head at a certain angle in a certain light and welcome them into a country like his own.

## AUGUSTINE RELIES ON MISHNA TO SAVE HIM

On Thursday night Augustine first sees the fields for Saturday's races at Moonee Valley, but he has to wait until Friday night before he can phone Goodchild and find out the name of their good thing. Long after Clement has gone to bed on Thursday, Augustine sits at the kitchen table trying to work out from the bare lists of names which horse is going to save him. Lying in the dark and reciting the words of the Memorare, the boy hears his father saying to his mother – you know what I reckon it is? there's a thing called True Orator in the three-year-old race that's trained by Peter Riley – he's supposed to be a mate of Goodchild's – that's the horse we'll be backing. Mrs Killeaton says – can't you just wait and find out when your friends are ready to tell you instead of peering at the paper all night? Augustine says – unless it's something called Penshurst Place that I think I remember Lennie went up to see running at Ballarat one day a few months back. Clement is almost asleep when his father comes into the room and whispers – say a little prayer son and ask God to bring home a winner for us soon – you never know – a little boy's prayers might make all the difference in a tight finish. After his father has gone, Clement says under his breath – please God help Dad to win enough money to pay back Therese Riordan's father. Then, because he has never found much pleasure in picturing to himself the races that his father goes to watch in Melbourne or even in northern towns where a band of sullen secretive men risk hundreds of pounds without even feeling the crinkle of money in their hands and watch the race that means so much to them without caring what stories of journeys or landscapes might lie behind the colours of their horse or any of its rivals and without noticing any more than a few of the hundreds of changes in patterns of colours that is all the spectators see of the field at the far side of the course and on the turn into the straight but only wanting to see the race over and done with and their own horse home under a flurry of blows three lengths clear of the rest, he falls asleep thinking of a race in which every square and diamond and spot and armband of a different colour brings to mind some detail of an heroic story of a horse and its faithful followers but no colour or shape stands for anything that Len Goodchild or his men have ever done. On the Friday morning Clement goes quietly up to Brother Cosmas before the Religion period. The brother leans down and puts an arm around Clement's shoulder while the boy whispers to him. When the grade stands up for the prayer before the Religion period, Brother Cosmas says – we'll all offer up our prayer this morning for Clem Killeaton's special intention. The other boys stare at Clement, who lowers his eyes and tries to see the finish of a closely fought race. On Friday night Clement forces himself to stay awake until his father arrives back from Riordans', where he has gone to phone Goodchild. Augustine comes into the kitchen and sits down. Mrs Killeaton says – well? Augustine says – it's a horse I'd never heard of – it's got no form at all. But Lennie says it's galloped well enough in a secret trial to win a Newmarket – the funny thing was he wouldn't tell me how much he wanted me to put on for him – I've got to ring him again at nine in the morning. Augustine spreads the racing pages of the paper in front of him. When Clement falls asleep his father is telling his mother stories of some of the good turns that Len Goodchild has done for him over the years. On Saturday morning Clement hangs around the house waiting for his father to come back from Riordans' place. It is nearly lunchtime before Augustine returns. He tells his wife that everything is all right except that Lennie only asked to have twenty pounds on the horse after he'd been talking for weeks as if he was going to have at least a couple of hundred on it. Augustine wonders aloud whether Goodchild might have another agent in Bassett and even whether he might not trust him (Killeaton) after all these years. He sits for a few minutes with his head in his hands, then says to his wife – you might as well know my side of the story – my credit's so bad here in Bassett that I had to ask Stan Riordan to put Lennie's money on for me – there's no question of me having any on for myself – I've done my dash completely – but I thought and thought and prayed too and I finally decided to tell Stan to have something on for himself to get back some of the money I owe him – you realise what that means don't you. Mrs Killeaton says – I've given up trying to follow you and all the trouble you get yourself into. At lunchtime Clement asks his father the name of the horse that he wants to win that afternoon. Augustine says – I'll only tell you if you promise to stay inside the backyard all afternoon and play by yourself and don't go near any other boys – not even the little snotty-noses from next door. Mrs Killeaton says – go on – if you'd stayed home a few Saturdays yourself you'd know the boy never has a soul to play with. Augustine looks over his shoulder towards the kitchen window then up at the clock on the mantelpiece. He says – there's still nearly an hour till the race – come back in about fifty minutes and I'll tell you then – we can't be too safe when there's thousands of pounds at stake. About half an hour later Clement asks his father again to tell him the horse's name. Augustine picks up the racing page and guides Clement's finger towards the name Mishna in a race for two-year-old fillies. Clement says aloud – Mishna – what does that name mean? Augustine presses a hand over the boy's mouth and says – do you have to blurt it out like that? how do I know what it means? unless it's something that Mr Goodchild's friend the Jew had dreamed up. During the last minutes before the race Clement looks out from the back veranda and wonders in what sort of country he might have tried to build the house where the people called Jews could have planned for their great day, but he knows so little about the Jews that he cannot see them anywhere in the landscape that stretches from the great racecourse to the quiet paddocks of Tamarisk Row. Just before the race his father calls him in and switches on the wireless. Augustine sits on a rickety kitchen chair with his legs crossed and no expression on his face. When the racing commentator says – they're going into line at the Valley, Augustine tells his son to get down on his knees and pray harder than he's ever prayed in his life and they'll soon see whether all the boy's fussing over rosary beads and altars in his bedroom and drawings of saints in his schoolbooks was worth anything or just a sham. Mishna is one of the first horses out of the barrier but the commentator does not mention her name again until the field is approaching the three-furlong post. By this time the filly is about tenth in the field of fourteen. As the field approaches the turn, the commentator (following a long-established custom which Augustine and Clement know well) names only the leading few and tries to predict which of them will eventually fight out the finish, except that if a runner behind the leading bunch happens to make a powerful run towards the leaders, he might suddenly break off his commentary to cry out its name in an ominous tone when its supporters had almost given up hope of hearing it again. Augustine, Clement and Mrs Killeaton hear how four fillies with names that mean nothing to the Killeatons sweep around the sharp Moonee Valley turn almost in line, with a gap of three or four lengths to the rest of the field. While one after another of the four threatens to draw clear in the short straight, Clement still expects to hear the name Mishna shouted once with a resonance that overrules all others' claims and promises certain victory. Until the last moments of the race he persists in seeing the filly bearing down on the leaders from an impossible position and so wide on the track that the commentator has still not noticed her. He finally hears the name Mishna when the commentator, after losing his breath in the excitement of the finish, recites in a flat, disparaging voice the names of the unplaced horses. Mishna has finished in the middle of the field. Mrs Killeaton laughs with an odd cackling sound and gets up to leave the room. At the door she turns and says to her husband – there's just one favour I want to ask you – I want you to sit down now with a pencil and paper and work out to the last penny just how much we owe everybody in this town – I'd just like to know before we head off like gypsies into the bush just what we're running away from. Augustine, still sitting in his chair, says quietly – there's something very wrong – something went wrong at the last minute and they decided not to try with the filly – I've done a terrible thing and it serves me right – I've ratted on Lennie Goodchild – the best friend a man ever had – it's the finish of me with all my friends in Melbourne – they'll never trust me with a penny of their money again. Mrs Killeaton stands staring at her husband. He says – you needn't ask what happened – Stan Riordan must have panicked and tried to get his money on hours too soon – he could have even let someone else in on our plans – the Master must have got wind of it and pulled the filly up – I'll never look him in the face again. Augustine turns to Clement and says – I don't suppose you've been blathering to little Ronnie Fitzgibbon and your mates at school that your father was going to back something at the Valley. Clement says – no of course I haven't, but remembers how he asked Brother Cosmas to ask the grade to pray for a special intention for Clement Killeaton and wonders whether some boy whose father is a bookmaker's spy might have worked out what the intention was. Augustine picks up a pencil and works out sums on the margin of the newspaper. After a few minutes he says to his wife – I can't think straight at the moment – say in round figures four hundred and fifty pounds – not counting the hundred or more that Stan Riordan must have put on Sternie and Mishna to try and get back what I owe him. That night Augustine refuses to eat any tea and goes to bed at eight o'clock. Next morning Mrs Killeaton tells Clement to go to Mass on his own because his father is too sick to get up. As Clement is leaving for Mass she says – if any of your father's friends see you and ask you where he is tell them he's gone to Melbourne and you don't know when he'll be back.

## AUGUSTINE AND CLEMENT HEAR
## MISHNA'S RACE AT FLEMINGTON

On the Sunday after Mishna's race, Augustine Killeaton stays in bed all day. He keeps the blinds drawn and the bedroom door shut, and warns his wife and son not to come near him and to tell anyone who calls that he has gone to Melbourne or the Western District. He refuses all food apart from a glass of milk at lunchtime. Towards evening he calls out feebly to his wife – for heaven's sake make sure the chooks get their feed. On Monday he stays in bed again and sends his wife to phone the mental home to say that he is ill. When Clement comes home from school his father is still in bed, but that night Augustine has a small meal of scrambled eggs on toast. After tea he sends for Clement. He tells the boy to bring from his father's wardrobe the old exercise book that he uses to write up the pedigrees of his best chooks. He tells Clement to sit beside the bed and listen carefully. He opens the book at the first page. When he finds that the page is blank he turns to the second page and then goes on turning blank pages until near the back of the book he finds a page with a few scribbled notes. He says – son – if anything ever happens to your father you'll find he hasn't left you much in the way of money – you'll find a lot of debts all right but I hope you'll understand that every bet I ever had in my life was only to get a bit of extra money so that you and your mother could live decently which was more than you could have done on the couple of quid a week I get as wages – but there's one thing I want you to promise me and that is that you'll do all you can to keep my Rhode Island Reds' bloodlines going – I've had a lot of time to think things over while I've been lying here sick and I've just about come to realise that the only worthwhile thing I've done with my life is breeding some of those beautiful birds out there in the yard – mind you I'm far from satisfied yet – I still haven't seen the perfect Rhode Island specimen – but if I get these notes in order while there's still time and if you remember all I've ever taught you about breeding you'll be able to carry on where I've left off and one day you can stroll out into your backyard and it'll be like a little kingdom all spread out in front of you all planted with green shrubs for shade for your birds and a few little paddocks of barley and lucerne in one corner to grow the green feed they need to keep their eyes bright and golden and if you're old enough and sensible enough to really appreciate the way God does things you can even feel a good keen pleasure watching your best rooster mating with all his perfectly shaped hens. Clement says – won't you ever write all the names out clearly and make it one long story starting with the first birds you ever had? Augustine says – I'll see about it – what I really wanted the book for was to work out which birds I'll have to get rid of if we shift to the Western District. On the Tuesday morning Augustine gets up and goes to work at the usual time. He says nothing about his book of poultry pedigrees. That night he spends a long time at the kitchen table trying to write a letter to his brothers at Kurringbar. He tells his wife that he's as anxious as she is to get away from Bassett onto a farm where they can start saving money for once in their lives but he'll be damned if he's going to let them think he's running away from Bassett or depending on them to do him a favour. He finally tears up the letter and drafts a telegram to send the next day. When his wife says that a letter would be cheaper, he says – let them puzzle out for themselves how I can still afford to send a telegram. He reads out to her the words of the telegram POSITIVELY NO WISH PARTNERSHIP OR WAGES ON FAMILY FARM STOP WILL ARRANGE OWN FUTURE AS MANAGER SUITABLE PROPERTY THANKS AUGUSTINE, and tells her to send it first thing next morning. On Wednesday night he sits silently for a long time after tea. At half-past eight, the time when he usually rides his bike to the Bassett Post Office to phone Len Goodchild, he walks over and stands with his back to the stove and says – I wonder if it really was my fault after all that they pulled that filly up – a man'd be a fool to be worrying all this time over nothing – the least I can do is ring Lennie and find out the worst. Mrs Killeaton says nothing. Augustine goes out. His wife and son hear him fiddling with his bike. After a few minutes he comes inside again and sits at the table. His wife still says nothing. Augustine says – I don't think I'll ever be game to ring Len Goodchild again and find out the true story. On Thursday night Augustine points out to his wife the name Mishna in a race for two-year-old fillies at Flemington. She says – can't you get it into your head that I never want to hear another word about racing as long as I live? He says – I'll have to listen in to the race at least to hear how the filly goes – it'd be lovely wouldn't it if next Saturday was the day and last week was only to try me out to make sure I was still solid. Mrs Killeaton says – are you trying to say that your friends wouldn't trust you after all these years when you've been running messages for them all over Victoria? and come to think of it when is Mr Goodchild going to send you the money that you had on for him last week – it strikes me he's got a lot more to be embarrassed about than you if you ring him. Augustine says – you'll never understand will you? The Master and his men have bigger fish than me to fry – when they plan one of their really big plunges they send messages all over Australia – still it only needs one weak link like me to ruin the greatest scheme that a racing genius could dream up – no wonder they never really took me into their inner circle – a man'd need a lifetime to prove himself with them. On the Saturday afternoon Clement is playing in the backyard when his father comes out to the veranda and beckons him inside. Clement goes into the kitchen and hears from the wireless that the horses are at the barrier for Mishna's race at Flemington. Augustine sits down and lifts his son onto his knee. Mrs Killeaton pushes furniture around in one of the front rooms to show that she never wants to hear another race broadcast. Far away across more than a hundred miles of grassy paddocks sloping this way and that regardless of the long road and the railway line that crosses them from Bassett to Melbourne and the forested hills and gullies that only the sunlight can take in at one glance, at the Flemington racecourse which Clement has never seen the field jumps away and the race is on. It is the first race that Clement has ever heard in which the very tone of the commentator's voice tells the listeners clearly, even in the first few furlongs, that one horse is destined to win. From the moment when they hear that Mishna has taken up a position just behind the leaders, Clement and his father are sure of the result. And when, with more than a furlong still to go, Mishna hits the front and starts to draw away, Augustine pushes his son from his knee and says – hurry up outside and pray to God that you never get mixed up in racing. A few minutes later, while Clement is wandering aimlessly around the yard, the boy sees his father go quietly into the shed where he keeps his choicest breeding poultry. When Augustine has still not come out from the shed a long while afterwards, the boy creeps up to the wire-netting at the front and peeps in. His father is sitting on the fowls' perch with his head between his knees. The rooster named Orange-Eyes, Augustine's favourite bird, tilts his head and looks up curiously at the man sitting silently in the corner, then struts forward, calling to his hens to follow, and scratches fearlessly with his toes only inches from Augustine Killeaton's feet.

## THE TRUE STORY OF MISHNA'S RACE

On the Sunday morning after Mishna's win at Flemington, Augustine tells his wife that he can't go into hiding forever and it's only Stan Riordan that he doesn't want to see so he'll go off quietly to ten o'clock Mass just like the old days and hope he doesn't run into Stan. He takes Clement with him. After Mass the Killeatons are walking across the gravel yard towards Fairbairn Street when someone calls out – look at him sneaking home to count his winnings. Augustine looks around and sees the little group of racing men in the shade of one of the date-palms. He strolls over to join them. Frank Hehir says – no wonder you've been lying low Gus – admit you were the brains behind this Mishna business. Hehir has a Sporting Globe in his hands. Augustine leans across and reads the headline – *Filly Lands Australia Wide Plunge*. A man says without smiling – you can tell us at least whether you had something on it Gus. Augustine sees them all looking at him expectantly. Another man says – someone in Bassett must have backed her – they say Horrie Attrill got hit for nearly a thousand. Augustine says quietly – well gents I won't deny that I was mixed up in it in a small way. Someone says – good luck to you anyway Gus – no one can say that you don't deserve a break – I wouldn't mind having a few friends like your Melbourne mates to put me onto an eight to one winner. Augustine tries to hide his surprise, and asks Hehir to show him the paper. He begins to read the story on the front page *Illegal S.P. operators in all Eastern States are believed to have paid out a fortune after the shock win of the filly Mishna in the Acorn Stakes at Flemington today. Caulfield-trained Mishna, whose form before today's race had been very mediocre, had a little support on the course, firming from 12s to 8s late in the betting. But while few punters at Flemington wanted to back the bay daughter of Caithness, an army of well-informed commissioners, apparently* working to a carefully rehearsed plan, swamped S.P. men all over the country with a deluge of bets. While off-course operators were trying frantically to lay off their bets, supporters of Mishna had few worries as the filly looked the winner from barrier rise and scored by two lengths in fast time. Trainer Cec. McGarvie denied after the race. Augustine feels a hand on his shoulder and hears Stan Riordan saying – Gus please don't forget to have a word with me before you go home. Clement sees that his father is preoccupied with his racing friends and says politely – Dad can I have the money for a milk-shake please? One of the men says – spend up big son and tell the lady in the shop Mishna's paying for it. Augustine gives his son a two-shilling piece and tries to laugh. Clement hurries across the road and buys a chocolate malted milk and an ice-cream. He takes great bites from the ice-cream to finish it before he leaves the shop. Then he wipes all traces of it from his lips and goes back to the churchyard. His father and Stan Riordan are talking quietly together apart from the others. Clement slips the change from the drink and the ice-cream into his father's pocket before Augustine can count it. Stan Riordan says – so I did a little investigating on my own around the town and rang up a mate of mine in Melbourne and put two and two together and realised they must have pulled the filly up at the last moment at the Valley – then when I saw she was entered for Flemington I kept my ear to the ground and heard the faintest whisper and worked out the rest for myself – I waited for you to get in touch with me Gus but I didn't dare ask you – after all it was none of my business and I guessed you were waiting till the last minute for the right information about her at Flemington – anyway the long and short of it is I took a risk yesterday and backed my judgement and had quite a decent bet on the little filly and I want you to know that you don't owe me a penny now – I've more than cleaned up your little debts with what I won from Horrie Attrill – tell me now

Gus did you have a good win yourself? Augustine marks out a long aimless road through the dusty gravel with the toe of his shoe. He says – I'll be honest with you Stan – I had a very modest bet – I'm too far under these days to get out with a single bet anyway – but I'm very glad to hear you did so well yourself – and I'll never be able to thank you for all you've done for me in the past mate. Riordan sees that Augustine is anxious to get away from him. He pats Augustine on the back and says – keep up the good work Gus. Then he goes over to join the men in the shade of the date-palm while Augustine and Clement set out for home. When he reaches home Augustine says to his wife – the Master has pulled off the plunge of his life – yesterday was the day he and I used to dream about all those years – the Jew must have helped him of course but the Master was the brains behind it. Augustine waits for his wife to ask him what he is talking about, but she does not even look up from her work.

## CLEMENT FOLLOWS THE CREEK THROUGH BASSETT

On what may be the last Saturday morning that he spends in Bassett, Clement Killeaton listens carefully while his father explains that he has an important message for the boy to take to a man on the other side of the city. Augustine hands Clement a sealed envelope and tells him to guard it carefully. Then he writes on a scrap of paper the names of the streets that the boy must follow to reach the house where the man is waiting for the message. Clement goes down McCracken's Road then into Cordwainer Street, which is the same route that he follows to school. Not far from St Boniface's school he enters a confusing system of streets that he has never seen before. A mob of strange boys follows him for a few yards and he remembers the story that a nun once told the First Communion class of the little saint Tarsisius who was sent by a priest to carry the Blessed Sacrament through the streets of Rome to a Christian dying in prison but who met a gang of pagan boys on the way and refused to tell them what he was carrying under his shirt and against his heart and ran for his life when they threatened to grab his hand and find out for themselves but was caught in a dead-end street because he didn't know that suburb of Rome very well and was beaten to death by the boys but died with his fingers locked together still protecting the body of Our Lord, and prepares to run. He finds the house and delivers the message to the man who opens the door. The man says – I suppose you know your way home youngster. Clement says – yes thank you – the main streets of Bassett are over there aren't they? and points. The man says – no bloody fear they're not – they're over that way – you must be bushed. Clement shows the list of streets that his father has written down for him. The man only glances at them and says – look it's a lot easier than that, and then describes streets that Clement has never heard of and landmarks that the boy cannot remember passing on his way to the house. For the sake of politeness Clement agrees to set out for home along the streets that the man suggests. But soon after leaving the house he tries to find his own way by following streets that seem to lead back towards home. He soon finds himself in a set of streets that neither his father nor the man in the house has mentioned and that he himself suspects are leading him the wrong way. Then at the end of the most perplexing street of all he sees a sign reading NO ROAD and looks down over a post-and-rail fence at a narrow drain, walled with cement and open to the sky, that must surely be a part of the creek that flows through his own quarter of Bassett and then heads vaguely northwards, although he has always supposed that the creek passed on its way through places far

different from the jumble of streets where he now finds himself
and led in the end to a place quite different from any part of
Bassett. He climbs through the fence, slithers down the grassy
embankment and starts to walk beside the drain in the direction that he believes will lead him home. After he has rounded
the first bend in the creek, he no longer knows which part of
Bassett he is passing through. Above him, on both sides of the
gully or cutting that the creek follows, are the back fences of
yards behind strange houses. At one point he scrambles up the
slope and looks through a gap in the palings. He sees a backyard
with a parched lawn and a few stunted fruit trees and no place
where a child could mark out a road or a farm that might lie
hidden from the adults who walked across the yard from the
back door to the lavatory, but the sight of a few shrubs leaning
together and partly blocking the view from the street at the
front towards the backyard suddenly suggests to him that he
may be looking at last into the backyard of Barbara Keenan's
house – the same yard that he used to wonder about on all the
Saturday afternoons when he played alone among the weeds
and dust in Leslie Street and in which he believed that the girl
he loved built out of broken glass and flowers and scraps of
satin, or drew in her own purer dust, or simply arranged from
the leaning boughs of ample shrubs something that a boy
would only have to see once to understand what it was that
girls knew about or hoped for so that they had no need to
bother about boys like himself who believed, despite all the
scorn of ordinary boys and the anger and incomprehension of
their parents, that they were in love with girls of their own
age. The sight of a few tree-tops in the street beyond the shabby
house and even the roofs and chimneys of the houses around
makes him even more sure that this really is Barbara Keenan's
house. He looks all round the yard but sees nothing to suggest
how Barbara might have spent all her Saturday afternoons.

Then, as he clambers back down the slope to the creek, he looks up again and sees half a dozen wide gaps in the fence and realises that on any Saturday during the past few years any boy or gang of boys who knew how the creek wound its way past hundreds of backyards could have climbed up from the drain and watched for hours any secret things that the girl tried to make in her yard. Walking further he discovers what he has never even suspected – that the creek follows a course through Bassett which seems, to anyone looking along it from one of its bridges, to confine itself to the obscure parts of a few suburbs but which in fact finds its way through almost every quarter of the city by a route which could almost be that of a journey which Clement has always wanted to make through all the places that he has only seen beyond strange patterns of streets or at the ends of fenced yards thick with shrubs, and during which he could have paused again and again and looked towards a certain street or the front of a certain house and known that he was looking along a vista that had often troubled him but this time at last from the remote distance back towards the place where he had stood so often and only stared and wondered. At one place, where the embankments are steep and the houses above seem a long way off and where an untidy weed has spread all over the flat ground beside the drain and formed a jungle of greenery taller than a child and cut through by a maze of narrow pathways leading to hidden clearings at its centre, Clement believes from a few signs that he sees in the direction of the nearest road that he may have discovered the place where the boys of Barry Launder's gang used to take their girlfriends after school. He follows a few paths into the green stuff and sits down in the first clearing that they lead him to, although he knows that there are probably many other clearings still further in and more secluded. He looks up and finds that the green fronds around him are so tall and the place itself is so far beneath the level of the streets nearby that all he can see is a green wall around him and the blue sky above and, where the two merge, a few grey panels of iron roof or wooden palings in some backyard behind a house that he would probably never recognise if he saw it from a street in Bassett. He stands up, then sits down again, and finally throws himself onto his back on the ground to learn what is the last thing that a girl would see after she had agreed at last to follow some swaggering boy from Launder's gang down from the street to the place where, so he had told her, she would find out some of the secrets that adults kept hidden from children and before she realised as he fell on top of her and snatched at her pants that he had tricked her into showing some of her own precious secrets and that afterwards, even when she was alone in some dark private place in the depths of her backyard she would have to admit to herself that somewhere in Bassett was a boy who had seen and touched her naked. He seems to have penetrated to the bottom of a green well or tunnel in a place far different from Bassett yet, because a hint of a backyard is still visible far above him, whose entrance lies among the ordinary houses and yards of the city, he decides that if only he could have persuaded some girl to come to such a spot with him he might have proved to her that what he had always believed was true after all and that there was deep within their city a much stranger place whose green entrance could be reached from its streets. Farther still along the creek, which is the first pathway he has ever followed through Bassett that seems likely to disclose the things that any traveller may see all round him on the long roads through the country towards Tamarisk Row, Clement Killeaton finds in front of him a huge shaggy pepper tree which he decides must be the true hide-out of the Protestant gang from Shepherd's Reef State school that he went in fear of for years although he met them only once and whose hide-out was supposed to be in a remote secret place safe from discovery and well protected against Catholics. He walks boldly through the curtain of foliage and sees that the place has been abandoned for a long time. He searches for some trace of the secret non-Catholic lore which Protestant children share and which enables State-school boys to do whatever they like to almost any girl they choose. In a hollow where the lowest bough joins the trunk of the tree, at a height that he can reach without any trouble, he finds a a rusted tobacco tin. He opens the tin and spills out some broken lengths of a rosary. He leaves the place wondering whether the Protestant gang tortured Catholic children to make them give up their religious treasures or whether they might have stolen things like rosary beads because they had after all few mysteries and rites of their own and wanted to copy from Catholics and might even have envied boys like himself because they could go whenever they wanted into buildings with altars and confessionals. He expects to walk a long way further before he reaches his own part of Bassett, but around the first corner past the abandoned hide-out he notices a familiar row of streets beside a street above the creek. He climbs up the embankment and finds that he has already reached Cordwainer Street and is only a few hundred yards from home.

## CLEMENT KNOWS HE WILL NEVER ENTER THE WALLACES' AVIARY

Clement Killeaton searches all day in his backyard for marbles or small toys that might have been forgotten beside back roads through the weeds and rubbish. Just before tea-time he walks around the yard once more and drags his feet through the dirt so that not even a single one of all the stones that used to stand for horses in the neat paddocks of stud properties is left standing near another in a way that might suggest to a stranger days or weeks afterwards that someone had put it there on purpose and start him searching around the yard for other signs of the pattern that was once laid out across it. He goes inside satisfied that the next boy to live at 42 Leslie Street will never discover anything to tell him what sort of games the boy Killeaton used to play there, although he suspects that deep under the soil there may still be some things hidden from the days when the boy Silverstone used to play there. After tea Clement's mother sends him to Mr Wallace's shop. Mr Wallace says he hopes to be moving to another part of Bassett before a month is up. Clement tells him that the Killeatons will be gone long before then. The birds in the aviary are settling on their roosts for the night. Margaret Wallace cannot say what will happen to the birds after the Wallaces have shifted. Clement asks whether Mr Wallace has thought of taking them all to some patch of bush north of Bassett and letting them go so they can find their own way to the places where they belong. Clement admits that some of the birds might take a few years to find their way home, but he reminds Margaret that birds are able to find secret routes away from roads and towns and that if the birds from the aviary don't live long enough to reach home again they will build nests along the way and have young ones and bring them up so that they or their young ones will one day find their proper home somewhere far away in the heart of Australia and recognise it because it reminds them of a place that a man once built for their parents or grandparents because he believed he could make a landscape so pleasant that a family of birds would live there contentedly for years thinking it was their true home. Clement tells Margaret that he will be leaving Bassett for good in a few days. She says – wasn't there some part of the aviary you were always dying to see and you'd still like to see it before you go? He says – there's something else I'd much sooner see than the aviary. She picks up a tin half-full of conversation lollies and says – I've found a new way to get lollies from the shop without my father knowing. Clement starts to open his fly. He says – I'll go straight and tell your father you've been pinching stuff again unless you pull down your pants for me. For the first time in all the years that Clement has known her, Margaret Wallace seems almost afraid of the boy who has tried for years to convince her that he is just as strong and manly as the boys in her brother's gang that she follows home from school along McCracken's Road and sometimes through the bulrushes near the creek where the State-school boys will not allow Catholics to trespass because that is where they pull down the pants of all the girls who walk home with them, and who has always stopped talking about the birds in her father's aviary as soon as he suspected that she thought he was a cissy who wanted to cuddle the soft feathers of birds or finger their downy nests or admire the colours of their eggs because he always hoped that when she admitted at last that he was no different from the tough Shepherd's Reef boys she would let him do to her what the State-school boys must have done hundreds of time. She tries to dodge past him towards the door of her playhouse, but he moves quickly to block her. He grabs at her dress. She knocks down a long shelf stacked like the shelves in her father's shop with jars and tins and boxes. Out of one tin a heap of broken biscuits spills down onto the dirt floor. She says – give me time to pick up the bickies and I'll let you have a handful. He says – I suppose you pinch them from your father too. She says – no I've just been saving them. He says – I'll give you fifty to pick them up, and starts counting aloud. Then, while she is bending down with her back to him, Clement pins her arms against her sides with his left arm and with his free hand struggles to tear down her thick white pants. He and she roll over together on the floor, upsetting the flimsy shelves and tearing down the grubby white curtains. She kicks and punches him silently and savagely, but for just two or three seconds while her knee is lifted to aim a kick at him he sees clearly among the biscuit crumbs clinging to her thighs and belly a low white ridge split by a narrow unpromising fissure but with nothing else to distinguish it from the pale slopes around, so that any man or boy who chanced on such a place after years of searching would probably still go on looking for the strange shape that he was really after. Then she escapes and crouches in a corner out of his reach with her knees pressed tightly together. A sign that once stood in her father's shop lies beside her, and Clement sees, beneath a picture of a beautiful dark-haired woman, the words YOU TOO CAN HAVE THE FLAWLESS COMPLEXION OF THIS HOLLYWOOD STAR. He says – now I've seen what I always wanted to see when I used to ask you to take me in and show me the secret parts of the aviary. She says – you must be nuts – I've got things hidden in there that you'll never see as long as you live. He asks her will she take those things with her when she shifts or do they have to stay inside the aviary. She tells him that he'll never know what happens to them because he doesn't know what they look like and it doesn't matter if he comes back to look for them every day after she has gone and searches for them in every corner of the aviary, he'll never know whether he just missed finding them or whether he was looking at them for hours and didn't know it. She pulls her pants up tightly under her dress. He says – goodbye Margaret and if I ever come back to Bassett again I'll come and visit you because then we might be old enough to do grown-up things with each other. Clement walks home wondering why he waited for so long to look at Margaret Wallace when all he had to do was twist her arm behind her or push her over backwards. Then he remembers that somewhere in a country that is almost a perfect copy of Australia there are places where even a stupid helpless girl like Margaret Wallace can leave things out in the open exposed to the sunlight and yet know that no one might know what they mean because even the ordinary hills and plains in that country are not really what they seem to be.

## THE KILLEATONS REST ON THEIR WAY
## TO THE WESTERN DISTRICT

During their journey back from Bassett to the Western District, the place that they think they belong in, Mr and Mrs Killeaton decide at last to stop for a rest. They ask the driver of their furniture van to pull up in the town of Skipton. In a scanty park beside the main street they sit beneath English trees and look out across the plains where the oldest and wealthiest families in Victoria live in sprawling bluestone mansions out of sight on their huge properties. The husband and wife think only of the journey ahead of them across the plains towards the coast, but the boy Clement sitting between them remembers the empty rooms of the house in Leslie Street, Bassett, and the last few minutes before the Killeatons climbed into the furniture van, when his parents were looking into every room to see if they had forgotten anything and he suddenly looked behind the kitchen door and found the St Columban's Calendar hanging there with the outermost page still headed *January 1948* because no one had remembered to turn the pages for several months. He lifts the calendar out of the basket on his mother's knees and stares at the nameless place somewhere between Palestine and Egypt on an afternoon when the Holy Family are already miles away from their true country. While his parents believe he is watching only Jesus, Mary and Joseph resting on their journey thousands of miles away the boy Clement wonders at which point in his journey the child scans a region of the plains so far ahead of the family that even a large city there might seem only a vague pattern of streets or rooftops and yet so like the colour of many an afternoon or a street that he has known that he knows clearly what a child there might see when he looks to where a family wanders and knows what another child would see if he looked across the distance towards him.

## THE GOLD CUP RACE IS RUN

A boy suspects all along that he may only be pushing a handful of marbles without knowing where they might finish while a rider lifts his arm again and again and brings the whip down savagely and the horse Sternie who was once the hope of the Jew the shrewdest punter of all goes on slowly improving his position in a field of plodding country gallopers he sees a racecourse where silks of a certain red promise a man that he might soothe at last the restless cock between his legs when he looks out above the roof-tops of an inland city that he has never understood while he spends years training for the day when he comes from behind to win a famous foot-race in the straight now it's still anybody's race *Lost Streamlet* is the leader but *Passage of North Winds* is coming out after him studying pictures in the Sporting Globe of horses a few furlongs from home in races that have already been decided while people in the crowd gape at their fancies bunched indecisively near the rails and the horse Clementia comes down the outside rail alone and almost unnoticed and his owner wonders why he never guessed that he was training a champion where white silk may stand for the soul of a man with God on his side far across the great northern plains that he has never ventured into he tries for years to discover a place where Protestant and pagan girls walk naked and never care who sees them *Hills of Idaho* is looming up suddenly *Veils of Foliage* is not to be denied shoving stones along a dirt track between crude fences of chips of wood while a woman stands with her ear pressed against a crackling wireless set and the horse Skipton that her husband has backed for hundreds of pounds leaves the rails and begins his run from absolute last in the Melbourne Cup field where orange reminds someone in the crowd of the gritty footpaths and yards in the city that he always returns to past the heart of Australia that he admits he has no claim to he searches for years for a backyard where a pure girl knows an innocent game that he and she will never tire of *Hare in the Hills* is coming into the picture *Proud Stallion Den of Foxes* is in the thick of things and *Captured Riflebird* is trying to get through straining his muscles and gasping for breath trying to come from last in a foot-race while the filly Mishna draws clear at the furlong and two or three men in the crowd glance at each other but so discreetly that no one would guess they were about to bring off one of the greatest betting plunges ever planned in Australia where every shade of blue hints at the awesome mysteries of Our Lady and the Catholic Church over the woods and fields of England filled with birds that breed and nest without fear in sight of the people there he sees for years above his calendar a land of sombre colours where saints and holy people go gracefully past on journeys of their own past the furlong and *Hills of Idaho* shows out in front but challenges are coming from everywhere listening through the wall of his bedroom to learn what his parents are planning while the horse Silver Rowan with a few huge strides asserts his claim and a man whose ancestors once built a stone castle with a tower that looked out over miles of green country that they never wanted to leave knows that Ireland is about to be avenged at last where pale gold is meant to be the colour of a delicate freckle hidden beneath a woman's dress on a secret part of her body between the dark hills of Europe that the gypsies found their way out of at last he reaches the very borders of a land where great herds of cattle graze on shining prairies and men return across great distances to find their sweethearts *Lost Streamlet* is refusing to give in *Veils of Foliage Hare in the Hills* is swooping on them wandering through a maze of streets in a city whose map he could never draw while the people of Melbourne are talking about Bernborough a mighty horse from the north who is on his way down from Queensland winning race after race and Augustine Killeaton solemnly tells his son that a greater horse than Phar Lap has appeared in the land where the least glimpse of a certain pale green may mean that a man has discovered a country that no one else will ever see beyond the enormous prairies of America that will be remembered forever in films and hillbilly songs he comes as near as he dares to a green-gold land where creatures set out from intricate cities over plains that may take a lifetime to cross or may suddenly close over the travellers and all trace of their journeys a mighty wall of horses *Hills of Idaho* is about to be swamped and *Springtime in the Rockies* sees daylight at last watching plains and hills and more plains rushing past the window of a train or a furniture van while the professional punter Len Goodchild and his inner circle appear in the crowd on yet another provincial racecourse and a knot of people follows them to see what they fancy where a rare silver sometimes appears like the rain above a coast where a man first dreamed of following the races even further than the desolate lands between Palestine and Egypt and he believes he has reached for once a different city although it still seems familiar *Veils of Foliage Hare in the Hills Springtime in the Rockies* emerges from nowhere and never able to foresee the end of it all far out on a plain three or four horses are bunched together about to take up the positions that will be preserved for years to come but their riders jerk their arms or thrust with their heels or raise and lower their whips with a graceful action as though they cannot hear the screaming crowd and know nothing of the thousands of pounds depending on them and do not realise that any one of them with a last desperate effort might lift his mount and himself into the one position that will make them famous but are already figures in a faded photograph showing the finish of a great race in which one horse triumphed and the rest were soon forgotten by all but a few faithful followers and where a colour that no one has yet been able to copy onto any silk jacket the colour of the most precious milk-stones might tell of a traveller who can find his way back from lands it is hopeless to try to cross in the direction of the district of Tamarisk Row he sees what may still not be the last place of all yet he knows at last that he will never leave Tamarisk Row and *Tamarisk Row* is coming home when it's all over.

Dear readers,

As well as relying on bookshop sales, And Other Stories relies on subscriptions from people like you for many of our books, whose stories other publishers often consider too risky to take on.

Our subscribers don't just make the books physically happen. They also help us approach booksellers, because we can demonstrate that our books already have readers and fans. And they give us the security to publish in line with our values, which are collaborative, imaginative and 'shamelessly literary'.

All of our subscribers:

- receive a first-edition copy of each of the books they subscribe to
- are thanked by name at the end of our subscriber-supported books
- receive little extras from us by way of thank you, for example: postcards created by our authors

## BECOME A SUBSCRIBER, OR GIVE A SUBSCRIPTION TO A FRIEND

Visit andotherstories.org/subscriptions to help make our books happen. You can subscribe to books we're in the process of making. To purchase books we have already published, we urge you to support your local or favourite bookshop and order directly from them – the often unsung heroes of publishing.

## OTHER WAYS TO GET INVOLVED

If you'd like to know about upcoming events and reading groups (our foreign-language reading groups help us choose books to publish, for example) you can:

- join our mailing list at: andotherstories.org
- follow us on Twitter: @andothertweets
- join us on Facebook: facebook.com/AndOtherStoriesBooks
- admire our books on Instagram: @andotherpics
- follow our blog: andotherstories.org/ampersand

# Current & Upcoming Books

GERALD MURNANE was born in Melbourne, Australia, in 1939. He is the author of eleven works of fiction, five of which will be published by And Other Stories in the coming years. He has won multiple high-profile awards across Australia including, most recently, the 2018 Prime Minister's Award for *Border Districts*. He lives in the remote village of Goroke in the north-west of Victoria, near the border with South Australia.